GHOST CHASE

A dead man running

Second
In
'The Needle's Eye' Series

By

Simon Hinton-Bates

**Grosvenor House
Publishing Limited**

This book is published by
Grosvenor House Publishing Ltd
Link House
140 The Broadway, Tolworth, Surrey, Kt6 7Ht.
www.grosvenorhousepublishing.co.uk

A CIP record for this book
is available from the British Library

ISBN 978-1-78623-051-5

'The Needles Eye' Series featuring Jack Ramsay

RANDOM ACT – A deadly chain reaction

GHOST CHASE – A dead man running

LANGTON HALL – A case of murder

To J.P.

Hope you like the
second book !

13/12/17

This book is dedicated to
Philip Arthur Bates
1924 – 2016

PREFACE

At fifteen thousand feet, the water looked flat and calm between the clouds. He fell, tumbling toward the sea far below, the wind screaming in his ears and clawing viciously at his face. It was cold, so much colder than he ever imagined it would be. He tried to move, to gain some control, but his arms and legs were powerless and forced backwards by the speed at which he was dropping. Eventually, and with sheer determination, he was able to stabilize himself and passed quickly through a layer of cloud at ten thousand feet. The moisture had soaked his clothes, and now he was really beginning to feel numb. With every second that passed, the cold air sucked from his body what little warmth and life remained.

At last, and at five thousand feet, he could see the sea coming up to meet him; there was *just* sea, nothing else. He looked in all directions, *just* sea! It wasn't blue; it was a dismal grey with white spume, blown by the biting wind. It wasn't flat either; it was a mass of heaving peaks and troughs. He was losing sensation and the want to go on — the will to live. If he could only wake up now, then it would all be a dream.

He knew he had to do it and do it now. Slowly and with an extreme effort, he moved his hand to his chest and tugged hard at the cord. For the first time in his thirty-eight years, he felt so very alone.

CHAPTER ONE

It was Monday 7pm and a fine summer evening, the sun still high in the cloudless western sky and the air was warm with not a whisper of a breeze. Jack looked at his watch. He was early! As he rounded a shallow bend in the lane, he saw the long trimmed hedging and the sign that indicated he was at his destination. He turned off the road and through a large arched gateway onto a winding gravel drive, the house still out of view. The drive meandered its way through a small copse, which then opened out and curved past a large and immaculately manicured lawn. Jack could see a car, a large Mercedes parked near to the house. He parked his car, or rather, the hire car he had for the next week, in a convenient space to the side of the entrance porch.

The large and well-proportioned house sat comfortably on rising ground. The walls were of soft red brick with stone arches at the windows, the whole mellowed by a hundred summers. The original part of the house looked to be early 1900s but with later sympathetic additions. Looking up, Jack could see a high level of security had been installed. There were two cameras pointing down at the gravelled area to the front and side of the house, as well as a clearly displayed alarm box.

Crunching gravel underfoot, he made his way to the entrance. He was feeling less than comfortable. His right arm was badly bruised and sore, and his chest was giving him considerable pain, the result of two cracked ribs. His head was a mess. A neat line of twelve stitches on a shaved area above a badly bruised and swollen eye clearly indicated that Jack Ramsey had spent some time in accident and emergency very recently. Less than three days was insufficient time to repair the damage that had been inflicted, and it was clearly apparent he'd done more than trip over! Given the choice, he'd have preferred an early night. He'd spent hours in Newport Hospital, having X-rays, stitches, and countless examinations to establish that he was well enough to then spend all of the Saturday at the police station. The day was spent making statements, being questioned and, most of all, proving his innocence. When Jack got back to the hotel in the early evening, he was shattered. There he remained, not leaving his room and sleeping through the best part of Sunday.

Jack pressed the ornate bell push with the finger of his left hand and waited, expecting the door to be opened by Catherine. He was slightly taken aback when a young girl's figure appeared, framed in the now open doorway. "You must be Mr. Ramsey. Would you like to come in?" She stepped back, smiling sweetly and still holding the large door handle as Jack entered the hall. Jack guessed she was about seven years old. "Did you fall over? I'm Amelia, by the way." She was looking at his face. "I fell off Gypsy last year and broke my arm."

2

She held up her left arm. It looked perfect to Jack. "It's mended now. See!" Clearly, Gypsy was the grey Welsh pony, a photograph of which was displayed on the wall. There was Amelia in full riding gear, wearing a big red rosette and an even bigger grin.

Away in the distance at the far end of the hall, a door opened. "Hello Jack, how lovely to see you. You appear to have met Amelia already." Amelia smiled at Jack and held out her hand as a formal introduction. Catherine walked or glided, as it appeared to Jack, the twenty feet or so to meet him. When he turned his head, she gasped, "Oh my goodness, what *have* you done to yourself?"

"It's nothing really," said Jack, lying best he could. "It was just a little accident the other day." Jack knew it would be all over the papers by the end of the week. He just hoped he could keep his name out of it! There'd been reporters outside the police station, waiting to interview the private investigator who'd discovered and blown wide open the drugs organisation on the Isle of Wight!

Catherine led Jack through to the drawing room, where her father-in-law was seated in a wing chair, listening to a radio programme through a pair of small headphones. His wife, Catherine's mother-in-law, sat close by on the leather chesterfield. She tapped her husband's ankle with her foot, and at once, he removed the headphones. Catherine spoke. "This is Mr. Ramsey. Remember he helped us when we were on the ferry?"

"Please call me Jack." He went forward and took Mrs. Blanchard Senior's hand. She looked at his face, his swollen eye, and gauze patch, with disapproval. Jack then turned to Mr. Blanchard and, remembering he was blind, gripped the hand that was waving in limbo in

3

front of the elderly gentleman. "I'm very pleased to meet you both again."

"Mr. Ramsey, sorry, I mean Jack is staying on the Island on business. He's staying at the hotel." Pleasantries over; Catherine prepared drinks for her in-laws. Turning to Jack she smiled. "What may I get you, Jack?"

"Well, I'm driving; so I'd better. . ." He stopped talking when she forced a large gin and tonic into his hand and poured herself the same.

"Jack, we've spare rooms for guests here. But if you insist on going back to the hotel this evening, I'll get Frederick to come and collect you in the hotel taxi. He can drop you back in the morning to get your car."

Jack couldn't argue, especially as he'd have had to do so with the owner of the hotel at which he was staying, and she was standing before him! He graciously gave in. "In that case, cheers!" He raised the glass to her; to the seated pair as well; and to Amelia, who had just entered the room clutching a lurid red drink in a long glass.

"You'd better not spill that drink on the carpet. Your father certainly would not have allowed it. Allowing children to walk around the house with drinks and spill them all over the place!" Mrs. Blanchard Senior looked most disapprovingly at her granddaughter. Amelia sat quietly on the edge of a two-seater sofa, as far away from her grandmother as she could get.

"I'm sure she'll be fine, won't you dear?" Catherine smiled at Amelia, who'd not yet mastered the art of making a drink last. She'd gulped down half of it already, leaving a red moustache on her top lip.

Amelia smiled at her mother. "I will be very careful, Mummy." She looked sideways at her grandmother, with whom she always felt ill at ease.

4

"Dinner will be in about fifteen minutes." Almost immediately, there was the crunching sound of wheels on the gravel drive followed by a muffled chime of the doorbell. Catherine turned and placed her drink down on the coffee table. "That'll be dinner arriving now. Please, Jack, sit down and make yourself comfortable."

Jack sat in the vacant wing chair and discussed the weather, the economic climate, and other random but fairly safe topics with the Blanchard's Senior. Mr. Blanchard did his best to respond, but his wife was hard work. Jack asked how long they were staying.

"Another week I believe," said Mr. Blanchard with a smile, but his wife immediately contradicted him.

"We'll be going home tomorrow." She looked sternly at her husband who, being blind, felt no pain from the daggers in her eyes. "My husband has an appointment at the hospital," she huffed. "He'd be hopeless left to his own devices!"

Jack clearly got the impression he'd quite enjoy being left to his own devices once in a while.

* * *

Cleo had been frantic with worry. He'd promised to call her Friday, the previous evening. Jack's phone was not being answered, and when she called George, he'd no real idea what was happening. Eventually, he rang from the police station at midday.

"I'm fine Cleo, really, I'm OK." Jack's head was thumping like a bass drum. "The case is basically closed, as far as I'm concerned." Jack brought Cleo up to speed with a précised account of the events of the previous twenty-four hours. "George wants to pay my expenses, but that's not going to happen; so don't send him an invoice." Ramsey, Dawkins, and Bell Investigation Services were not going to make a fortune with this case. Cleo held the partnership together — acting as secretary, advisor, receptionist, tea/coffee lady, cleaner, and lastly and most recently, the new woman in Jack's life. "I need to get back to the hotel. I need to shower, grab a bite to eat, get some rest and a replacement phone. I'll call you when I'm there."

He phoned her again after he had arrived at the hotel in the evening, feeling a little refreshed having showered and eaten. She'd already arranged for a new phone to be delivered by special courier the following day. They talked for quite a while, Jack talking in far greater detail about what had happened.

"I'm so glad you're all right Jack. You are, aren't you?" She paused, waiting for his reply. "I could come down to be with you. I could leave now and be there in about three hours."

"That would be nice! But listen, Cleo, I'm really shattered and will probably sleep most of tomorrow anyway. On Monday I have to see George and collect my car. I have to tie up loose ends at the police station, and I also have this dinner at the Blanchard's house in the evening." Jack's voice was beginning to drift off. He was lying on the bed, sleep beckoning him. "Why don't you come down here on Tuesday?" He yawned uncontrollably.

"OK Jack, Tuesday morning, I'll be there," she answered quickly, knowing he'd be fast asleep any second. "I'll be on the 8:30 a.m. from Portsmouth. Goodnight Jack. Love you!"

She knew it was her mind working overtime. She knew Jack was honest and faithful. She knew she loved him, and he, her. *'Why does this woman want Jack to have dinner with them?'* She wished she was going with him.

* * *

Exactly fifteen minutes later, the four were seated in the dining room. The in-laws seated across the oval table, Jack and Catherine at either end. Amelia had eaten earlier and was already in bed at this time. "She's probably watching the television in her room," her mother said when Jack enquired as to her whereabouts.

"You're far too soft with that girl," Mrs. Blanchard Senior said to Catherine. "A television in the bedroom whatever will it be next? She clearly thought Amelia was spoilt and intended to raise her disapproval at any and every opportunity that presented itself. Catherine caught Jack's eye, aware of the tension within the room.

Mr. Blanchard Senior was clearly oblivious to the rising tension but, remembering there was a guest in the room, started talking about the attractions on the Island. "Have you seen much of the Island, Mr. Ramsay?"

His wife fired a salvo across his bows. "Put your napkin on your lap. You'll drop dinner all over your trousers, and then we'll have to get them dry-cleaned!" He immediately stopped talking and concurred with his wife's wishes.

The mimosa eggs were a perfect first course, but the conversations were somewhat stilted for a while. The pheasant arrived next and was a wonderfully rich main course. The conversations began to flow more easily like the excellent Merlot, the in-laws talking and smiling as they warmed to Jack. The sweet course was a fine lemon syllabub, and by this time, Jack had been elevated to the rank of perfect dinner guest by Catherine's in-laws. Jack finished his plate and placed his knife and fork together. He was about to open his mouth to speak.

"Before you congratulate me on producing a wonderful meal, I must tell you it's courtesy of meals-on-wheels!" Catherine laughed and Jack looked somewhat confused. "Sometimes I get the kitchens at the hotel to prepare a meal and send it out to me here." She looked at Jack. "Is that awful?"

"Not at all, if you're prepared to inflict it on the hotel guests, it's only right you eat it yourself!" Jack raised a glass. "I propose a toast; compliments to the chef." All four raised their glasses and toasted The Weston Manor Hotel kitchen staff!

The Blanchard's Senior declined coffee and made their excuses. They had a guest suite on the ground floor and were going to take an early night. Jack stood up and helped them to the dining room door.

"Jack, would you like to take coffee in the lounge?" Catherine had stood up and was holding the tray. "Please don't try to be a martyr and offer to carry the tray. I can see you're in no fit state!" Jack followed her into a room smaller than the drawing room. This room was so much more comfortable with deep leather chairs and a large coffee table in the middle. Catherine placed the tray down and poured the coffee from an elaborate silver coffee pot. From a cabinet she produced a bottle of twelve-year-old Islay Malt Whisky and poured two large glasses, handing one to Jack.

Jack had certainly consumed more alcohol than he'd intended even if he was getting taken back to the hotel by taxi! "I don't know whether I can manage a whisky, Catherine." But Jack took the glass all the same and placed it on a circular leather coaster.

"I expect you're probably wondering why I invited you for dinner, Jack" Catherine leaned closer to Jack. He could smell her perfume. It was something expensive, the name of which he did not know. However, combined with the coffee and whisky, it proved a powerful and intoxicating concoction. "Don't worry. I'm not going to jump on you!" She laughed and settled back in the leather chair tucking her now bare feet under her.

For an instant, Jack felt a slight tinge of disappointment. Cleo's face was suddenly before him looking into his eyes. He felt guilt. He was confused. He was feeling hot. He'd had far too much to drink and wasn't feeling as if he were in charge of himself anymore. He wondered if he'd been in charge at all since arriving at this house. He was at a total loss as to what to say in response, but the silence was only short lived when Catherine spoke again.

"You don't remember me, do you, Jack?" Her voice was almost a whisper but made Jack's blood feel hot and the hairs on the back of his neck tingle. Catherine smiled and took a sip from her whisky.

Jack tried to think quickly, but his mind was racing with all the possibilities of where he might have seen her. "You have me at a disadvantage, Catherine. Have we met before?" He stumbled over his words. "I mean before I met you and your 'in-laws' on the ferry and you invited me here."

"Well, obviously I made no impact on you whatsoever!" She pouted at him, and there was an awkward silence, which lasted for just a few seconds. "OK. Let me put you out of your misery. When we last met, I was Catherine Williams and it was nearly fifteen years ago! I turned up at your house with Peter, who was my boyfriend at the time, a friend of your brother. You were just leaving. You were on your way to the airport or something. It was only a very brief hello and goodbye."

Jack tried to recall the event without success. "I'm sorry Catherine, I don't remember. . . "

"It's no big thing, Jack. Anyway, I recognised you on the boat immediately and, at the time it, was easier not to get into trying to explain the link. I knew what your line of business was, and I assume it still is?" Jack nodded. Catherine continued, "Giving you the hotel business card and hoping you'd stay there was a way of getting to see you so that I could talk to you." She put the glass down and considered her next statement. "I know what you do, I mean, what your business is. I need your help, Jack, your advice. I need someone with your experience to help me." She let the statement sink in.

Jack waited for her to continue, but she'd stopped talking. He looked at her and could see a tear rolling down the side of her face. She stood and walked across the room to fetch a tissue from a box sitting next to the drinks cabinet. Jack, as quickly as he could, got to his feet. He wasn't sure what to do but felt he needed to do something. He walked across the room to where she was standing and gently placed a hand on her shoulder. He could feel the warmth of her skin through the thin silk dress she wore.

"I'm sorry, Jack. I'm a bit overcome." She turned towards him, resting her head on his left shoulder. They stood quietly for what seemed to Jack a long time but could have been but a few seconds. "Do you want to sit down again?" He spoke gently into her ear. She nodded, and Jack eased her back to the leather chair, handing her the glass of whisky. "Catherine, what's wrong? Clearly, you're very upset. Can you tell me?"

"It's all to do with Paul, my husband." She looked down at her ring-less finger. "I mean the man who used to be my husband but not any longer." Catherine wiped her eyes. Jack could see she was trembling slightly. "Forever, 'till death do us part!" She looked up at Jack. "I'm not making a lot of sense really, am I?"

Jack could hardly say so, but he inwardly agreed with her. "It's fine Catherine, just tell me what you can, what you want to tell me." The good food, the three gin and tonics, the countless glasses of wine, and finally, the enormous whisky were all beginning to take effect. Jack was becoming very tired and finding concentration and focus difficult.

"Look, Jack, why don't I tell you all about it tomorrow? You won't go back to the hotel at this late hour. There's a spare room all prepared for you here. " Jack began to shake his head. "Please, Jack. Just let me explain it tomorrow when my head is clear. It'll be easier." Jack was tired, he had to admit. He sighed, and then nodded, slowly placing the now empty whisky glass down on the coffee table. Catherine rose to her feet and, leaving her shoes, padded across the room taking Jack's hand as she passed. "Come on then. Up you get. I'll show you to your bedroom, Mr. Ramsey."

Jack continued to hold on to her hand as they made their way up the wide staircase. He was concerned she may trip or fall, not that he was really capable with only one good arm of catching and saving her! "This is my room here," she said, pointing to a door on the left as they made their way along the landing. "And you, Jack, well, you're in this room." She opened the door and gestured for Jack to enter. She was still holding on to his hand as he walked in, and she followed behind. "You'll get the early morning sun in this room. I hope you sleep well." She was standing so close to him he could hear and feel her breathing. She put her arm on his shoulder and kissed him lightly on the cheek. "Sweet dreams, Jack." She let go of his hand and moved to the door.

"Thank you, Catherine, good night." Jack turned to look at the room in the darkness.

"There's just one more thing, Jack." He turned back to face her again. Catherine was back with him, close this time, her arms round his neck and her mouth on his, kissing him with passion. He felt her tongue hot against his lips and her fingers softly caressing him. "I've wanted to do that for fifteen years!" she whispered in his ear. He could feel her body moving under the thin dress as she pressed against him.

* * *

Chapter Two

The journey from London had been pleasant, if uneventful, as the train pulled into the station at Portsmouth, the end of the line. She placed the paperback, which she'd been reading, in her bag. Cleo walked along the platform and out of the station where she found a taxi to take her the short distance to the car ferry terminal. She chastised herself for not checking that there'd be a connection by rail and simply booking as a foot passenger on the ferry that Jack had used to make the trip. However, she soon found herself in a shuffling queue of passengers boarding the ferry, which would take them across the strip of water that lay between the mainland and the Isle of Wight. Once on board she headed up the steep stairway to the main lounge and joined yet another queue, this time for the café, where she purchased just a coffee. At exactly 8:30 a.m. the ferry cast off and slowly made her passage out through the narrow harbour entrance and into the Solent.

A short while later and in the less restricted waters outside of the harbour entrance the ferry turned to starboard and started to pick up speed. Cleo continued to read her paperback whilst half listening to the chatter of those around her. A young family, sitting nearby, were in discussion as to where they might go first. The many attractions in the Island guide spread out before them on the table. As well as holiday makers, there were people in suits with mobile phones clamped to their ears, their murmured conversations almost inaudible. The deep vibrations, constantly running through the ferry, caused crockery to rattle on the plastic trays and tabletops.

As the end of the crossing drew near, Cleo remembered she'd intended to call Jack to confirm which ferry she was on. The book had been devoured; its story so totally compelling Cleo had completely forgotten about calling him. She felt sure he'd be there to meet her as she took out her phone, scrolled down the names, selected his, and waited. Jack's phone was not on. She left a message. People were leaving their seats and starting to make their way down to the lower levels to be ready to disembark as soon as the ferry arrived.

Cleo followed the small procession of foot passengers as they filed off the ferry, eventually drifting away in different directions as they continued on with their individual journeys. She couldn't see him. She looked beyond the passengers' heads, hoping to see Jack's face looking in her direction. Once again on the solid ground and able to stand where she wasn't in the way of those following, she phoned again. His phone was still off. She left another message.

* * *

Jack opened his eyes, the sun's rays streaming in through the open window and the birdsong welcoming him to the beginning of another day. He couldn't actually remember getting into bed, and it was a few seconds before he remembered where he was. With a slight feeling of panic, he checked the bed to discover with some relief that he was and had been the only occupant. He lay there for a while longer, piecing together the events of the previous evening. He remembered the meal, the wine, the whisky, and lastly, the strange conversation with Catherine. Then, as he lay there staring up at the ceiling, he remembered just about everything!

Throwing back the silk sheet, he got out of bed and walked naked across the room to the open window. The view of the grounds merging softly with the woods beyond was both peaceful and tranquil. It was like a perfect photograph from an expensive country house magazine. There was small stable complex off to the left, and Jack could just make out a grey head peering out over a stable door. A diminutive figure appeared at the corner of the building with a carrot, and Jack watched as Amelia fed the pony.

It was just 6:20 a.m. It seemed to Jack there were no other sounds coming from the rest of the house. He found shaving gear, toothbrush, and all manner of guest items in the en-suite bathroom. Jack showered, shaved, and quickly got himself dressed. Looking at his watch, it was now 6:45 a.m. He closed the door and made his way along the landing. He stopped and listened but could hear no sound coming from Catherine's room. On finding the kitchen, Jack filled a kettle and switched it on. While it boiled, he discovered a cupboard with mugs and another with instant coffee. A drawer near the sink supplied a spoon and the refrigerator, the milk. Just as the kettle came to the boil, the kitchen door opened. Some women have the ability to look stunning even when their hair is uncombed and they're wearing just a baggy pink T-shirt. Catherine was one of them. Jack held up a mug towards her. "Hope you don't mind. I helped myself!"

Catherine smiled and took the mug, holding it carefully in two hands. She leaned against the kitchen worktop to reach a packet of sweeteners and Jack was suddenly aware of how short the T-shirt was. He was trying to stop himself admiring her legs and in doing so found himself staring at her body. "You're spilling it!" she said and reached for a piece of kitchen towel to mop up the coffee Jack had poured on the work surface.

"Catherine. Last evening . . . last night, I hope I didn't, I mean I was . . . ," he started to say.

"Wonderful!" she replied as she took a sip of the hot liquid. Jack was unsure whether she was referring to the coffee or what had happened seven hours earlier!

"Did I.... we. I mean ..." Jack's mind was in overdrive — that last part of the evening was a blur.

She looked up at him over the rim of her mug and smiled. "Don't you remember?" Catherine carefully placed the mug on the surface and stretched her arms up spreading her fingers wide. "Was it *that* much of a non-event Jack?"

Jack's heart thumped wildly in his chest and he could feel himself blushing. His throat was dry. He swallowed and tried to speak. "No, I'm sorry Catherine if I . . . it's just that I'm not . . ."

She cut his reply short. "Jack for Christ's sake stop winding yourself up like this. If you want to know you were the perfect gentleman." She paused to let it sink in and smiled. "Nothing happened!" Catherine took a loaf from the bread bin and a bread knife from the drawer. "You escorted me to my room, opened the door, saw me to my bed and then left kissing me good night. I slept soundly until about ten minutes ago." The toaster was duly fed four slices. "That, by the way, was the best night's sleep I've had for three years!"

They sat, the two of them at the breakfast table, ate toast, drank coffee and unaware of the depth of each other's thoughts considered what might have been. Jack wondered why this beautiful woman was living here, alone but for her daughter. Whether she was divorced, widowed, separated. Jack looked over Catherine's shoulder at the kitchen clock; it was 7:15 a.m. "So, what did you want to tell me, Catherine? Last night you said you would tell me tomorrow. Do you want to tell me now?" He placed the now empty mug down on the table. Catherine finished hers and did likewise.

"It's difficult to know exactly where to start Jack." She made them both more coffee and sat back down at the table. There was a pause while she collected her thoughts looking around the room waiting for some signal. Catherine cleared her throat and started talking about her life during the previous fifteen years. She told him about meeting her husband Paul, her marriage, her daughter Amelia, the success of the hotel, and Paul's business interests. She went on to describe how everything was looking so promising for her and her family. Jack listened intently not wishing to interrupt. "Paul died, in a flying accident, three years ago, Jack. I've got over it now, the shock I mean. Well, you never get over a thing like that you just learn to live with it.

But Jack I need to find out the truth about how he died. I just don't know what really happened. You see his body was never discovered. It's just assumed that he died, was killed. I don't know nobody knows but it was assumed he was killed in the accident you see." Jack didn't see but he was trying to follow. "I won't believe that he's dead!" She waved the last piece of toast in the air as she talked, honey running down her wrist. Jack handed her the paper towel and she continued. "He flew off to a meeting and was never seen again." She placed the paper towel in the bin. "Oh, they found a few bits and pieces floating in the sea but nobody Jack. Don't you think that very strange?"

Jack replied. "Not necessarily Catherine but what do you want me to do? I'm sorry for your loss but I'm not sure there's anything more I can find out. Three years ago?"

"I need to know the truth Jack about what happened to him." She licked some honey from her wrist. "The hotel was in his name. He left no will, it's all a mess still and until that's all cleared up I'm in limbo, Jack." Catherine looked out of the window toward the stables. "It's not just for me. I want Amelia to know what happened to her father as well. She needs to have closure as well, doesn't she?"

Jack glanced again at the kitchen clock; it was 7:15 a.m. It was *still* 7:15 a.m.! He removed his wristwatch from his trouser pocket and looked at the dial showing 8:47 a.m. He suddenly remembered Cleo and that he was meeting her from the boat. The boat that was due in very soon, fifteen minutes by Jack's reckoning. "Look, Catherine, we will need to talk some more but not right now. I'm sorry. Give me a call later today will you?" He took a card from his wallet and handed it to her. Jack was doing frantic mental calculations in his head, trying desperately to establish whether he could get to the ferry in time. "I have to meet somebody. She's arriving on the ferry very soon!" He paused, looked again at his watch. "Thank you for the meal it was lovely but I really have to go now." He and Catherine got to their feet. "By the way," he pointed at the clock on the wall, "your kitchen clock's not working!"

"That's the least of my worries Jack it stopped working two months ago!" She saw him to the door and waved him goodbye as he manoeuvred the car to face back down the drive. As Jack looked in his mirror he caught a glimpse of her standing in the doorway. Her face was outwardly smiling but there was sadness also. Her eyes although looking in his direction were looking not only at him but through him. Her eyes seemed to have just the merest touch of a glaze about them, as someone peering at the future and not sure whether the future was a place she wanted to go.

* * *

She'd been standing there for what seemed like ages. People were now walking past her in the opposite direction to board the ferry ready for the trip back to the mainland. She looked at her watch again, sighed deeply and peered off into the distance.

"Are you all right Luv?" The voice that startled her came from an orange fluorescent jacketed member of the shore crew.

"I'm fine thanks, I'm waiting for someone. He shouldn't be long." With that, Cleo picked up her bag and walked slowly towards the main car park. Cars were being directed down the jetty and she had to pick her moment to cross to the other side of the road.

A blue Astra appeared at the top of the road and the driver flashed the car's headlights. She knew it was Jack and waved back as she walked purposely towards the car. Jack parked the car in a vacant space got out and held out his arms as she ran up to him.

"Sorry, I'm a bit late." He kissed her and took the bag she was holding with his good arm.

"Jack! Your face, your eye! My god Jack, you told me it was just a few scratches!" Cleo touched his face lightly. "What else did they do to you?"

"Just a couple of cracked ribs Cleo. Don't worry it'll mend. Jump in and I'll tell you all about it." Jack walked to the back of the car and placed the bag in the boot. Cleo climbed into the car and stretched her long legs as far as she could, realised she couldn't stretch them very far and adjusted the seat as far back as it would go. "Let's go and have coffee and I'll bring you up to speed."

Cleo was unsure whether she was in 'work' or 'girlfriend' mode and turned to Jack. "Is this trip business or pleasure Jack?" She leaned across and kissed his cheek.

"Well this morning it's pleasure," he grinned at her, "but not until after I've told you about why I'm staying down here a little longer." Jack turned right out of the car park and headed for the main road.

* * *

George Clark sat in the old wooden framed deckchair outside the hut which served as his office and looked out over the small airfield. It was warm the sun was up it was a cloudless sky but it was quiet. It was unusually quiet for the time of year and unusually quiet for 10:00 a.m. Normally there'd have been a couple of flights booked for today, trips around the Island and the like. But today it was quiet, the lesson arranged for 3:00 p.m. had cancelled at short notice but George didn't mind. He'd sit for a while longer, finish his coffee and if there were still no punters, he'd give his chum Charlie a call. He fancied a pub lunch. Far more desirable than the cheese sandwiches he'd thrown together at 7:00 a.m. The bread was past its best and dry, to say nothing for the cheese which was of a vintage George couldn't recollect. He knew it must have been in the fridge for about two weeks or even longer. He emptied the last of the tepid coffee from the thermos into a plastic mug and picked up the newspaper from the small wooden table at his side. The local press had been quick off the mark. There on the front page was the story or at least the press's version of what had happened. *'Private investigator blows open Island drug ring'*. George read the sketchy information which amounted to very little. There was just the one blurred, long distance photograph but no mention of Jack Ramsey. It just said there'd been a successful operation involving the police and an un-named private detective to smash a drug organisation at a local farm. Another small photograph showed a line of blue and white police tape strung between trees and the blurred shape of a farmhouse which had been taken with a long-range camera lens. George smiled as he read the five paragraphs. The thinnest of information spread almost to the point of transparency to cover a quarter of the front page. George had been great friends with Jack's late father. He'd been virtually adopted and in his early years, Jack had been introduced to George as 'Uncle George'. George smiled thinking how much like his father Jack had unknowingly become. He was glad the friendship had been rekindled during the summer months. George had no family of his own. He'd been married but his wife had died many years ago. With no children of his own George held Jack's friendship in great esteem.

His interest in the newspaper was abandoned when he heard the sound of an engine. A plane was taxiing out to take off. George watched and listened as the engine's sound increased to a roar and the plane sped down the runway. As it left the ground it banked to the right and proceeded to turn slowly gaining height in clockwise spirals until at about 4,000 feet it levelled out. George discarded the newspaper which he'd left on his lap and took the binoculars from the table at his side. He watched as a small black speck emerged from the plane's open doorway, falling away and down. Then in a sudden flash of brightness and colour the canopy of the parachute opened and the figure suspended beneath twisted and turned its way back down to earth. Landing just feet from a large white cross staked out on the grass in the adjacent field.

* * *

Jack parked the car on a grassed area just off the road. The elevated position allowed a view of a large portion of the Island which included Sandown Bay. The two seaside towns of Sandown and Shanklin spread out below. The van selling burgers also sold drinks and Jack walked back to where Cleo was sitting on the grass. "Here you are." He handed her a coffee and placed his down on the grass.

"It's truly lovely here." Cleo peered out from under the brim of her sun hat. "I could sit here all day," having kicked off her shoes, she gently rubbed her bare foot against his leg, "but only if you're here with me!"

Jack was of the same opinion and indeed could have easily spent the entire day sitting with her watching the world go by. He sipped at the coffee, which was remarkably hot, and between sips he recalled the visit to Catherine's house, meeting the 'in-laws', meeting Amelia and having a delightful meal. He was economical with the details regarding the events later in the evening, mentioning that he'd been invited to stay and so was able to have a drink.

"So she put you up for the night did she Jack?" Her dark brown eyes fixed on him. "I hope you behaved yourself!" She said with just a hint of humour but insufficient to put Jack at ease.

Jack could feel his face glowing and he tried to move the subject on. "Apparently we'd met before, about fifteen years ago. She was the girlfriend of a friend of my brother's. They turned up at my parent's house one day. I have to say I don't remember." He finished the coffee. "I didn't recognise her but then again I'd only met her once, all that time ago!" Jack screwed up the paper cup. "She's asked me to try and find her husband or rather to find out what happened to him three years ago. According to the papers, he's dead killed in a plane crash. I think she believes he's still alive".

They walked along a footpath over a style and into an enormous field the lush grass dotted with countless thousands of yellow meadow buttercups. Cleo let Jack talk about his injuries and how he was feeling. His eye was less puffy but the bruised area was really putting on a multi-coloured display. He found his chest less painful, his breathing easier and his arm although still hurting was improving. She put her arm around him trying not to press on his ribs and rested her head on his shoulder. He turned his head towards her and kissed her gently on the lips. "It's so very good to have you here Cleo." They kissed again. "Stay down here while I try and sort out this case, will you?"

"I'd love to but only if the boss lets me, Jack. You know what a tyrant he is!" They laughed together, forgetting about everything else but being with each other.

* * *

Chapter Three

He sat there most mornings sometimes outside at the small table under the canopy when the weather was good. When it was cold he'd be inside by the window. It was a fine warm day with no clouds or breeze to spoil the weather. He was sitting outside and reading the local newspaper. He'd been living here for just over two years and his daily routine was beginning to imprint permanence to his life in this quiet town. Owning this small café made him feel as if he belonged here. There were few people about even though it was the holiday season. It was early in the day, the village never stirred until 8am. The only reason the small café bothered to open its doors for business was to catch passing trade headed for the beach during the summer or workers making their way to the railway station. He finished his coffee placed the cup neatly in the centre of the small circular table and got to his feet putting the paper under his arm.

"Bonjour Monsieur Michael" The young woman was crossing the narrow road towards the café.

"Bonjour Mademoiselle Katrina comment ça va?" He raised the brim of his hat as she approached.

She smiled sweetly as she walked toward the café entrance. "Ça va bien merci beaucoup." She skipped lightly through the open doorway and immediately fell into conversation with an older woman working behind the counter. Their dialogue lost partially drowned by the music from the small radio behind the counter and the coffee machine doing a fine impersonation of a lorry's airbrake system.

As he owned the place there was no need but he left five euros by the empty cup. He crossed the road and made his way back up the hill toward the village. There were a few more people about now. He spoke briefly to an elderly woman at the junction before crossing and an elderly man emerging from the boulangerie three loaves under his arm. He too purchased a small loaf and carried it up the long steep stepped alley which led to his flat. He placed the key in the door and went inside closing it quickly behind him.

The flat was on the ground floor but elevated slightly because of the hill on which the building stood. It was typical of the region with stone floor and plain walls. There were two bedrooms and a bathroom leading off the wide hallway and another door leading to a large main room serving as kitchen dining room and lounge. The shuttered windows were still closed and the room was in semi-darkness but there was an aroma of fresh coffee. He threw the newspaper into a waiting chair and crossed the room to the small kitchen area. She turned towards him and smiled as he wrapped his arms around her naked shoulders. He kissed her tenderly while reaching for two mugs from the shelf behind her head.

"Michael you have been down at the café? I woke and you were not here, could you not sleep? I made coffee for us. You want some now it's still hot enough yes?" Even in broken English Maria was perfectly capable of putting together a multi questioned sentence.

"Yes, and yes, and yes!" He placed the two mugs on the worktop and poured from the cafetière. "Katrina was late again but just a few minutes. It's not a problem really."

"She's too lazy you must sack her." Maria was a woman who spoke her mind and if Michael agreed with her she'd go down to the café and sack her there and then. "Yvette can manage the place and we'll save a wage." She sipped at the hot liquid cradling the mug in her hands.

"It's not that easy having mother and daughter working in the same kitchen and anyway Yvette doesn't let her get away with much. She's only sixteen. Maria has much to learn about work and life. If I let her go Yvette would probably give her notice as well and then who'd run the place?" Maria scowled slightly disapprovingly imagining the young girl had some invisible hold over him.

"I could run it for you then we'd save two wages!" Maria was tapping her long fingernails on the work-surface with a mechanical staccato rhythm.

"Let's see how it goes over the next few weeks. She's getting better with her timekeeping." Michael placed the coffee mug down and pulled her closer to him. "It means we can spend more time together."

"OK you can have your way with it but let me say this..." She didn't get the chance to say anything more as Michael planted a kiss on her lips.

The café now had three customers, a local woman who was sitting inside at the bar cappuccino in front of her on the counter, the elderly man with the loaves of bread and now a pastis seated in the sunshine by the doorway and a younger man, not local seated with a black coffee at the table where Michael had been sitting just thirty minutes earlier. He was well dressed, not overdressed but casually smart. He wore fine Italian shoes with a matching leather belt for his chinos, a tailored linen shirt, an expensive Tag watch and Ray-Ban sunglasses completing the ensemble. The man was clearly not a local. He'd ordered his coffee in French but Katrina had recognised an accent which she assumed to be English. He'd been coming every morning for a couple of weeks, sitting and drinking coffee for about an hour and then leaving. He was watching the street, watching the people from the village going about their daily routines. He had a newspaper on the table in front of him, a local paper. Today both the coffee and the newspaper were as yet untouched.

* * *

Lunch had been a pleasant and unrushed affair in a small café found by chance when they'd turned off the main road to avoid joining a procession of vehicles behind a slow moving tractor and trailer carrying an early hay crop. They were walking back to the car as Jack's phone chirped into song.

"Hello, Catherine... Yes, I'm fine thanks... Yes about 4:00 p.m? OK see you then. Bye for now." Jack put the phone back into his pocket. "That was Catherine, she'd like to see me and to. . . "

"I bet she would! Hasn't she seen enough of you already Jack?" Cleo interrupted. Her enjoyment and the spell of having Jack to herself had been suddenly broken. She inexplicably felt threatened. She didn't know how to react and she'd let her feelings show in no uncertain terms. She was angry with herself for showing her feelings in that way but it was too late.

"She wants to see *both* of us she wants *you* to come as well." Jack smiled at her. "Look you silly, pretty, one and only gorgeous girl." He waited to let that sink in. "This is simply business, it's just another job as far as I'm concerned. So stop worrying, will you? Anyway, I'm not even sure we'll find out anything even if I take this on." Cleo accepted Jack's reasoning. She trusted him really. Deep down in her heart she trusted him; but not her. She was an unknown and Cleo didn't much like the unknown. "So we have another couple of hours. What do you want to do?"

"Well, Jack I need to find somewhere to stay. I suppose we'd better find me a B&B."

"I rather thought we could..... What I mean is my suite at the hotel is very generous." He flushed and faltered. "Sorry perhaps I'm presuming too much but I thought that we were at a stage in our relationship ......" He faltered again. "I'm making a complete mess of this aren't I?"

"Yep, you certainly are Jack and I'm enjoying every second of it!" She gave one of her warm smiles that melted him. They climbed into the car and Jack started the engine deafening the birdsong.

"OK we'll go back to the hotel, you can settle in and after that, we can go and talk with Catherine."

* * *

Catherine had dropped Amelia at her friend's house for a few hours. Amelia wasn't particularly fond of her grandparents having said her polite goodbyes earlier. Catherine carefully turned the car on the drive and opened the boot ready for the two suitcases. "Dad, would you like to sit in the front?" Catherine too was not close to her in-laws but felt obliged for Amelia's sake to try her best to maintain some warmth towards them. Having established they were both safely belted up and all items of luggage packed she made her way down the drive to the road.

The journey to the ferry had been somewhat eventful, the normal vehicle manoeuvres without signals to be anticipated and consequences avoided. The driver of one old car pulled out of a side road without looking. Another driver opened a car door without looking and causing a car coming the other way to swerve out of the way directly into the path of Catherine's Mercedes. They arrived at the ferry terminal with about thirty minutes to spare. Sitting in the car whilst listening to Radio 3 they could view the ferry as it slowly approached the landing stage and was made fast. The passengers and vehicles were streaming off within minutes and almost immediately cars were being directed on. The crossing was calm, not too busy and a comfortable table was found. Two teas and one coffee were consumed and before long they were making their way back down to the car deck ready to disembark.

She stayed long enough at her in-law's small bunga-low to make sure they were sufficiently comfortable and well provisioned for the next few days. 'Good-byes' were exchanged and she was soon on her way home. She started the engine and checked her mirror looking for vehicles coming down the narrow lane. There were two cars parked behind hers and she noticed that one of them moved off shortly after she'd pulled away from the kerb. It was the fact that the driver had done so without indicating that had caught her attention. She was recalling in her mind the number of occasions during the day where drivers had made a manoeuvre or opened a car door without either looking or warning anyone else. 'Tutting' quietly to herself she turned onto the main road and headed for the ferry.

The driver stayed as far back as he could and tried to keep a couple of cars between him and the Mercedes. It wasn't easy when the cars between kept turning right and left and leaving him staring at the back of the car he was supposed to be following covertly! He was concerned she'd notice the car as the same one that had followed her in the morning. He wasn't sure if his cover had been blown. He slowed to allow the driver of a car waiting at a side road to slip between them and immediately felt some relief at not being in direct view again. This undercover work had lost its excitement many years ago. It was just monotonous and boring following somebody going about their daily tasks going shopping, an appointment at the dentist and hair salon, collecting daughter from school, taking daughter to school again, noting times, routines and patterns and recording everything.

* * *

At exactly 4:00 p.m. Jack and Cleo arrived to be greeted by Catherine at the front door. With introductions exchanged between the two women all three then sat in the comfortable leather chairs of the cosy room that Jack and Catherine had retired to the previous evening.

Jack felt somewhat uncomfortable remembering the soft lights, the music and Catherine in that thin silk dress. Catherine offered tea and poured three in delicate bone china cups from the tray which was already on the coffee table in front of them.

"Thank you, Jack, for agreeing to help me, I mean us. Amelia is with Gypsy at the stable in the paddock at the moment."

Jack was looking or rather staring at her face and trying to remember their first and very brief meeting fifteen years earlier. She was certainly an extremely attractive woman and Jack found it difficult to imagine having met her and for it not to have had a greater and lasting impact. He realised he'd not replied and Cleo was looking at him also now. "Sorry! ... What I mean is I'm not sure I'll be able to do much especially now that so much time has elapsed. Three years!" Jack paused, collected his thoughts and spoke again. "OK, so Catherine if you can try and tell us about what happened and what you know." He looked at Cleo briefly and continued. "Do you mind if Cleo takes notes and records our conversation?"

"No, go ahead." Catherine placed her cup and saucer on the tray with care and sat back allowing the sumptuous brown leather of the chair to embrace her. There was a faint click as the Dictaphone recorder started. "It was nearly the end of May and Paul said he'd a meeting in London on that Monday morning. He was to fly the plane to the mainland. He had a private taxi booked to take him the rest of the way." She looked at the two visitors. "Paul had a private pilot's licence and wanted to get some hours in. He shared the plane with two other business colleagues; they kept it at the airport near Bembridge." She paused briefly got to her feet and walked to the doorway from where she could look through the kitchen toward the stable. Amelia was grooming her pony.

"You said that debris from the plane was found floating in the sea. That must have been in the Solent between the island and the mainland." Jack inadvertently scratched at the stitches on his head and winced. "Any plane going down in the sea would have been seen by countless people it's one of the busiest stretches of water in the world."

"That's not where the wreckage was found, Jack. The plane went into the sea about fifty miles southwest of the island, more than half way to Cherbourg!" Catherine returned and sat back in the chair.

"Could the wreckage have floated there?" Cleo's input broke the sudden silence.

"I suppose it could eventually but it would probably have taken days to end up there." Jack turned back to face Catherine. "How long was it until the wreckage was discovered?"

She sat staring directly ahead her eyes unfocused. At the same time, her mind was playing back the events of three years ago. She held the leather arm of the chair, her fingernails making impressions in the soft surface as she tensed and then relaxed her hand. "Sorry!" She was back with them again composed and ready to recount the painful details of the search. The phone calls she received first from the airfield then air traffic control. The calls she'd made to Paul's mobile over and over again and the messages she'd left on his voice mail. The panic she felt, the sick feeling deep down inside her. Amelia's questions, her distress at seeing her mother in tears. The slow and tortured realisation there was something so terribly wrong and that from that moment on lives would be forever changed. She wanted so desperately to talk to him to hear his voice telling her that all was well. She remembered how for hours she called the mobile number just to hear his recorded message, the voice of a ghost. One who has moved on from this life but has not yet arrived at the hereafter. She recalled the telephone call the following day. Some floating debris had been spotted by a ship in The Channel but it was thought to be too far south to be the plane. The phone call later that day to confirm that it *was* his plane. The stark realisation that he'd probably perished alone in the cold water was the catalyst, the final straw.

Catherine described in cold hard detail her descent into the depression that followed and how she managed eventually after three months to claw her way back to again be a mother to Amelia. She spoke of the loneliness the deterioration in the relationship between her and her mother-in-law and the desperate financial state that had to be addressed before she could access money to pay bills and the like.

Both Jack and Cleo had listened without interruption to Catherine's story. The three sat there in silence until it was broken by two events. The tape in the recorder came to its end the machine gave a click and stopped. The three all turned to stare at the small box responsible and then turned their heads to look towards the open door where Amelia stood clutching her favourite red drink. Catherine smiled at her daughter. "Come in darling and say hello to our guests."

"You're Mister Jack, you were here yesterday." She carefully placed her now empty glass amongst the bone china on the silver tray and looked at Cleo. "Are you Mister Jack's wife? My name's Amelia, I've been grooming my pony Gypsy. Do you ride? You could come and see him. Would you like to?" The barrage of questions had caught Cleo completely off guard and as a result she was at a loss as to how to respond to this young girl. It was Catherine who spoke and introduced Cleo.

"This is Cleo who works *with* Jack, Amelia. I'm sure they'd both love to see Gypsy but not today darling another time would be good." Amelia was just a little disappointed at not being able to show the pony to the two guests but nodded her head before leaving to go and change out of her wellingtons. They all watched as the girl skipped out of the room leaving just a small piece of caked mud and a short length of straw as a witness to her presence in the room.

It was Jack who steered the conversation back to the death of Paul, Catherine's husband. "I will then if you wish, make enquiries and see if I can find anything more. I would suggest a week to start with it'll be enough time to establish if there's more to be discovered. We can take it from there should you want me to continue. How does that sound?"

"Yes, that's fine Jack and thank you. You see I need to know what happened. He has no grave that I, I mean *we,* can visit. It's so hard for us and of course his parents. They need closure as well."

There was another silence, it was clear that the meeting had run its course. The three duly got to their feet and Catherine was thoughtfully quiet as she showed Cleo and Jack out. Reliving the events had taken its toll and she was thankful that it was now over. She exchanged the normal pleasantries as they left but did not stand in the open doorway to watch Cleo and Jack as they drove away down the gravel drive.

The dark blue car parked in the gated field entrance just down the lane was passed unnoticed by Jack as he turned to glance at Cleo. "There, that wasn't too much of an ordeal was it?" He smiled at her but was aware that the expression on her face clearly indicated she was not entirely convinced. The occupant of the blue car noted the time in his book and slapped it closed.

* * *

Chapter Four

Katrina enjoyed the attentions of this rather nice foreigner. He'd visited the café each morning for about three weeks, smiled at her when she took him his coffee while seated at the small table just outside the doorway. He'd always sit at the same table. Katrina had made sure that the table remained vacant and that it had a fresh flower, a rose in the small vase. She'd blushed slightly when he'd first called her by her name. No big deal really as it was clearly printed on the small badge clipped to her blouse. But he'd taken the time to note her name. She wondered what his name was and what he did for a job. He was certainly wealthy he left her a one euro tip every day. Katrina had a number of names she'd conjured up in her mind while daydreaming at the counter. Her mother scolded her for standing idle while there were glasses, cups, and plates to be cleared and washed. She smiled back at her for it wasn't her mother that *he* smiled at, it was *her*! She looked at her watch he was late today but she was sure he'd come. He hadn't missed a day yet and he'd order his coffee and sit by the doorway and smile when she brought it to him. She stood at the entrance to the café and looked up the road but there was nobody in sight. She sighed to herself and sat at the table, *his* table and waited.

She'd probably been sitting for five minutes when she was aware of somebody standing in front of her. "Katrina." The voice she recognised immediately.

"Pardon Monsieur," she jumped to her feet and in her best schoolgirl English, "I am sorry I did not see you were already here." She beckoned him to sit and he obliged her with a smile.

"Café noir, s'il vous plait Katrina." He placed the unopened newspaper on the small table, adjusted his sunglasses and leaned back into the chair. Less than a minute later she reappeared with the coffee and placed it on the table. "Would you sit and join me for a little while, I can see you're not busy?"

She looked quickly back inside the doorway and couldn't see her mother. She was probably out in the back room. "OK, yes please." She blushed, hoped he'd not notice and quickly sat opposite him at the small table with their knees almost touching. "Just for two minutes, I can sit with you." He removed his sunglasses and placed them in the leather case he took from his bag that he'd placed on the table. She smiled and melted into his grey eyes.

They talked for what seemed ages to Katrina but in fact only about ten minutes. His name he told her was Jason and he was on business and renting a room in the town. She asked him about his job but he seemed a little vague and said something about being on a working holiday. She didn't quite understand but smiled sweetly at him and he smiled back. He seemed to be asking most of the questions but she didn't mind she enjoyed the company of this foreigner. He asked how she'd come to be working here when she obviously should be running her own business. He flattered her and she bathed in the attention. She told him about the owner and the woman he lived with. She told him she lived with her mother and that her father had died when she was five. She spoke of her mother's constant nagging and how she'd like to leave and go and live in a big city someday. Their hands were on the table fingers tantalisingly close and Katrina longed for him to reach forward and take her hands in his.

Two things happened simultaneously. His phone rang and Katrina's mother appeared at the doorway holding a tea-towel which she flicked like a whip. The spell now being broken, she jumped to her feet and went about her job clearing the adjacent tables. Her mother chastised her for fraternising with the customers while Jason saying nothing rose from the table holding his phone to his ear. He picked up his newspaper, bag and walked off down the road in the direction of the town.

* * *

From the elevated section of narrow road, the small airfield looked hardly big enough to accommodate a landing strip yet there before the two of them lay countless brightly coloured planes lined up as if for inspection. The road twisted and turned as it made its way down the hillside and soon they were through the gates and into the airfield car park.

Jack and Cleo found George asleep in the deckchair; a newspaper lay open on his lap, his left hand resting upon it. His right hand was hanging at his side and the coffee mug held by one finger of his right hand had long since tipped its contents onto the grass. His mouth was open and he was softly wheezing. He woke not with a start but in a slow and measured way first looking up then down and eventually at his two visitors. He tried to scramble to his feet to greet them properly but Jack interrupted his efforts.

"Stay in your chair George no need to jump up on our account."

"Well pull up a couple of chairs, lovely to see you, Cleo". George pointed towards his shed or office as he preferred to call it. "So what are you doing out and about? I'd have thought you'd be taking it a bit easy Jack old boy!" He looked at Jack and studied his head for a while. "Are you OK, fit for service and that? You could be 'Excused Boots' as they say." George lowered his voice. "You took a bit of a pasting back there old chap!"

"You should have seen the other guy." Jack smiled. "Anyway, we thought we'd come and take you out for a bite and a drink and bring you up to speed on events." Jack needed to fill George in with the details of the drugs case as well as warn him that he'd probably be asked to make a statement as well. It was George who'd asked Jack to look into an incident that had resulted in smashing wide open one of the largest drug operations on the Island. It was really just a formality, Jack had stressed to George, but 'forewarned is forearmed' as they say.

"I was intending to call Charlie and go for a lunch with him," George looked at his watch and raised an eyebrow, "I must have fallen asleep. I haven't even eaten my lunch, cheese sandwiches!"

George required very little in the way of further encouragement and twenty minutes later found them pulling into the small gravelled car park of a pub just a couple of miles down the road. It was warm and the air was still although the sun had risen to its highest and was beginning its final descent towards the west. The three sat at a wooden table in the beer garden. Cleo and Jack with fruit juice and lemonade and George with a pint of local bitter. While they enjoyed their drinks Jack started to tell George about his dinner with Catherine Blanchard but leaving out some of the details which would have clearly upset Cleo. He didn't want to do that!

"I remember that incident, the plane crash." George put his pint down and licked his lips. "Fine pint of beer is this Jack!" The two glanced at each other and waited for George to gather his thoughts. "Yes, it was about three years back. I didn't know his name until after the accident when it was splashed all over the local paper but he and some others each had a share in that plane at the airfield."

"What was he like George, Paul Blanchard, can you recall?" Jack was kneading his head around the wound area with his fingers. Cleo put her hand on his shoulder looking concerned. "I'm alright, just my head aching a bit. Too much sun today I expect!"

"If it doesn't feel better soon I'm taking you back to the hospital Jack, you could have a concussion. They did x-ray you didn't they?" Although his head was thumping Jack was secretly reassured by Cleo's concern for his wellbeing.

"Thanks, but I'll be OK, and yes they did check me out completely!" He held her hand and smiled at her. George coughed and continued.

"As I said old boy, never really spoke to the chap. He turned up flew off, flew back again and I rarely saw him. Never saw him talking to anyone here at the field."

"How long had he been keeping the plane at the airfield George? Was he taking flying lessons with anyone?"

"I think about six or eight months, but I can't be sure." George was thinking hard and it made him thirsty. He took another gulp from his glass and placed it down again. "He'd already got his flying ticket I believe so all he needed to do was log his hours. As far as I know nobody ever went up with him." The glass was picked up again. "I don't know whether the other chaps had their tickets they seldom ever came near the place!" George's glass was empty and it went down with a thump. "I think I found out more about him and his cronies from the newspaper than I did all the time they had the plane there. Mind you, they concentrated on this Paul fellow the others didn't get a mention in the paper other than to say they shared the plane."

"Let's order something to eat, I'm starving!" Jack picked up the menu and handed it to Cleo to peruse.

The topic of conversation moved on to food and after short deliberations, orders were placed, and a numbered wooden spoon adorned their table along with replenished drinks. George steered the conversation back to Paul Blanchard.

"So Jack, you're going to try and find out how this poor fellow perished?" He cradled the pint glass in both hands his elbows resting on the bleached and weather-beaten oak table top.

"I think so George, for a week anyway for starters. That should be sufficient time to establish what happened." Jack's eyes moved from George to Cleo. "I'm not convinced it's quite as clear-cut as it first appears, and if something is wrong somewhere then I'd like to know what it is."

"You're not convinced are you, Jack? I can tell you're getting the bit between your teeth." George smiled. "You're just like your dear old dad, he could never let go until he discovered the truth."

* * *

Michael sat with his coffee, his newspaper open on the table. Katrina had been on time today which pleased him. The town was awake with traffic noise percolating through the narrow streets along with the smell of diesel fumes and the aroma from the patisserie just a few hundred yards away. The bell on the town clock declared it to be 9am and all was well. Michael checked his watch and was suddenly aware of a shadow cast across the table. He looked up blinking and looked directly at the silhouette of a figure standing between him and the sun.

"Hello, Michael." The voice sounded strangely familiar.

Michael's eyes were squinting against the fierce rays of the sun. "Sorry? Who is it?"

"Perhaps you'll answer better to Paul. Is it Paul or Michael or are you one of a twin? And have you got some other names tucked away for later use?" The man sat uninvited at the table pushing the newspaper to one side with his hand. "You owe me my share of an aeroplane," he leaned slightly forward and lowered his voice to a whisper and with a calculated degree of menace in his voice added, "and more to the point you owe me an explanation!" Jason leaned back in the chair and smiled in a sardonic manner awaiting some response. "Think fast Paul or whatever you want to call yourself. I'm waiting and it'd better be bloody good!"

Paul was shaken and couldn't believe this was happening. He did indeed have to think fast to stall to give himself time, to get himself out of this enormous hole that had just opened up and swallowed him. Jason wanted answers *and* fast! "OK yes, we need to talk Jason but not here. Can we just go somewhere else?"

"Oh yes, we need to talk alright, or rather *you* need to do the talking. You need to explain where our plane went Paul. I want back my share of that plane." He got to his feet. "I want to know how and why you vanished and I want to know why you've been hiding from me all this time. I thought we were friends Paul, friends don't treat each other like this!" He leaned forward placing his hands down on the table and lowered his voice to barely more than a whisper. Paul sat motionless like a trapped animal that had given up the fight and awaited its fate. "I knew you were alive and *you* knew I'd find you eventually. I wouldn't give up until I found you." His eyes, steely grey were focused and piercing. "You know, you're lucky I found you, Paul. You're certainly lucky *I* found you *first!* It'll give you a chance to practice your story before you tell it to the police!" Paul stood up and without thinking picked up the newspaper from the table, he was shaking inwardly. He'd been taking the newspaper with him every morning since he took over the ownership of the café. It was more a conditioned act than a considered one. Jason gestured with a wave of his hand as he straightened up. "You lead Paul I'll be right behind you!"

* * *

The morning dawned bright with the promise of a fine day ahead. The season was at its peak and holiday makers were clogging the roads on their way to all the attractions the Island had to offer. Car-parks were filling up everywhere, buses punctuating the lines of cars crawling along at snail's pace. This was a time of plenty for the holiday trade but misery for the locals who were caught up in the chaos trying to do their shopping or on other domestic business. Cleo had made her way by bus to the Island's principal town Newport and had found the offices of the IOW County Press. After a wait of some twenty or so minutes, she'd eventually been taken through to a small office where a computer containing electronic files of all back issues of the newspaper were available for her to read. She lost little time in finding the article and having read it through requested a printed copy which was brought to her within minutes. Jack had agreed to meet up with her around mid-day and so she decided to wander the streets of the small market town and while away a couple of hours.

Jack was just a few miles away at the hospital to have the dressings changed to the wound on his head. Having waited for nearly an hour, and also having read the Island Life magazine from cover to cover, eventually his name was called. He looked up to see a smiling nurse in blue beckoning him into a small treatment room. He was ushered into a chair alongside which a trolley with instruments was positioned. The nurse consulted the file, Jack's record. She looked at him and smiled again.

"It *was* you in the paper! The undercover detective who'd discovered that drug dealer's place over the western side of the Island." She'd clearly seen the local paper or heard the local news radio account both of which were full of exaggeration if not pure fabrication with regard to the finer details which the police had not as yet released. "You're a bit of a hero I've heard." She set to work on the stitches. "This may sting a bit!"

Jack smiled but remained silent. For him, the case was closed but he didn't want to jeopardise the continuing police investigations. He winced as the old dressing was removed.

"I understand you're staying at The Weston Manor Hotel near Yarmouth," Jack's sudden head movement caught her unawares and the next stitch was pulled with unceremonious haste, "I read it in your notes in your file."

"Sorry yes. For a minute I thought the entire population of the Island had been told." Jack had been relieved there had been no reporters hounding him. As yet they didn't know where he was staying.

"Weston Manor, that's owned by that bloke who flew off in his plane and was never seen again!" She resumed the stitch pulling. "My grand-dad says it was a bit like that Lord Lucan in the 1960's. He vanished, never to be seen again you know!" Jack sighed inwardly and was fast realising that people on this Island seemed to know anything and everything about just about anybody who set foot on the place! "He was in here about three months before he vanished, thought he'd broken his ankle."

"Who, you mean Lord Lucan?"

"No, Paul Blanchard silly! I was working A & E then." She completed the careful removal of the last piece of dressing. "There, that's healing nicely! Just keep an eye on it to make sure it stays clean."

"How did he break his ankle?" Jack was suddenly interested in the nurse's small talk.

"Oh, some accident parachuting, apparently he landed heavily and thought he'd broken it but he'd only sprained it, quite badly, though!" She carefully cut and placed new clean dressings on the head wound and was now clearing away the tray. "Anyway ice packs and support bandaging did the trick and he hobbled off. Never saw him again after seeing his picture in the paper when he was killed. Shame, all that money, and there he was, gone in a flash! He was a good looking bloke too. What a waste!"

"All what money, what do you mean?" Jack was trying to sound simply conversational and mildly interested but he was intrigued by this woman's knowledge. He wanted to know more without appearing to question her.

"Oh, I don't know. He was quite a well-known businessman owning that big hotel and a few other enterprises. I suppose we all assumed he had lots of money. He had that big house and a flash car. You know all the things us normal mortals can only dream about." She was finished now and suddenly looking at her watch. "Look, I'm sorry but I do have to deal with another patient in a few moments. It's been very nice to meet you, Mr. Ramsey."

Jack found himself back in the waiting area and the next patient's name being called. An elderly lady slowly rose to her feet and began to shuffle her way towards the treatment room. He queued again and eventually handed his yellow file to the receptionist who in turn placed it amongst a pile of others awaiting their return to the bank of filing cabinets that lined the back wall. Two minutes later he was back in the fresh air and sunlight. He looked at his watch, it was noon. Remembering he'd agreed that he'd meet Cleo he made his way through the maze of paths which eventually brought him to the visitors' car park. The one and only piece of dual carriageway on the Island linked the hospital with the town of Newport and being lunchtime it seemed to Jack that every car, bus, lorry and motorbike that the Island possessed wanted to use this piece of road. With increasing irritation, Jack had managed only fifty or so yards along this stretch of road in about ten minutes. Frustrated by his lack of progress he turned off at a roundabout, parked against the kerb and called Cleo. In the hope, she could catch a westbound bus and they could meet a couple of miles out of the town. He explained his predicament.

"Great Cleo, I'll be parked near the bus stop just down the road from that small pub I've been promising to take you. Today is as good a day as any. What do you think?"

* * *

CHAPTER FIVE

George parked his old car in the corner of the car park and started off toward his wooden office, then he stopped and turned back to look at the main building. It was quite early but there were a few other cars around. He walked to the opposite end of the building where he knew Sam would be sitting in his small room on the ground floor. Little more than a broom cupboard the door had been re-hung to open outwards in an attempt to make full use of the very limited floor space. George could hear the tinny sounds of pop music, distorted though over amplification, emanating from the room long before he reached the open door. Sam sat hunched over the small desk which was awash with paperwork and turned as George tapped his finger on the door.

"Hi George, don't see you up at this end of the building much these days. You come for a parachute jump lesson?" Sam swivelled the chair around to face George.

"Not bloody likely! No, I wanted to pick your brains, can you spare a couple of minutes?"

"Sure thing, grab a perch!" Sam cleared a pile of papers from the other chair and deposited them unceremoniously on the desk amidst the others. "Paperwork, I seem to spend more time at this desk than I do actually teaching!" The slight breeze playing at the open window coaxed the top three or four pieces of paper to flutter and slide off the table directly into a waste paper bin. Sam grabbed the bin, papers and all and used it as a temporary paperweight placing in atop the pile on the desk. He turned to George. "So what can I do for you?"

"Did you ever give lessons to a Paul Blanchard, that chap who had the plane here? He flew off, crashed, never found him remember?" George eased himself into the office chair.

"Paul Blanchard?" Sam repeated the name to himself a couple of times. He was trying to recall the name. He rubbed at his temple pressing the skin and leaving a smudge of chocolate from the bar he'd been eating. "Oh yeah, I remember him. Never gave him lessons, though, didn't know he knew anything about parachuting. He kept that very quiet." He popped the last small square of chocolate into his mouth. "Why do you ask George?"

"Oh, nothing really just that the accident came up in conversation the other day and knowing that he was based here wondered if .... you know!"

"Sorry old mate can't help you."

"But this *is* the only airfield they jump from isn't it?" George was trying another tack but it was clear Sam knew nothing that would further his personal investigation. He rose from his chair. "I'll let you get on with your work, *Roger and out!*" George mock saluted Sam and turned to go.

"He probably took lessons on the mainland somewhere. We're the only school on the Island"

"Thanks, old boy!" George's turn of phrase somewhat misplaced in view of the fact that Sam was barely thirty!

* * *

He led Jason down the street to a small open park like area where there were some seats facing a pond. A young girl who was feeding the ducks emptied the bag and walked off as they arrived. The two men sat down, Paul clearly trembling, his hand still clutching the rolled newspaper. The seconds of silence accumulated, it was a couple of minutes before Jason spoke.

"So start at the beginning and tell me everything. No, wait, start *before* the beginning. I want to know if you planned this all along!" Jason's demand was urgent, the sound of the words cascading around in Paul's head made him feel violently sick.

"I didn't do it to cheat *you* really. I *had* to get away, believe me, Jason." Paul was breathing hard his mouth dry and he was sweating, and not because of the ambient temperature.

"Why, who or what did you *have* to get away from?" Jason had half turned on the seat, he was facing him. "Was it your wife and child?" He let the words sink in for a couple of seconds. "She was absolutely devastated you know. Oh, actually you don't know, do you? She was convinced you'd died, but now I think she's not so sure." Paul's head turned slightly, he was looking at Jason.

"How is she, how is Catherine? .... And what about Amelia, how's she?" Paul's voice was so faint it could have been whisked away by the flapping wings of a duck on the pond racing another competitor for a last remaining morsel of bread.

"What the fuck do you care, you haven't contacted Catherine in three years. You don't give a shit about either of them!" Jason's words were like hammer blows. "She's managing. I only saw her at the inquest three years back, but talking to people at the hotel recently, it seems she's getting her life back together."

"I *had* to get away, you don't know what I've ...." His words trailed off. Paul leaned forward and buried his head in his hands dropping the newspaper to the ground. A wisp of a breeze caught the pages turning them one by one like some unseen hand. Paul was sobbing so silently it could have been easily missed, drowned by the distant hum of vehicles on the main road that bypassed the town.

Jason eyed him with some caution, he'd trusted Paul and he'd let him down. He'd lied, schemed and cheated on all of them. How could he believe one word that this man was speaking? For three years everyone thought he was dead, had gone down in the sea along with his plane. For three years he'd been living and building a life somewhere else. Another name, another existence with new friends who'd trust and believe this man was who he said he was. Jason now knew he was alive, he'd thought so and now he'd been proved right. He kicked absently at the grass by his feet not knowing what to do. Did he trust him or should he turn him over to the police now? Leaning forward he rescued the newspaper as it started to escape, blown by another gust of breeze. Jason knew Paul was about to lie to him again. And yet he felt some sadness for what he had found here in this small French town. This man, once his close friend, seemed so much older now. Much more than the three years that had passed between them. The twin burdens, guilt, and terror had clearly eaten away at him. He seemed to Jason to be almost a shell of his former self, certainly not the astute and successful businessman he had once known him to be. Even though he sat alongside him he appeared distant, unreachable and to have no substance. A virtual being, a holographic image that might at any time disintegrate before his eyes.

Both men sat there for a full minute, staring directly ahead unspeaking, each with their thoughts. Jason's voice now calmer and quieter than it had been and also with just the merest hint of warmth spoke, breaking the silence.

"So Paul let's have the truth. What in hell's name made you do what you've done? You can tell me, you can trust me…. you *have* to trust me!"

Paul slowly turned his head toward Jason, took a deep breath and nodded. "OK, I owe you that at least." The two men sat in silent contemplation.

* * *

Lunch had been pleasant, the meal only mediocre but the company wonderful as far as Jack was concerned. Cleo was radiant, attracting admiring glances from the locals who used the pub for their liquid lunches. Over the meal, they'd updated each other on their morning's activities and were just finishing their drinks when Jack's phone chirped into life.

"Hello Catherine, how are you?" Jack was blushing slightly, remembering his mug of morning coffee and

Catherine's tee shirt. Just as quickly the colour drained from his face as he held the phone to his ear. "Catherine, take a breath! …. Now tell me what happened." Cleo imagined some dizzy scenario in which Catherine had locked herself out of her car or some such thing and that Jack in shining armour would be there in an instant, to rescue her from excess parking charges or the like.

"Oh Jack, what's happened? Has there been an accident?" Cleo put her hand on Jack's shoulder. He turned just slightly to look her way raising his eyebrows in disbelief. His phone still at his ear, his eyes were wide and staring.

Cleo couldn't make out what was being said but she could feel the hair on the back of her neck standing on end. Something was terribly wrong, something so terrible that she felt a knife turning in the pit of her stomach. "Yes now, we're leaving now. Stay there, we'll come to you. Don't go anywhere, you understand?" Jack returned the phone to his shirt pocket and picking up his glass, drained the remains.

* * *

"All I knew Paul was that you were making trips over the Channel. What you took or collected I'd no idea, didn't want to know if truth be told." Jason and Paul sat on the bench the physical distance between them less than half a metre but the damage caused by three years had made any real building of bridges almost an impossible task. Jason was trying to pick elements of truth and piece together the events of Paul's disappearance and the reasons why he'd chosen or been forced to act out his demise.

"I didn't want to do it, any of it. You have to believe me. I had no choice." Paul took a deep breath and continued. "Drugs, it had started with a few thousand pounds worth at a time. Passports, real ones, probably stolen, I don't know. Then it was bonds, shares. Fake or legitimate again, I don't know, I didn't ask." Paul rubbed at his eyes. He was telling Jason things he'd kept bottled up for over three years. He was shaking slightly.

"Who was behind this Paul? Partners others who owned the plane?"

"Yes and no! You see that was all a con as well! I didn't have the money to buy a share of the plane in the first place. You'd put up a quarter, I theoretically had put up the same and two others paid the rest."

"Yeah, I know that! But we never saw the others I don't know why they bothered." Jason leaned back feeling the rays of the sun on his face. "Did they know what was happening?"

"I had no money. I was in debt, I'd gambled away bloody thousands and I owed these guys big time. Loan sharks call them what you will, I was in their debt and the amount was going up with each month that passed. It was a way to earn my way out of the red, or at least that's what I thought. They put up the money for 75% the plane and I did the runs, taking and bringing back as required. I never asked too many questions, I was in enough shit as it was!"

"Did you pay them back?"

"What do you think? No way! The interest was so high I didn't stand a chance!"

"Did you meet them, explain the problem. Ask them to give you longer to pay them while you sorted yourself out?"

"Are you mad? They wouldn't meet me, I couldn't explain anything. They wanted their money *and* they wanted me to work for them! That's all there was. There was no compromise, that's not how they work Jason." Paul was gripping the bench with his hands, his knuckles white. "I was working for them and getting deeper in their debt with each month. There was no way out so I faked my death." He took another deep breath. "I knew I was carrying about five million in cash and shares so I jumped out of the plane near the French coast, let it crash into the sea. I'd arranged and paid some French fisherman, someone, I could trust to keep quiet for a few thousand euros, to pick me up. I was in the bloody water for nearly an hour. Almost froze to death! Anyway, I kept low, paid cash for everything so as not to leave a trail and started a new life."

"All planned out then?"

"Not really! I didn't expect to meet Maria. I thought, probably stupidly, that I could lay low for a year or so and then just turn up back on the Island and carry on as if nothing had happened."

"You bloody idiot Paul! Surely you knew that wasn't going to work?"

"I know that now. Don't you think I'd do things differently if I could start again?" Paul leaned forward on the bench placing his elbows on his knees and his head in his hands. "So there we are. That's the shit I'm in and I don't see a way out!"

* * *

George was in his element. He'd sat in the clubhouse and using the club's laptop and the wireless connection had been 'surfing' the internet. The small notepad at his side now scrawled with countless names and telephone numbers as well as websites. All the schools in the south of England offering parachute lessons. He sat back in the chair and stretched his legs forward to relieve the cramping muscles. The cold, half full mug of coffee on the table by his side was a testament to the effort, time and enthusiasm that had been sacrificed in pursuing this end. He rubbed his eyes and scanned the page before him. It would be a long job but the sooner he started, the sooner he'd be done, he convinced himself as he eased himself out of the chair and made his way over to the bar.

"Any luck George?" She beamed across at him as he handed her the laptop and then placed the coffee mug on the counter. Millie was nineteen, sun tanned and very attractive. She looked totally out of place wearing rolled up dungarees and an oil-stained tee shirt but she was happy to fill in wherever help was needed. She was working at the airfield while waiting to go off to university to study engineering. Working on engines was her passion. "Want another coffee? On the house as you only drank half of that one!" Not waiting for a response she took the mug and within half a minute had returned with a fresh one.

"Thanks, Millie, Jolly good show." He took the replenished mug gratefully and leaned forward lowering his voice. "I don't suppose the house phone could run to a few calls, I'm P.A.Y.G, costs me a small fortune!" He held up his battered old mobile phone and raised an eyebrow questioningly.

"I don't see why not George, after all, you're a paying customer!" She reached down behind the bar and placed a cordless phone on the counter. "There you go." She grinned and headed off to busy herself with cleaning tables and the like.

George sat again in the comfy chair and started to work his way down the list. Some didn't answer, the phone ringing and ringing for minutes on end. Others had answering machines; George didn't leave any message. Two numbers were unobtainable, George suspecting that the schools had folded. Four others where he did get a person at the other end of the line seemed somewhat unhelpful and suggested he call back later and speak to the manager, a delaying tactic in his view. He stretched back in the chair and pushed his legs forward, at the same time rubbing his eyes. This was proving rather disappointing, he'd hoped to be able to help Jack by doing a bit of delving himself, but it seemed he was wasting his efforts. George looked at his watch and declared it to be lunchtime. He'd spent the entire morning chasing his theory and was more than a little fed up. Millie was clearing a table nearby.

"I don't suppose there are any ham rolls left? I'm a bit peckish after all that hard work."

"I'll go and find you something George, it may not be ham. Are you willing to take pot luck?" Millie collected the empty mug and the now redundant phone. "I take it you're finished with this?" She held the phone up. "And you'll want another of these?" She waved the mug.

"Splendid!" George was suddenly interrupted by a chirping noise coming from Millie's pocket where the phone now resided. She pressed the green button and listened as a voice she did not recognise spoke.

"Could you hold the line for a second?" She handed him the phone. "I think it's for you George, probably one of the calls you made earlier."

"Hello, you called this number. I couldn't get to the phone in time. Who am I speaking to?" The voice repeated the sentence for George's benefit.

"Oh, my name's George I'm making enquiries on behalf of a Mr. Jack Ramsey." There was silence at the end of the phone. George was not sure whether he'd hung up. "Are you still there?"

"Yeah, yeah I am!" There was a slight pause. "Are you police, or tax office or something?"

"No, no old boy, nothing like that. A friend of mine Jack Ramsey is looking into the circumstances of an accident that happened about three years back." George thought and then added. "I'm doing some of the phoning around on his behalf."

"Not bloody injuries at work! What sort of accident? How did you get this number?" The voice was becoming both angry and nervous.

George was new to this and he decided the best way forward was to come clean. "Do you recall a chap called Paul Blanchard? He died in a plane crash about three years ago." He continued. "Flew off in his plane and was never seen again. Debris was found in the sea, but nothing of him, it was assumed he'd drowned or whatever." There was silence, a pause long enough for George to ask. "Are you still there?"

"Yeah I am. Interesting, how did you know I knew him?"

George's heart skipped a beat. He tried to remain calm but his next sentence came out somewhat garbled. "Did you teach him, I mean give him lessons. Did you teach him how to use a parachute?"

"Hold on a minute ...." There was a clunk as the phone was placed on a table or similar surface.

George thought for a second that he'd hung up but he could hear muffled voices in the background. A few seconds later he was back. "Sorry! We're talking nearly four years ago when I was running the jump school. That folded last year."

"Your number came up when I did a search on the computer." George suddenly realised he didn't know who he was talking to. "Can I ask your name?"

"Yeah, no worries …….. It's Ross. I owned and ran the 'Miles High Jump School' in Wiltshire, but that's all in the past, the school I mean."

George quickly scanned down his list and found the name, underlining it with his pen. "So did you give this Paul chap lessons?"

"Yeah, I did, just a few, four or five. He was good, you know, a capable sensible kind of bloke, did it all by the book. Wanted to do some AFF but never got round to it. He was very keen to have a go but couldn't arrange the time to spend on the training."

"What's AFF?" George changed the phone to his other ear and picked up his pen to scribble the three letters down.

"It's short for 'Accelerated Free Fall' you know, skydiving you'd know it better as. You jump from fifteen or twenty thousand feet. Get good at it and you can start doing tricks and the like. It's serious stuff, you've really got to know what you're about or you end up pizza, splat!"

"So *you* didn't teach him how to do this AFF then?"

"Nope, never got round to it as I've already said."

"Did anyone else at the school give him AFF lessons do you know?" George was asking all the right questions and beginning to enjoy his little detective work.

"No........ But that guy was into so much, I'm surprised he'd the time to do what he did with us. He was always on the phone arranging meetings for this and that, you know work type meetings." Ross thought for a second and added. "Shame, though, he was a talented bloke. I heard about the accident on the local news, didn't know it was him at the time. Discovered it was him when I read all about it in the paper, well what there was to tell anyway. He left a wife and kid I understand."

"Yes, it's on their behalf we're making the enquiries, albeit three years on." George was now pretty sure that this Ross couldn't shine any more light on the demise of Paul Blanchard. "Thanks for what you've been able to tell me, Ross. Can I contact you on this mobile number again?"

"Sure thing, but look I do now have to go." There was the sound of a baby crying in the background and a woman's voice impatient and stressed.

"Thanks once again Ross, we may be in touch soon. Bye for now."

"OK, cheers. It's funny though you phoning like that and asking about him, the second call this month!" There was the shortest of pauses then he spoke off the phone. "Yeah, I'm coming now...."

The throwaway remark hit George like a sledgehammer. "*What!* ..... You're telling me you've had someone *else* asking about Paul Blanchard?" George stood and looked disbelievingly at the phone in his hand when he discovered there was nobody there. He'd been talking to a dialling tone, the line had gone dead. He redialled the number immediately and waited, drumming his fingers on the coffee table impatiently. All he was rewarded with for his efforts was an answer-phone message.

* * *

The traffic was typically busy and progress slow and it was nearly 3pm before Jack and Cleo arrived to find Catherine standing at the doorway. Her eyes were red with crying and her hair, normally so finely controlled, was hanging limply. She was wearing an expensive cream tee-shirt and khaki shorts along with deck shoes, all of which were clearly designer labels. She ran to the car as it came to a rest, scrunching on the gravel.

"Jack, Jack she's gone. Amelia, she's vanished. I don't know where she is. I don't know what to do Jack." She clung to him as he got out of the car. Jack held her close and she gripped him so hard his damaged ribs sent searing stabs of pain through his body. Just when he thought he'd have to ease his own discomfort she released her hold on him.

Cleo had quietly got out of the passenger seat and came round to join them. Her emotions still close to the surface and confused, even more now as she watched this rival woman clinging to Jack.

"Let's all go inside." Jack looked at both of them in turn but making sure he held Cleo's gaze just long enough to express his concern. Catherine stood for a moment staring all around and half expecting Amelia to suddenly appear. Then she nodded acceptance and turning led the way back towards the still open door of the house.

They were some twenty feet from the open doorway when Jack was suddenly aware of a ringing noise. Catherine started running and both Cleo and Jack took up the pace. They followed Catherine into the hall where they found her clutching the telephone to her ear. She was silent but staring straight ahead, the sound of the dialling tone seemed to be reflected and amplified in the hall.

Jack stepped forward and gently eased the handset from Catherine's trembling fingers, she was visibly shaking. He dialled 1471 and waited. *"You were called today at 15.10 hours. We do not have the caller's number."* The automated voice was unconcerned and cold. He replaced the handset, turned to face Catherine and Cleo and shrugged.

"Was it someone...?" Her voice trailed off.

"We don't know Catherine. Amelia could just be lost somewhere. We don't know if that call was anything to do with her." He tried to smile. "Let's be positive!" Jack motioned with his hand and the three made their way through to the back of the house where Cleo busied herself preparing three mugs of tea. Catherine sat at the kitchen table her elbows perched on the edge and her face buried in her hands, her sobbing was just audible above the unconcerned singing of the electric kettle. Jack sat opposite and took out a small notepad and pen. He'd already noted the time of Catherine's call and now he added the time of the missed call to his list. "Catherine." He spoke softly, there was no response. "Catherine, listen! I want to get a bit more information down while it's all fresh. I'm going to ask you some questions and I want you to think carefully. OK?" There was just a pause in the sobbing and she slowly lifted her head to level her eyes at his. They were red and wet and her mascara had smudged badly. Cleo passed a box of tissues and she took one to wipe at her eyes and face.

"She was down the bottom of the garden at the stable and I thought she was a long time so I walked across the…" She stopped to blow her nose. Catherine's voice was quiet and somehow distant, speaking as if she were not there, not in that bright sunny kitchen with birds singing just outside the open window. She was in a cold dark and terrifying place, a place she'd never been before. She was scared, so scared of what might be. She didn't want to think of what *might be* because just thinking it might make it all happen, might make it all come true.

"Catherine, listen to me! What time did Amelia go to the stable, can you recall?" He looked at her and tried to get her to focus her thoughts. He knew she was in a terrible place, a place where all your worst nightmares live. A place your mind sucks you down and into, where you live out all the wicked scenarios that tear at your heart. He felt for her, he'd seen many, too many, people suffering as she was now, yet he couldn't help, he didn't know what to do. He reached out and took both her hands in his. "Catherine, listen! You must try to talk to me. I need to know so I can help."

Very slowly she began to compose herself, her shallow breathing began to deepen and she closed her eyes for a few seconds. Jack released her hands and she picked up the tissue again and held it as if it were some kind of comfort blanket. She turned to Cleo. "Thank you for the tea." Picking up the mug she took a sip. Jack and Cleo waited the few seconds which seemed an eternity before Catherine spoke. "It was just after lunch, we'd had an early one. It was about a quarter to twelve. She pointed to the kitchen clock. "I put a new battery in!" With a slightly unsteady hand, she lowered the mug to the table. "Amelia wanted to go down and groom the pony, she got changed and ran off down to the paddock, I was just doing some work in the study."

"So when did you realise Amelia was gone?" Jack felt anxious about the clumsy way he'd worded the question, but whichever way he tried to form it in his head he couldn't say it any other way. It was going to be upsetting to say the word *gone*. He just hoped Catherine wouldn't fall apart even more.

"I got tied up with some business work, a call. It was someone wanting to book a party of people for an event. And suddenly I realised the time." She pulled another tissue from the box and wound it round her finger. "It was just 2pm. I decided to walk down and see how Amelia was getting on at the stable. She must have finished grooming him by then." Catherine pulled at the twisted tissue until it broke. "She wasn't there! I called, expecting her to come walking round the corner of the stable but she was nowhere to be seen." It was at this point the terrible realisation returned and her face crumbled under the overwhelming helplessness she felt. "Amelia has been taken, hasn't she? If I hadn't been on the phone I would have been watching her from the window. Why did I have to deal with a business call? I know it, she's been abducted so don't try and tell me otherwise. She wouldn't just go off on her own."

Catherine lowered her head into her hands and started to sob. Cleo leaned forward and placed her hand on Catherine's shoulder, feeling her body trembling beneath her palm. Cleo could only imagine the utterly shattered world into which Catherine had been so cruelly and suddenly dropped. She had no words with which to comfort her, for there was nothing she could say. The loss of a child and a mother's grief were the deepest of wounds for which there was no cure. It was the cruellest pain ever to be inflicted and ever to be endured. The three were motionless, as if in some stage set that had become frozen in time, only the birdsong giving the lie to the scene.

The bird song became louder. It was but a fleeting moment before anyone recognised that the song was that of the telephone. Jack silently motioned for Catherine to remain at the table while he reached for the receiver. He listened! Silence! .... It had begun.

* * *

Chapter Six

"I still can't believe it, Paul. How in god's name have you managed to get yourself into this mess?" Jason put his head back, the full intensity of the sun scorching his face. The breeze had dropped and the full heat of the mid-day sun bore down on them seated on the bench in the small park.

"It just happened! I let things get out of control, and then there was no way back. You have to believe me when I tell you, Jason." Paul was beginning to relax just a little. The relief, at last, being able to tell somebody about the nightmare he'd endured for so long. "They're going to kill me if they find me if they discover I'm still alive."

"So how much do you owe?" Jason being unaccustomed to the heat was withering.

"I don't know. They wanted two million, but that was just before I took the other money and ....." He trailed off but then continued. "Before I had the *accident* and died! I had to do it, Jason, don't you understand? With them thinking I was dead I was in the clear and they, Catherine and Amelia would be safe, it was the only way!"

"Depends what you mean by safe, once they *know* you're still alive Paul." He let the thought sink in. Jason got to his feet picking at his shirt which had stuck to his back. "Look Paul." He was feeling uncomfortably hot. "I … *we* need to get out of this sun and I need to drink some water or something, I'm dehydrating!"

* * *

Within ten minutes of Jack's call to the police station at Newport one unmarked car and three area cars were parked on the gravel drive outside. Jack whispered to Cleo. "If anyone *is* watching the house, they'll know now that the police have been called. Talk about subtle!"

The police had certainly been thorough. Statements made, recorded, checked, and double-checked. House searched twice! Grounds searched. Catherine's friends had been telephoned. Neighbours albeit a long distance away, contacted and their gardens searched. The day had dragged on and no sign, nothing at all to indicate where Amelia may have gone. Catherine's doctor had called, she'd been prescribed a sedative which at first she'd refused to accept but as the day progressed she was eventually persuaded to take it.

The telephone rang a couple of times during the afternoon and everybody froze in expectation. Friends whom Catherine had telephoned earlier were simply phoning back to see if Amelia had been returned or been found wandering about somewhere. Eventually, the police left, the two CID officers in the unmarked car were last to leave. They would return tomorrow morning and explain how they would proceed, assuming Amelia had not been found or had returned home.

Catherine sat in the kitchen staring out through the window and down to the stable. The house felt cold and grey although the sun was shining and it was a warm day. Something had been lost, the sound of a laughing child. Amelia, who seemed to be part of that house, was missing and the house was in mourning. The minutes and hours moved slowly on, the sun was already well on its decline into the western sky and the shadows were lengthening across the garden. It became darker and Jack eventually went around the house locking and checking doors and windows. Jack and Cleo were at a loss as to what to do. Catherine certainly could not be left on her own. She was incapable of anything more than monosyllabic responses whenever she was faced with a question. *'Did she want a drink or anything to eat?'* It simply caused welling up and dissolving into tears. The officer who'd been assigned to remain with her was pleasant enough but, understandably remaining professional, appeared somewhat cold.

It was Cleo who arrived at a decision. "I'm going to stay here with her tonight as she appears to have nobody else she can call upon. Do you think that's a good idea, Jack?"

"Yes, it's a good idea Cleo if you don't mind. She certainly can't stay here on her own." Jack took Cleo's elbow and coaxed her away from the kitchen where Catherine was still seated on a stool. "It's possible Amelia has been abducted for some kind of ransom, there may well be a phone call Cleo. You need to be on your guard."

69

Jack turned and walked across to Catherine and put his hand on her shoulder. She jumped as if being violently brought out of a deep trance.

"Sorry! … Jack: any news? Is she safe?" Catherine's eyes were red and moist.

"No Catherine, no news as yet." Jack knew of no words that would ease her pain. He looked into her face. "Cleo can stay with you tonight; you need to have someone here with you. You can't be on your own."

Catherine nodded and looked towards Cleo. "Thank you. That policewoman is nice enough but I'd be pleased if you'd stay too."

Jack and Cleo walked out to the hallway. "Use the Dictaphone in your bag to record any phone calls Cleo." He kissed her. "Call me, whatever the time, if you get a call. I can be here in about ten minutes. Love you."

* * *

The room was very quiet. She couldn't tell how big it was because it was in total darkness. Her ankles were held together with metal rings. She felt them, they were cold and smooth with a short chain between them. She'd seen things like this on the television. They were handcuffs like the police used. *'Why was she handcuffed, she hadn't been bad?'* She started to cry. *'Had she been locked up by the police?'* Amelia could not understand why she was here, she was frightened, she wanted her mother and she wanted to cuddle Gypsy. She listened, she knew she'd been asleep but she didn't know for how long. She'd taken her watch off when she was mucking out Gypsy's stable and that was a long time ago. *'Was it night time already?'*

She was on the floor. There was nothing, no furniture but there was carpet! She rolled one way until she found she was against the wall. She carefully got to her feet and reached along the wall. There was a door! She felt for the handle but there was none. There was a hole where the handle should have been. She got down and rolled the other way, another wall! The room was not very big, much smaller than her bedroom at home. She carefully got to her feet and reached out to touch the wall. There was a recess, it was a window but the glass wasn't glass! It was wood, like the wood that lined Gypsy's stable. Thick heavy wood fixed to the window frame. She banged her hand on the wood but in doing so made only a little noise. The wood was thick and securely fixed with large screws.

Amelia sat down and put her hand out to the side. There was a tray on the floor with a bottle of water and a sandwich wrapped in a triangular cardboard pack. She opened the pack, difficult in the dark because she couldn't see her hand in front of her face! She smelled the sandwich, it was cheese. That was OK, she liked cheese. She was hungry and thirsty but didn't know whether to eat and drink the food on the tray. But she was very thirsty! She removed the cap and put her nose to the open bottle. It didn't smell of anything at all. She put her finger in the top of the bottle and felt the liquid. It didn't sting her finger. She took the finger out and slowly touched it to her tongue. It tasted of nothing, it was just like water! She drank from the bottle, just a little, she had to make it last, she didn't know how long until she might get some more water. She carefully replaced the top and screwed it tight. She ate one of the sandwiches and tried as best as she could to cover the other one in its wrapping to stop it going dry, she'd save it for later. She remembered the book her mother had read to her when she was younger. The story of Alice in wonderland, the drink that made you big and of the cake that made you small, or was it the other way around, she couldn't remember. She thought of the water and of the sandwich. She curled herself up into a small ball and lay on her side on the floor listening in the darkness.

* * *

The relief at being able to tell someone was tempered by the loss of control over what could now happen. Paul now had to keep Jason *'on-side'* which he could probably do. All this time only *he* knew the truth of his existence, but what if Jason decided to tell Catherine he was still alive, she'd be in danger, Amelia too. He had to keep the lid screwed firmly down.

They'd gone back to Paul's, *or Michael's,* apartment where Maria was making preparations for their evening meal. Maria was introduced to Jason as an old friend from school days and she accepted him with a shrug of her shoulders. "So am I now cooking for an extra person this evening?"

"Thanks, Maria," said, Jason. "*Paul* and I have a lot of catching up to do. It will be nice to do it over a meal."

"So if that's OK Maria, Jason will eat with us this evening."

"Why are you calling *Michael* Paul?" She said his name with a questioning look in her eyes. "His name *is* Michael."

"It's a long story, goes back to school days when I was a kid." He looked at her for reassurance.

"OK, if you say so, buy I do not understand why you have to change it. I am, how do you say, *unsure*." She looked at the two of them wide-eyed and accusingly as if she had just found then stealing apples from the tree the branches of which were less than a metre from the open window.

"Jason and I will explain everything tonight Maria. Don't worry yourself, it's all fine."

"OK if you say so." She repeated again but shrugging her shoulders. "So long as I know, then I will make the meal." She sighed and picked up her purse and an old string bag. "I go down to the market and see what else there is if it has not all been sold first, back later." With that she was gone, the door slamming shut behind her.

"Feisty one you got there." Said Jason as he sat in the chair and took the glass of water from his host. "Bet she's a goer, though!" Jason looked around the apartment. "Not a bad little set-up you've made for yourself Paul." He took a long drink from the glass. "Where did you get the money for this? Let me guess! ...... And you bought the cafe too?"

"Look Jason *your* money, your quarter of the plane. That money is safe, I haven't touched it I promise, it's *all* there!" Paul wiped at his face with the back of his hand. "I was stupid, I know ...... I'm sorry Jason."

"Stupid! It doesn't come bloody close! What was I to think eh?"

"I didn't properly think it through Jason, how was I to get your money back to you without you realising I was still alive. Once I'd done that they'd come after me. Don't you see I had to do it this way?"

"All I see is that you're in a complete fucking mess and I don't see how I can get you out of it." He drained his glass and held it out for Paul to refill. "Also I paid half the cost of running and maintaining that aircraft. The bloody insurance company has coughed up peanuts, nothing like the true value. I'm spitting blood and feathers here and all you can do is to say you're sorry!"

"I can give you your money and you can go back, just keep quiet about me. What about that? I could sort it all out in a couple of days. Just give me a few days."

"Oh fine, swan off back home again and forget that you're here making a new life for yourself. How the hell can I keep this to myself, Paul? And what about Catherine and Amelia, don't they deserve to know the truth? Are you so bloody heartless Paul, are you?" Jason got to his feet, the two men facing each other. "For Christ sake Paul, she has to be told that you're *still* alive!"

"You could just take your money and go back Jason it would be for the best. Don't you see I *can't* go back not now it's impossible? It's all gone *too* far."

"Consider this Paul, carefully consider what I'm about to say. It took me a while, but in the end, I found you, I traced you to here!" Jason turned to leave. "Think about it, if *I* managed to find you then the others, the ones you've told me about eventually will. Make no mistake about this Paul you're in a very dangerous place." Jason handed Paul the glass. "I'll see you this evening."

Paul stood holding the glass in his hand. He'd known this day would come and now it was here. He looked at the glass, his hands shaking uncontrollably. They'd come for him, find him. He had to get away, the question was away to where?

* * *

Birds were chirping their cheerful repertoire of morning songs in the hedges that bordered the gravel drive as Jack turned off the engine. In the distance, crows were adding their voice with less skill but greater volume. He closed the car door and walked slowly across the short distance to the porch. No call had been made to the Blanchard residence. Catherine had taken a sleeping pill and was still asleep when Jack arrived at the front door. Cleo opened it and let him into the hall. "I know it's very early Cleo I couldn't sleep."

"Jack, it's only six o'clock!" She took his arm and led him towards the kitchen.

"Have you had breakfast?"

"I've had a coffee but I could manage another." He sat at one of the stools. It felt strange to see Cleo standing there wearing not a lot more than Catherine had twenty-four hours earlier.

"She's still asleep." Cleo pointed a neatly manicured finger to indicate that Catherine was upstairs. "No calls, nothing at all." She sipped at her coffee and looked at Jack over the rim. "Why, do you think she might get a phone call? Amelia may have been abducted by someone wanting to ……" She couldn't finish the thought, it was too terrible to consider. "Oh Jack, this is awful, I can't even begin to imagine what Catherine is going through, it's all so cruel."

"It's possibly Paul the so-called 'dead' husband. Perhaps he's taken Amelia, or got somebody to do it for him." Jack put the mug on the worktop. "Think about it Cleo, his body's never been found, he could easily be behind this."

"You know Jack I almost hope you're right. At least she'll be looked after and not harmed."

They both turned as a figure appeared in the doorway. Catherine looked as if she'd aged twenty years in twenty-four hours. "What's happened, what have you found out Jack?" She moved toward him. "Have they found her? Oh God is she safe? Why did no one wake me?"

"There's nothing Catherine, no news as yet. But the police are coming back this morning and a search has already started." Trying to take her mind off what may be happening later Jack took her arm and led her to one of the kitchen stools. "Tell me again about your day yesterday."

"Amelia was taken for Christ's sake, what else is there Jack? I want her back. I want her back safe and unharmed." Catherine began to sob, Cleo passed the nearly empty box of tissues across and she took one. "I'm sorry I know you're only trying to help." She blew her nose, wiped her eyes and looked up at Jack.

"I want you to try and remember everything that happened yesterday. I know it's going to be painful but it may just give us something, some kind of clue." Jack suggested they all go into the lounge, the soft leather chairs affording a deal more comfort than the stools upon which they were currently perched. The three sat and Catherine started to recall yesterday's events while Cleo made notes. Jack asked questions which occasionally required Catherine to go over the event again. She was surprised how much detail of the day she had subconsciously remembered.

"How long were you working, when you were in the study yesterday?" Jack looked at Cleo who caught his eye. The recalling of events was getting now very close to the time when Amelia vanished and they knew this could result in Catherine dissolving again into tears.

"Well, I can't remember exactly."

"Was it half an hour or longer?" Jack was treading very cautiously, picking his words with great care trying not to cause more stress.

"It was probably about an hour, although I hadn't intended to work at all yesterday. You see we had this possible booking." Catherine wiped at her eyes with another fresh tissue from the box which seemed to accompany her now.

"Do *you* deal with the bookings for events and things?" Jack began to sit up in the chair. "Don't you have an events manager or someone who does that for you?"

"Well yes, I do, but they were insistent that I deal with them personally. They wanted to know a whole range of prices for corporate functions. I don't know why they could have just got all the information they wanted from the website. Jane on the switchboard at the hotel transferred the call to me here."

"What was the name of the company Catherine, did you make a note of the person calling you?"

"It's on the desk, I'll get it." She jumped to her feet and within half a minute was back with a piece of paper. "Here, 'Ragan Electronic Components' and the address, he didn't tell me exactly, but I think it was somewhere in Wandsworth. The person said his name was Hardeep Gupta." She handed Jack the piece of paper, her hand trembling. "Do you think it important Jack?"

"At the moment, Catherine, I don't know. It could well just be coincidence but I will check it out." He copied the information and handed her back the piece of paper. "I don't suppose they gave you a telephone number?"

"No Jack. Sorry. We can check to see if it was taken at the hotel but I very much doubt it." Catherine seemed a little more composed, feeling she was perhaps being of some use.

"Did they make a booking over the phone?"

"No, after all, the talking about prices and available dates, in the end, he just said he'd phone again to confirm arrangements."

"OK Catherine, so after you had concluded your conversation on the phone, what did you do next? Can you remember how long it was until ..." Jack considered his words carefully but found no easy way. "Until you noticed Amelia was missing?"

"I think about ten minutes or so, I filed a couple of papers, put away the prices and tariff printout I had been referring to and then went back to the kitchen." She started to tremble. "Then I looked out the window and she wasn't there!"

"But you didn't know she had gone then surely!" Jack spoke softly.

"Not immediately, no. I walked down to the stable and when she wasn't there, I looked in the paddock. The pony was out and Amelia was gone!" Catherine screwed up the damp tissue breaking it into shreds. "It's that booking! If only I'd just told Jane to deal with it."

A car's wheels crunched on the gravel outside the window and from where Jack was seated he could see the two CID officers who'd been at the house yesterday emerge. The next stage was about to begin. Jack knew this was going to be a difficult day for Catherine. Before he could start to speak Cleo raised her face towards him.

"Jack, go and do what you need to do. We'll be alright; I'm going to stay with Catherine. We spoke last night and she wants me to stay here with her.

* * *

She had her arms around his neck and kissed him passionately, the knife in her hand dropping to the floor narrowly missing her bare feet. "Why do you always want that I kiss you when I am busy doing the things in the kitchen?" She broke away and turned to face the vegetables on the worktop. "I have to get on," reaching down she picked up the knife and threw it into the sink, "you go and sit, I'll get this finished." Paul reluctantly moved away and, sitting down, picked up the local paper. "Tell me about your friend Jason. What time is he coming this evening? I need to know for the meal." She spoke while keeping her back to him, busy with washing the vegetables under the running water from the tap in the sink. "And I don't like that you keep the big secrets from telling me also. It's not a good thing to keep the secrets about your name not being yours. I am not sure anymore, about so many things." She turned from the sink and looked across the room. "What name are you really called? Is it Michael, as you have told me or Paul as Jason calls you?"

"Does it really matter at the moment? Call me what you like, they're *both* my names." Paul was irritated; he was off guard and just wanted to keep his thoughts to himself.

"OK then *Michael*. So what time do we expect your Jason friend?" She emphasised his name, the one *she* knew him by.

"Not sure, later sometime." Paul remained focused on the paper holding it like a shield between himself and his interrogator.

"But when exactly, I need to know for the cooking?"

"He's coming in about an hour I think." Paul raised his voice to a volume higher than needed in the confines of the room. "Look I don't know exactly what time for god's sake! ..... Does it bloody well matter what time he comes eh?" Paul threw the newspaper down and put his head in his hands. A few seconds later he raised his head to look at her but she still had her back to him. "Look, I'm sorry love. I don't mean to snap at you. I'm just a bit tired that's all. I've had a bad day and things have got on top of me a bit."

"I don't like you using swearing at me, it's not good and you shout also. And snaps to are bad, so don't do the snaps at me." She turned to face him now. "Jason. There are things he is going to be telling us that perhaps I don't want to know. You will go away and leave me. Is that what this is all going to be about Michael, is it? You are leaving me now?"

He couldn't tell her 'no' and he couldn't say 'yes' either. "Look, Maria, it'll all be much clearer to you after we have talked tonight, the three of us. Wait until then OK?" He wasn't reading the paper but he picked it up again simply using it as a distraction from what was racing through his mind. Dealing with Jason and keeping him 'sweet' and trying to stop him from bringing his world tumbling down around him. He didn't know how he was going to go about it. He didn't know whether when Maria was put in the picture she'd stand by him. It was all so complex. "Do you want me to help you?" Paul looked up from behind the paper.

She didn't answer, just sighed and turned again to her tasks. Her eyes were moist. The spell of happiness she'd known in recent months was to come to an end. Her mother had warned her about being let down by men who promised everything. It had *'turned her head'* her mother had said. It hadn't stopped her, she'd left everything to come and live here with him anyway. Perhaps she should have paid more attention to her. It was too late now. She knew that things were about to change, she didn't know how much or how great the changes were likely to be. But she certainly now knew things would change! A shiver travelled down her spine and the hair on the nape of her neck felt as if it were standing on end. She wouldn't tell him, not now. Not if things were going to go bad. *'A bad situation is no place to be bringing a baby into.'* A tear slowly formed in her left eye, she wiped it away with the back of her hand. "I'm OK. The onions, they always make the eyes go wet." She said out loud.

* * *

CHAPTER SEVEN

Jack made the phone call to his office and left a message on the answer-phone. Hearing Cleo's recorded voice, *'This is the office of Ramsey, Dawkins, and Bell, unfortunately, there is no one to take your call at the moment, please leave a message after the tone and a contact number and we will get back to you as soon as the office reopens. Thank you.'* reminded him of the recent tragic events that had led to the death of his friend and colleague. The partnership was now just the two, himself and John Dawkins.

Jack had the piece of paper in front of him bearing the name of the electronics company which Catherine had been speaking to at the time Amelia was taken. He was convinced she'd been abducted and he needed this company checked out. If it was legitimate then it could be disregarded as pure coincidence. But Jack had a feeling about it. It was too much of a coincidence, too convenient that Catherine was tied up talking to a potential client when it could, and should have been dealt with by the staff at the hotel. He tried John's mobile but it went straight to answerphone. Jack left a message and address of the company. He was at a loss to know what He could do next. He had no leads, nothing to go on. His phone chirped into life, the call was George.

"Hello, George. What can I do for you?" Jack tried to sound keen but really he could have done without him calling just at that moment.

"Done some digging old chap, on your Paul Blanchard fellow." George slammed the door of his old car shut as he shuffled into the driver's seat. "Thought we could meet up and I'll fill you in on the details. What do you say, nearest watering hole?"

"OK George, you tell me where." Jack had no plans, no ideas and no leads so he thought that thirty minutes for a spot of lunch and a chat with George was preferable to sitting in his car and just waiting for something to happen.

The pub was nothing special, which suited both of them because it meant that it was disregarded by both holiday trade and locals alike. They were able to buy a drink, find a table and order a round of sandwiches all within ten minutes. Jack filled George in the happenings at the Blanchard's, the disappearance of Amelia and the police instigating a search.

"Oh dear Jack, I am sorry. I hope the police find her soon and that she's OK. It's a terrible ordeal for a mother to have to suffer." They sat in silence for a few minutes, each considering the possibilities.

"So George, what was it that you uncovered?" Jack was trying to lighten the mood.

George explained his findings to Jack, who was both surprised and pleased at what he had found out about the businessman Paul Blanchard. While George recalled his numerous phone conversations and the discovery of the parachuting lessons Jack listened intently, not interrupting with the many questions that were forming in his mind as the story unravelled.

"I'm afraid it doesn't shed any light on how the poor chap perished." George took a drink from his glass, licked his lips and began to devour the first of his sandwiches. Speaking again, but this time still with semi-masticated chicken salad in his mouth. "Mind you, Jack, if he'd had a parachute with him he might have ended up in the drink, but alive! Eh? By all accounts, he'd done quite a lot of parachuting leading up to his disappearance".

Jack was listening to what George said the glass in his hand half way between table and lips was motionless. "You know you're on to something George, I don't quite know what as yet, but we seem to have some pieces of a jig-saw. We just have to work out how to fit them together," Jack drained the last of his drink, "assuming that the pieces we have are from the same puzzle!"

"Not with you old boy! What do you mean; the *same* puzzle?"

"George, I'm convinced there's a link between the disappearance of Paul Blanchard three years ago and the disappearance, or call it abduction of his daughter yesterday." Jack placed his glass on the table with slightly more of a thump than he'd intended, making George jump. "What *you've* discovered about Paul Blanchard's skydiving activities may just give us the key to that link."

"Oh another thing," said George, "it may just be a coincidence but when I was talking to this Ross chap he just happened to mention that he'd had someone else asking about Paul Blanchard just a couple or so weeks earlier."

"If somebody else is looking for him George then that means there's a strong chance he *is* still alive! Paul Blanchard is hardly likely to kidnap his own daughter. It's more likely she's been taken as a means to get information of his whereabouts."

"So there are others looking for him Jack!" George's face contorted in deep thought.

Jack's phone rang and taking it from his pocket he put it to his ear. "John, that was fast work, I didn't expect to hear back from you quite so quickly!" He listened to the voice on the phone, punctuating the breaks with affirmatives. "Yes, OK John and thanks for the information. Talk soon, bye." He replaced the phone in his pocket and picked up the two empty glasses. "Would you like the same again George? And I'll tell you a little story about non-existent electrical companies."

* * *

There were questions, more questions, tissues and endless cups of tea. Catherine was exhausted and Cleo was becoming more than a little annoyed at the slow speed with which the police investigation appeared to be going. At one point she was able to talk to Annie the woman CID officer assigned to the case who assured her that a search of the area had already begun and that houses in the area were being visited. The telephone line had been tapped and any calls made to the house could be recorded and hopefully traced. Cleo was unsure how to react to the fact that there'd been no news. She considered trying to comfort Catherine by saying that no news was good news, but decided not to use such worthless platitudes. Catherine was an intelligent woman, to say such things would be pointless. The comments would have no worth and offer no comfort. She wanted her daughter back and nothing else would put a stop to the unbearable pain that tore at her insides.

Cleo had made yet more mugs of tea and handed one to Catherine just as the telephone rang. In her haste to get to the handset Catherine sent the mug flying to the floor, the hot liquid splashing against Cleo's legs. The woman CID officer raised her hand to allow the phone to ring three times before Catherine picked it up.

"Hello? ...." Catherine's voice was trembling. "Hello, who is it?"

The automated voice spoke through the loudspeaker positioned alongside the telephone, it was distant and cold. "Have you been mis-sold a loan or mortgage protection policy in the last ten years? Did you know that ...."

"Christ all mighty!" She threw the receiver back into its cradle and fell into a heap on the sofa sobbing. The others in the room just looked on helpless.

* * *

She was riding over open grassland where sheep in the distance were busily nibbling at the lush green grass. The sun was beating down, it was hot but the air was cooled as it rushed past as Gypsy cantered up the incline to where her mother was sitting on a blanket with a picnic. She called out, but her mother was looking out to sea. She couldn't hear her. She called again, louder but her mother didn't look in her direction. Gypsy was slowing to a trot then a walk. She tried to kick him on but he stopped walking altogether. She was shouting at her pony, she was shouting at her mother but no one could hear her. *'What was the matter with them, were they deaf? Couldn't they see her?'* They were fading, getting harder to see clearly. The colours were weakening, bleaching. She tried to blink but her eyes were fixed and the picture was vanishing. She called out again, louder, and this time she heard a noise. It was a noise unfamiliar to her, a scraping. A voice, she thought, muffled. She couldn't make it out. It was a talking voice, talking quite loudly she thought, but coming from a long distance away. The voice had stopped. She opened her eyes but there was no Gypsy, there was nothing, only the blackness, the silence and the carpet against her face. She suddenly remembered where she was and started to sob uncontrollably, the tears running down her cheek and onto the carpet.

* * *

Jack followed George in his car, the two making their way to the airfield. They found it surprisingly deserted considering what a warm sunny and clear day it had turned out to be. The main office building was just a short walk from the car park and the two men fell into step making their way across the concrete area to the side of the building.

"I doubt we'll find much out Jack, being a few years ago now. Still, nothing ventured, as they say, old boy!" George opened the door and the two men entered the office.

Bill Tidy didn't live up to his name. The office was a complete mess with old half full coffee mugs used as paperweights to secure the masses of paper that seemed to occupy every horizontal surface. The office was empty. Bill was nowhere to be seen.

"He's supposed to be here to answer the blessed phone if nothing else!" George clearly had little time for the current incumbent of the office. He moved a cardboard box from one of the chairs and then finding nowhere to place it returned it to the chair. "Damn, I was hoping to sit down!" He pointed to a pair of filing cabinets at the back of the room. "Bill has only been here two years although to look at this lot you'd think differently!" He made his way over to the nearest cabinet. "Anything pertaining to more than two years ago and there's a good chance old Taffy, Bill's predecessor will have filed it in here."

George started opening and closing drawers, looking at files and then disregarding them. "This is all fairly recent stuff, but it's all over the place not in chronological order." He moved his attention to the other filing cabinet. He opened the top drawer and looked inside. "Some of this stuff is over ten years old." As he moved down the drawers the files became more recent. The third drawer yielded files from three to four years back. George pulled out a thin brown A4 file and passed it across to Jack. "Here you go old chap, I think this is what we're looking for." George closed the drawer and moved across the office to where Jack was studying the file. "Not a great deal of information I'm afraid. It's just maintenance stuff, refuelling costs and the like. I don't think there is anything here that is going to help us."

Jack studied the file, looking down the lists, the maintenance schedules, a log of hours flown and fuel purchased. "I think you may be right, there's nothing here which is out of the ordinary." He handed the file to George who placed it back in the filing cabinet. "Bit of a dead end George, I don't think we're going to find anything that suggests it wasn't anything but just a terrible accident." Jack looked around the office taking in the pictures of the light aircraft, mainly photographs of planes that had used the small airfield. "You say this Paul Blanchard kept very much to himself, didn't really have much to do with anybody here. Am I right?"

"I think so Jack, there are very few people still here who even remember him. He would usually turn up on his own and off he'd go. I think only the control tower ever held a conversation with him."

Jack placed his hand in his pocket and took out his phone which was vibrating. "Hi Cleo, is there any news?" Jack listened as Cleo brought him up to date on the police visit, the further questioning and search update. "George and I are just at the airfield clutching at straws trying to find out anything which may raise a question mark over the disappearance of Paul Blanchard. We seem to be drawing a blank at the moment, but I'm not convinced there isn't more to this story. I'll call by at the house later today. Try to keep her positive Cleo, and do take care, let me know the moment anything happens." Jack placed the phone back in his pocket and turned to George. "Let's go, I don't think there is anything here that is going to help us."

* * *

Jason decided to walk after all it was only a short distance from where he was staying along the main road to the turning where Paul had his flat. The air was still warm even though the sun was now low in the western sky. The residents of the small town were going about their daily chores. A game of boule was in full swing in the small square. The smell of French cigarette smoke seemed to hang in the air above the players. Jason had been thinking about this moment ever since Paul had vanished that fateful day. He'd been questioned by the police investigating the accident. He knew that plane and it was in tip top condition. He was able to show them the maintenance log book and prove the plane was A1. He attended the inquest, listened to the theories and saw the photographs of the flotsam that had been found floating in the sea. The accident was blamed on a mechanical failure in the end, but Jason knew different. He now knew the reason behind the flight that day.

He was early and so decided to stop at the café for a drink. Katrina would still be working and it would be nice to spend half an hour in her company. He could see the café just along the road and started to increase his pace. The road was quiet with little traffic, the odd car or local scooter meandering along the streets. The café was on the other side of the road and Jason moved to cross. He stepped off the kerb just as the car accelerated. He turned to face the oncoming vehicle his eyes wide, his body frozen. He'd seen that car before! In that small moment of time, he understood his fate and the reason why his part in the life of Paul Blanchard had now concluded.

Katrina turned when she heard the collision. She saw the body being dragged along the road under the front of the car. She dropped the tray she was carrying and started to run screaming and waving her arms at the driver. The driver floored the throttle and the car bounced over the body in the road before vanishing down the hill in a cloud of dust. She reached the body and quickly knelt by its side. The body lay twisted and contorted looking like an abandoned mannequin's dummy. She recognised the jacket and the expensive watch. The face at first she did not recognise, but she knew it was him. He stared at her, his eyes wide open and fixed. The bloody pulp of his face peppered with tarmac from contact with the road. She felt for a pulse but she knew one would not be found. He was gone, and as the tears began to run down her cheeks others gathered round her in shocked amazement, staring first at the body and then in the direction the car had taken escaping the scene. There was nothing further to be done while they waited in stunned silence for the emergency services to arrive.

Paul looked at his watch and in the distance, he could hear the wail of sirens. The hairs on the back of his neck tingled. It was time, time to act. He closed the door and slowly turned the key.

* * *

When she woke the room was illuminated by a single unshaded light bulb set high in the ceiling. Lying still she looked about the room. The walls were plain, as was the carpet. She looked at the door, it was shut, locked. High up in the middle of the door was a small round spy hole. Just like the one in the front door at home. To the side of the door, she saw a square plastic plate screwed to the wall. She knew that was where the light switch should be. The light must have been switched on from somewhere else she thought to herself as she slowly got to her feet. There was a chair and a table, very plain, just wooden. On the table were a new bottle of water and more cheese sandwiches. Amelia sat up at the chair and unwrapped the sandwich. There were other items on the table, a small Dictaphone similar to the one she had seen in the office at home. Alongside it was a letter, not written by hand but word processed and printed. She picked it up and started to read.

If you want to go home use the Dictaphone to record the following message.

Hello, Mummy, I'm safe and am being looked after.

I will be released and can come home but only if they get information about where Daddy has gone.

Tell them where he is Mummy, and I will see you soon.

Amelia held the piece of paper in her trembling hands and with a faltering voice read it again, this time aloud and into the microphone on the machine. She placed the Dictaphone on top of the paper and unscrewed the cap on the water bottle. Picking up the Dictaphone she switched it again to record, "I love you, Mummy". She drank some of the water and ate one of the sandwiches. She listened, the room was quiet, no sounds from outside the shuttered window. She turned towards the door. The centre of the spy hole went from being bright to dark. She thought she heard footsteps fading away. Suddenly and without warning, the room was plunged into total darkness. Everything vanished from sight. Amelia put her arms on the table and rested her head on them. She sobbed quietly before drifting off again into deep sleep.

The sound of bolts being drawn and a key been turned in a lock did not rouse her from her drug induced slumber. The additive in the drinking water had done its job. The door opened slowly and quietly, the dim light from the passage illuminating the room. The figure entered the room and walked silently to the table. The hand reached out and picked up the Dictaphone. The door closed, the key again turned in the lock and the bolts slid back to secure the room.

* * *

CHAPTER EIGHT

What remained of that day slowly dragged on. The police again visited the house but with no new news, it only caused Catherine to fall deeper into her dark well of despair. Jack arrived in the early part of the evening. Cleo met him at the front door having heard his car tyres on the gravel. Catherine had taken one of the sleeping tablets prescribed by her GP and had taken to her bed. Jack placed the carrier bag on the table in the kitchen and started to unpack a Chinese ready meal which he placed in the microwave.

"It's not looking good is it Jack?" Cleo took two glasses from the cupboard and poured mineral water for of the two of them. "She's been taken, hasn't she? If she were just lost, wandered off, she'd have been found by now. Somebody's taken her." A shiver traced a pattern down Cleo's spine. "Oh my god Jack, what if she's......" She couldn't finish the sentence, the thoughts running through her head were two horrible to vocalise.

Jack took a sip of the water and carefully placed the glass down on the table. "Somebody knows that Paul Blanchard is still alive, and they are desperate to find him. Amelia is being used to get that vital information from Catherine."

"But Jack, Catherine knows absolutely nothing, I'm sure of it. She's no idea whether Paul is still alive or not. She was convinced he'd died in the plane crash." Cleo took two bowls from the cupboard and divided the steaming contents from the microwave between them. They sat at the table eating the meal, neither of them knowing what to say.

When they'd finished eating Jack rinsed the bowls and cutlery and placed them in the dishwasher. "It's all too coincidental Cleo. Tomorrow I'll try and contact the two guys who shared the plane with Paul in the hope they may know something that can help us. It's a long shot, but I have to try something."

Cleo and Jack walked to the door. He held her in his arms and kissed her tenderly on the lips. She stood in the doorway illuminated by the porch light and waved as Jack's car moved off and down the gravel drive. He raised a hand to wave at the uniformed officers sitting in the police car at the edge of the drive leading onto the road. The roads were quiet and the night was warm. Jack opened the driver's window and allowed the breeze to caress his arms and face as he made his way back to the hotel. His brain was full of thoughts about how he was going to proceed the next day. He looked at the clock on the dashboard and realised it *was* the next day!

* * *

Cleo had woken early and by 6.30am she was showered, dressed and downstairs making coffee in the kitchen. She was contemplating filling a bowl with some muesli or toasting bread when she heard the sound of the letterbox flap in the hallway being opened and post cascading onto the floor. She walked into the hallway catching sight of the fluorescent orange waistcoat of the postie through the window as she dragged her trolley across the gravel drive. Picking up the post, Cleo returned to the kitchen and placed it neatly on the table.

The sun was shining in through the kitchen window and she could hear birds singing in the garden. Cleo looked down the garden to the gap in the hedge where she could see Gypsy's stable. The pony was tied to a ring by the open stable door and happily pulling pieces of hay through the holes in a hay net tied high in the doorway. A wheelbarrow sat just inside the open doorway and Cleo could make out a slightly rotund female figure mucking out the stable.

She was suddenly aware of a presence behind her and turned to find Catherine had entered the kitchen. She was dressed in jeans, T-shirt, and espadrilles and although her clothes were casual, they were clearly very expensive designer items. Her hair and makeup had been carefully done. The sleeping tablets prescribed by her GP and taken the night before had done their job. Outwardly Catherine looked to be in command and ready to face the day. Cleo poured a mug of coffee from the machine and handed it to Catherine. She sipped at the hot liquid, smiled briefly and placed the mug down on the table.

Catherine was looking down the garden and after a few seconds of vacant silence she spoke, her voice sounding uncharacteristically upbeat. "That's Beryl she lives just a little further along the lane. She helps with Gypsy, mucking out and that sort of thing. I'll take her a coffee and some toast, she never gets around to eating breakfast!" She busied herself preparing a tray to take down to the stable. Cleo was a little unsure about Catherine's change of demeanour. She appeared different this morning as if a corner had been turned. It was unsettling, not the same Catherine she'd dealt with yesterday, the mother who'd lost a child and for whom her world had been torn to shreds. Cleo watched closely as Catherine buttered toast, busying herself with activity. Although outwardly Catherine looked strong Cleo could still sense the pain behind the façade. Catherine's hand began to shake and the knife clattered to the floor, the metallic sound amplified within the hard surfaces of the kitchen. "I can't do it! I need to be brave but I can't do it! I know they're going to ask me to appear and make an appeal on the news. How am I going to do that Cleo?" Her voice was hardly more than a whisper.

Cleo stepped forward and placed her arms around Catherine's shoulders. Catherine began to cry, silently at first. And then, as her emotions took the upper hand, she dissolved. The two women stood there, one in pain and torment, the other helpless other than to offer a shoulder upon which to cry. After what seemed to Cleo a long time Catherine began to pull herself together once again. The two women sat at the kitchen table and drank their coffee while the birds in the garden continued their songs.

For something to do and also to occupy her mind, Catherine started to look through the post which was still sitting on the kitchen table where Cleo had placed it earlier. She divided it into three distinct piles, a task she practiced each morning and today it was a routine upon which she focussed her mind in an attempt to blot out the reality of her situation. By far the largest pile was that destined for recycling, advertisements for pizza home delivery services, double glazing and special offers from the local garden centre. The second pile was post misdirected but intended for the hotel. She'd get somebody to come and collect it later. There were two items of post remaining both of which had her name and address. She picked up the first letter and recognising the postmark and handwritten envelope placed it to one side.

"It's just a *thank you* from my in-laws. They were staying with me for a few days. Her hand was shaking slightly as she picked up the last letter. It was a small white envelope with her name and address electronically printed. She carefully slit open the letter with a small knife and she'd taken from the cutlery drawer. She emptied the contents onto the table. The two women stared at the object before them, neither one speaking but both aware of the significance of the item upon which their interest now focused. Catherine moved to pick it up but Cleo realised a greater potential value in not allowing the item to be handled.

"Stop, don't touch it!" Cleo quickly moved her hand forward and rested it upon Catherine's wrist to stop her making physical contact with the item that was now the focus of their attention. She looked at Catherine and their eyes met. "There may be fingerprints Catherine! We must take care just in case." Carefully and without touching it, Cleo took the handle of the coffee spoon and pushed the flash drive back into its envelope. "Just sit there and drink your coffee. I'll take the tray down to Beryl." Balancing the tray on one hand Cleo opened the door and made her way down to the stable.

The woman was still filling the wheelbarrow as Cleo approached. She could hear a tuneless whistle but did not recognise the song. She turned as Cleo arrived at the open stable door. The woman looked older than her 50 years, her brown hair streaked with grey hung limply down to her shoulders. Her jacket dotted with hay and smudged with damp patches. She turned and smiled as Cleo placed the tray on an upturned bucket. "Thank you, my dear, how's Catherine, is she all right? I thought I'd tidy up the stable, put Gypsy out for a couple of hours." She picked up the mug of coffee, noisily sipped at it and placed it back on the tray. "Lovely, just the way I like it."

"I'm Cleo. I'm staying here with Catherine for a while. Until they find ...." Cleo's voice trailed off as she turned to look back at the house. The two women were quiet for a few seconds clearly deep in their own thoughts.

* * *

Jack was awake early, the sunlight streaming through the window and the distant sounds of the early morning traffic were sufficient to rouse him from his shallow sleep. It was not quite 6.00am but he showered, shaved and dressed ready for the day. It was too early for the hotel breakfast so he made do with a cup of coffee in his room. He'd managed to find the names and contact numbers for the two other partners who'd shared the plane with Paul Blanchard. The information was not up to date as it had been taken at the time of the inquest. But it was a start, Jack was sure that there was something more to be discovered. In Jack's mind there had to be a link between the disappearance of Paul Blanchard and the subsequent disappearance of his daughter Amelia. Jack took the phone from the bed and dialled the first of the two numbers. He waited but there was no answer, eventually, it went to answerphone. He left just a short message asking to be phoned back. He then tried the second number which he discovered was unobtainable. He threw the phone back onto the bed and drained the remainder of the coffee which was now only tepid. He looked at his watch it was 7.15 and he wondered whether it was too early to phone Cleo. It started to ring and Cleo's name appeared on the screen. He grabbed the phone and placed it to his ear. "I was just about to call you. Is there any more news?" Cleo filled him in with regards to the memory stick's arrival in the post. "Right, don't touch it Cleo and you will need to phone the police."

"It's already been done Jack I phoned them before I phoned you."

"Are you in the house at the moment?" Jack asked. He could hear noises but wasn't quite sure what they were.

"No Jack, I'm down at the stable, Catherine is in the house. I'm just talking to the woman who comes to help out with mucking out Gypsy in the hope so she may have seen or heard something. Unfortunately, she wasn't around at that time." Jack could now picture the noises he had heard as Gypsy pulled more hay from the hay net and began grinding it in his teeth.

"I'll come over to the house now. See you in about half an hour." Jack ended the call, placed the phone in his pocket and grabbed his jacket and keys.

Cleo walked slowly back up the garden path, the birds were still singing, the air was full of sweet scent from the flowers and shrubs that lined the route back to the kitchen door. The kitchen was quiet and empty. Not even the tick of the kitchen clock on the wall broke the silence. Cleo looked up at the clock then at her wristwatch and realised the clock had again stopped. She called Catherine's name but there was no reply. She called again louder this time a feeling of panic rising inside her. Looking at the kitchen table she realised that the small package containing the memory stick was missing. She ran from room to room but the entire ground floor was empty. She called again this time louder but still there was no reply. Looking out from the drawing room window she could see that Catherine's car was still parked on the drive. She made her way to the hall where she noticed the security chain still in place.

Climbing the staircase to the first level she tried Catherine's bedroom door. It opened quietly and Cleo entered the room. Although it was a bright day, the drawn heavy curtains rendered the room in dark shades. Glancing around she could see the door to the en-suite was ajar but that there was no light from inside. On the other side of the room was another door which was closed. Cleo quietly padded across the thick carpeted floor and stood with her hand poised to turn the handle. Closing her eyes and focusing her mind she was aware of voices from behind the door. Breathing deeply she slowly turned the door handle and pushed open the door. Cleo entered the room which was furnished with an office table and leather chair at which Catherine was sitting, her head resting on her arms spread on the table before her. She turned as Cleo entered, tears were streaming down her face and she was sobbing uncontrollably while the sound of her child's frightened voice filled the room.

* * *

Jack battled with the early commuting traffic, a number of holiday makers, a large coach – its driver clearly unaccustomed to Isle of Wight roads – and two tractors on his drive to Catherine's house. As he turned off the road and negotiated the gravel driveway he became aware of a number of cars parked at the house. In addition to Catherine's Mercedes were two vehicles he didn't recognise. He parked his car and walked over to the front door where he found his entry barred by a woman dressed in a blue casual top and jeans. Her dark hair caught into a loose ponytail, lack of excessive makeup and discreet trainers immediately indicated to Jack that he was being confronted by the CID. Before the woman had a chance to open her mouth Jack took a card from his wallet and handed it to the woman explaining his presence. She studied him for a few seconds and then nodded her acceptance, letting him through to the hallway. Jack found Cleo sitting at the table in the kitchen and as he entered the room she turned, stood and walked over to him.

"Sorry Jack I'm afraid she opened the file on the flash drive. I'd only gone a few minutes, taking a drink down to the woman who mucks out the stable. When I got back I couldn't find her, Catherine that is. I searched all around and eventually found her in the small office off her bedroom." Jack gently kissed her forehead and stroked her hair.

"It's OK Cleo don't worry, just as long as she hasn't wiped the drive."

"She said it was Amelia, she said also she thought she was reading from a script that had been prepared. She said she was clearly concentrating on just saying what was written and not speaking as she normally does at *'nineteen to the dozen'*. She was distraught Jack and I just didn't know what to do. I phoned the Police and they arrived within twenty minutes and took control." Subconsciously Cleo started to busy herself making Jack a cup of coffee. "She's still with them now." Cleo inclined her head indicating the lounge, or snug as Catherine preferred to call it. Jack could see that the door was closed. He took the hot coffee as Cleo passed him the mug and they both sat at the table. "You should have seen her Jack, she was in pieces. What cruel bastards are doing this?"

"At the moment Cleo I haven't a clue. But I'm convinced that there's a connection between what's happening now, Amelia being taken and what happened three years ago."

"But why take the child? Catherine doesn't know anything. She doesn't know whether her husband is dead or alive. After all, isn't that why she asked you to help, to try and find him?"

"Clearly somebody believes Catherine knows more than she's letting on." Jack took a sip from the mug. The coffee was still very hot and he placed it back on the table. "Amelia is being used by somebody who's determined to find Mr. Paul Blanchard and that, I am sure, is the reason she's been abducted".

Cleo was pushing the other pieces of post around on the table with her fingers and without looking up she spoke. "Why did she suddenly decide to ask you find out what happened to her husband? And why wait so long? That's what I don't understand Jack. Why so long, three years! Why wait for three long years not knowing the truth." Cleo stopped pushing the post and drummed her fingernails on the table, the staccato tapping amplified by the hard surface.

"I don't know Cleo. I have to admit it does seem a bit strange to leave it all this time. I suppose she just got to the point of needing to know. You know, to get some sort of closure. I'm sure her asking me to help was only prompted by that chance conversation on the ferry last month. I don't think it's that strange really." Jack decided that it was probably best if Cleo didn't know about Catherine's drunken pass at him. He felt slightly guilty keeping that from her but he was doing it with the best of intentions. He tried to steer the conversation back to the present. "I suppose the police have got the memory stick now."

"Yes Jack, they have but Catherine made a copy for you." She took from her pocket the small metal case and placed it in his hand. "There's a laptop in the conservatory that she said we could use."

"Come on then, let's go and see what we can find out." Cleo led him out through the dining room and into the large conservatory which was already becoming pleasantly warm. The laptop and was sitting on a small wicker glass topped coffee table against the wall. She fired it up and inserted the memory stick. There was only one file and upon opening it the recorded message sounded eerily tinny emanating from the small laptop's speakers and echoing on the hard surfaces within the confines of the conservatory.

They both listened without saying a word. Jack's eyes closed as he tried to focus on the voice of Amelia. Shaking his head slowly and opening his eyes he spoke. "I can't get much from this." He looked below the table's surface and noticed a pair of headphones on the shelf. "Ah, let's try these." Picking them up, he plugged them in and handed them to Cleo. "Close your eyes try and concentrate just on what you hear. Try to block out everything else and just listen and tell me what you think."

Jack replayed the voice and Cleo sat motionless cross-legged on the floor, her back straight and her chin slightly raised in concentration. She took slow deep breaths focusing on the sound of Amelia's recorded words in her ears. A small tear formed and began to trace a vertical path down her left cheek as she listened intently. Eventually, her head dropped forward as the child's voice fell silent. Tears now running freely down both her cheeks, Cleo removed the headphones, placed them carefully down alongside the laptop and wiped her eyes with a tissue she'd slipped from her pocket. After a moment she turned to face Jack, her deep brown eyes wet, wide and wild with anger. "You have to get this evil bastard, Jack." Cleo's shoulders started to shake as she descended into another sudden and uncontrollable burst of crying. "You have to find Amelia and get her back safe!"

Nothing Jack could say would soften the fear, hurt, and anger that were clawing at her. He knelt down at her side and put his arms around her allowing her to bury her head in his shoulder. She continued to cry, then to sob quietly for what seemed like an eternity but was only minutes. Jack's shirt felt damp, the tears, mascara, and lipstick had merged and left their token marks. He remembered he had a spare in the car. It didn't matter; he just stayed there and held her until the sobbing subsided, while in his mind wondering what the hell he was going to do, and where in all this mess he was going to start.

* * *

Chapter Nine

Katrina sat by the body sobbing quietly. She'd known him only a few days, not the time to allow love to blossom but time enough to want to know him better. All that had now been taken from her. She was sad, both for herself but also for the dead man at her side. He'd now never grow old. She wouldn't have the chance to get to know him, and perhaps even to marry him. She was angry, it had all happened so quickly. She didn't have a chance to stop it. So many emotions were swirling around in her head she felt as if it would burst at any second.

She reached into his jacket pocket and found his leather wallet. Slipping it carefully out and opening it she took out his driving licence. With the pad and pencil, she had for taking orders, she quickly copied the name and address down. She noticed there were a couple of other credit cards and about three thousand euros in notes. A small piece of paper fell out and was about to be blown away by a gust of wind but Katrina pinned it to the road with her foot before reaching out to pick it up.

There was a sudden noise as the ambulance arrived and within seconds she was being lifted to her feet and out of the way to enable the paramedics to establish what she already knew. Voices seemed to hum all around her, she was in a daze. More people had gathered and police were questioning the bystanders who were gesticulating in her direction. A senior police officer walked towards her and she passed the wallet to him. He grunted a brief 'thank you' almost inaudible above the noises all around. He stank of sweat and nicotine and Katrina took an involuntary step backward repelled by the affront to her senses. He too opened the wallet and removed the driver's licence. With his other hand, he removed his phone and took a picture of the licence. He then placed it back in the wallet and put the wallet into an evidence bag, sealing it and initialling it before handing it to another police officer standing nearby. Katrina gave her name to the second officer who appeared far more concerned and sympathetic as well as smelling of expensive cologne, which she instantly recognised but could not put a name to. He duly recorded her name, address and a brief account of what she'd witnessed.

Katrina became aware of her arm being gently held and being slowly walked back across the road to the café where she was encouraged to sit at one of the outside tables in the shade. It was one of the elderly gentleman customers who'd followed her when the accident had occurred. A jug of iced water and a glass appeared immediately and the elderly man poured, with a shaking hand, a glass for her to drink.

In what appeared to be no time at all, the ambulance and then the two police cars moved off. Katrina watched as if viewing a film, the plot of which she'd no interest or understanding about what was happening. It was as if nothing had occurred. Cars and vans drove past in both directions now. The road had returned to normal and people went about their daily routines, all except for those who'd seen the incident, unaware of the fatality which had so recently scarred that perfect summer day.

Katrina sipped the water and held the glass to her forehead, the cold numbing the pain, or at least causing her to focus on the cold sensation on her skin. She put the glass down and reached into her pocket for a tissue to wipe her eyes.

Unnoticed by her, the small piece of paper fell to the floor and was carried by the breeze into the doorway where it became lodged. She blew her nose and replaced the tissue in her pocket. The elderly customer, having seen the paper fall, got to his feet. He walked slowly over to the café entrance and stooped down to pick the folded sheet from the open doorway. With slow but deliberate steps he returned to where Katrina was sitting and placed it on the table in front of her. "Mademoiselle….." Touching his hat and tilting his head towards her he made his excuses and left her with her jug of water, the ice now melted, and the piece of folder paper now held in her trembling hands.

* * *

Maria had to keep changing hands, the shopping bag, heavy with food she'd bought for the meal, was hurting her fingers. She put the bag down massaged her hands and turning the handle pushed at the door which remained obstinately shut. Cursing under her breath she searched in her handbag for the key. She eventually found it. The place was empty and quiet. Maria called out Michael's name but there was no response. She was going to continue to call him Michael she'd decided, after all, it was Michael she'd fallen for not this Paul person who seemed strange to her. Dragging the bag through to the small kitchen she started to prepare the meal for the evening. Maria hated the quiet, it made her feel lonely, and because she disliked the emptiness all around her she switched on the radio for company.

* * *

Paul had thrown a few clothes into a small bag, insufficient to arouse Maria's suspicion but enough to get him by for the next few days. He'd pontificated whether to take *his* passport or that of Michael Collier, the pseudonym he'd been living under for the past three years. Undecided he took both, the decision too difficult to call. Leaving whilst Maria was shopping seemed a cowardly thing to do but it was too late now. He didn't want to face her. He couldn't listen to her tirade and he didn't want her placed in danger. She didn't deserve that.

Throwing the bag into the car he started the engine and negotiated the narrow streets leading south out of the town. As he drove along he looked down at the fuel gauge, the level of which he knew to be wildly optimistic. The car was only half full when he last used it and he couldn't remember how long ago that was. He did know Maria had used the car a couple of times. The gauge was showing just over the quarter mark, unlike the temperature gauge which was hovering dangerously near the red sector. He'd put 50 kilometres between himself and his life in the sleepy French village he'd started to call home. He knew running away was not the answer to his problems but for the time being, it seemed the only option open to him. He pushed on, 60kph being just about the limit for the old Citroen on the narrow road as he headed south. He hated the idea of leaving Maria without telling her why and decided to stop and call her. He'd say he'd been called away urgently. In his mind, he was convinced she'd see through any story he concocted so he may as well tell her the truth. He had grown very fond of her in spite of her fiery ways. Paul had noticed that she'd changed somehow. He wasn't quite sure how the changes were subtle. He couldn't say exactly why, but he remembered Catherine and how she had become a different person when she became pregnant with Amelia. The sudden realisation hit him like a sledgehammer. He jammed his foot hard down on the brake pedal and the old car groaned and eventually slewed to a standstill, the smell of hot tyre rubber and engine coolant erupting from beneath the bonnet.

* * *

It didn't make any sense to her. It was just a list of names, some with phone numbers and others with short notes added, place names too. She recognised some of them but others meant nothing. She thought she should take it to the police station as it wasn't hers. Katrina looked at the small neat handwriting, running her thumb along the lines as if she might somehow feel his touch. She sighed and carefully refolded the sheet, placing it into her pocket. She decided before she took it to the police station she'd make a copy to keep.

* * *

"How can she make contact with these people?" Cleo eased herself into one of the upholstered wicker chairs in the conservatory. "They haven't told Catherine how to contact them. Jack, there's no way she can get a message to them."

"They'll have to make contact again, clearly." Jack rubbed his chin with his hand. "We've both said *they*, it may well be just *him*....or *her!* We've no idea how many people we may be dealing with at the moment." Jack turned to Cleo and held both her hands in his. "We have to trust what was said on the drive and believe that Amelia is OK, that she is, in fact, safe."

"I know, I know. But there *has* to be something we can do. We can't just sit around waiting, not knowing if and when we are going to hear anything!" It's chewing *me* up! What it must be doing to Catherine god only knows!" She realised she was unknowingly digging her long fingernails into Jack's hands. He flinched slightly. "Sorry Jack!" She held both his hands up to her mouth and gently kissed them. "Better?"

"Look, Cleo. I have some lines of enquiry to follow regarding the plane. At least doing something will move this forward." Jack got to his feet. "You're doing a great job by keeping Catherine company and helping her through what must be hell." He made his way to the hall with Cleo and his side. She kissed him lightly on the cheek. Annie, the female CID officer was standing at the front door. It caused Cleo to suddenly become embarrassed by her act of affection. "Call me immediately if there's any news." He whispered quietly in her ear so as not be heard by Annie who was staring at them with a fixed but glazed expression.

Jack climbed into his hire car and started the engine. Manoeuvring carefully he turned the car and drove down the drive to the main road. He turned left and as he drove along he thought about all the possibilities. He decided he'd try and see George, to perhaps pick his brains or at least bounce some ideas in his direction. His phone was in his pocket and so Jack pulled into a small side road to make a call. He noticed a little further down the road a postman pushing his trolley of letters along the pavement. The beginnings of a possibility were germinating in Jack's head and he replaced the phone in his pocket and quickly jumped out of the car heading off in the direction of the postman. Wearing shorts, walking boots and fluorescent waistcoat, most posties look the same. It wasn't until Jack approached within 10 or 15 metres that he realised postie was, in fact, a young woman, her blond ponytail protruding at the back of her peaked hat.

"Hi, ya..." She said as Jack approached, smiling to reveal a set of perfect white teeth. "It's another nice day. Yeah....?" She said.

"Hi there and yes it is." Jack found himself looking at the tanned skin of her bare arms and legs and quickly tried to address the reason for him accosting her in the first place. "I hope you don't mind me asking but does your round include the big house down the road?" Jack gesticulated with his thumb over his right shoulder.

"Yes it does, why?" Her smile became slightly more inquisitive. She leaned on the handle of the trolley eyeing Jack up and down as if trying to ascertain his weight for express parcel rate.

Jack tried to sound casual as he considered how he might glean any useful information. "It's just we had a letter delivered with the post earlier and it didn't appear to have a stamp."

"Yeah, sometimes they do get through although usually they're picked up and you get charged the cost of the stamp plus the handling charge. You were very lucky then if you didn't have to pay." She pulled a bundle of letters from the bag held with an elastic band.

"It was early this morning, do you remember?"

"Yeah I do actually. I saw it in amongst the other letters and thought *lucky them!* It's no big deal really you know it's no skin off my nose."

The comment caused Jack to have to look at her nose. He thought it was a very attractive nose, placed perfectly on an equally attractive face. "Could anybody have slipped it into the bag while you weren't looking?"

"I can't really say, we're not allowed to let these things out of our sight." She tapped the handle of the trolley. "I'm legally responsible for delivering this post safely. If somebody tampered with the letters I'd be in the shit!" She started to tug on the handle as if to leave. "Anyway nice talking to you but I do have to get on."

"It's a long way to drag a trolley up the drive. Don't they allow you to leave it at the entrance?" Jack needed to keep her talking as he needed a clearer picture of the daily routine.

"Yeah if the path isn't too long and you can keep the thing in clear sight. But the driveway up to the Blanchard's place is long and goes through that wooded bit. I'm not allowed to leave the trolley unattended. I have to drag it all along that bloody gravel drive and back. I wish they had a post box by the gate." With that, she pulled again on the handle. "Nice talking but I have to get on. I've got to go." She gave him another of her captivating smiles, winked and turned away. "You can always come and talk to me again if you need more information on our wonderful postal service. I'll be finished and back at the sorting office by two." She said and laughed, taking yet more letters from the bag and vanishing through a small gate.

"I may well do just that. Enjoy your day." Jack ambled back along the road to his car trying to process the information and wondering whether it had any relevance to the disappearance of Amelia. Remembering why he had stopped in the first place Jack took out his phone and dialled George's mobile number.

"Hello old boy, how are things?" George's voice sounded tired. "Afraid I'm confined to barracks today, didn't have a good night so decided to take the day off."

"Sorry to hear that, George. I was planning on coming over to see you this morning. But no worries, we can catch up some other time. I just wanted to pick your brains."

"No Jack, I'd be pleased to have the company. Come over now if you like and have a cup of coffee. You're welcome to pick my brains although I don't know what help I may be."

"OK George, I can be with you in half an hour or so. Cheers for now." Jack placed the phone back in his pocket, took out his car keys and climbed back into the hire car.

* * *

Chapter Ten

He had to walk up the road trying to find the best signal. He telephoned her mobile but it went straight to answerphone. He tried unsuccessfully three more times, the signal strength was poor. He looked up and down the road but there were no houses or buildings to be seen. He walked back to the car, as he approached he could smell hot oil and coolant. There was steam coming out through the front grille and something was dripping under the car. He cursed loudly and kicked the door forgetting that his sandals were no match for the metal clad vehicle. He cursed again but this time for the self-inflicted pain. It was still warm; however, the sun was well on its downward track in the western sky. Paul opened the rear passenger door and retrieved his bag from the back seat. Pocketing the car keys he started to walk in the direction that the car was facing. The road ran straight and flat with nothing but open fields both sides. His foot was throbbing now and when he looked down he could see a dark discolouration caused by blood under his big toenail. He walked on, favouring his right foot and cursing the old Citroën.

After ten minutes or so Paul stopped and sat on the kerb stone. Unzipping the bag he removed a pair of socks and his trainers in the hope that the additional support offered over a sandal would ease the pain of walking with his injured toe. He remembered too late he'd left a bottle of water on the passenger seat of the car. His mouth was dry and his head was aching but he knew he had to keep walking. He took out his phone and looked at the screen. The signal was still poor but he tried to phone her again. He could hear it ringing. It continued to ring and ring and eventually went to answerphone. His head was buzzing, thinking through all the possibilities of why she was not picking up. He had no idea what he was going to say to her, he didn't know where he was going to start. He didn't even know if he would get a chance to talk to her, he imagined she'd probably just hurl insults down the phone to him. Paul decided, in the end, to simply say nothing and ended the call.

* * *

Jack parked the car in the corner of the gravelled frontage to the flat where George lived. He reached the communal entrance and pressed his button. Jack could hear George's voice on the small speaker and opened the door. He was waiting at the top of the stairs when Jack appeared. Beckoning him in, George busied himself in the kitchen making coffee while Jack went through to the small living room where he placed a bag on the coffee table containing Danish pastries he'd bought en-route. Jack noticed half empty bottle of rum alongside the chair where he was sitting.

"So how are you feeling George?"

"I'm feeling pretty rough, to be honest, old boy! Mostly self-inflicted I'm afraid." George walked slowly through carrying two mugs and placed them on the coffee table. "I stayed up late last night watching the old box. It was some old war film. Like a silly old fool, I fell asleep and woke up at about 2 a.m.! Of course, I'd had a few glasses off the old grog!" George reached down and picked up the bottle. "The trouble was that I couldn't get to sleep after that." George sat on the chair and peered into the paper bag. "Oh, what's this, breakfast?"

"More like elevenses! Help yourself George I picked them up on my way over here."

George brought two small plates from the kitchen and, handing one to Jack, took one of the pastries from the bag. The two munched on pastries and drank their coffee while Jack filled George in regarding the recent events.

"I'm getting nowhere with this. It all seems to be getting out of hand and I'm not sure if I'm the right person to be dealing with it." Jack placed his plate on the coffee table. "Perhaps I should suggest to Catherine that she leaves it to the police. Do you think I should do that?"

"You can't just walk away from it Jack, Catherine wouldn't have asked you for help if she didn't think that you were capable of doing the job." George took a swig from the now cold coffee in his mug. "What was it that old chap, I can't remember his name, had said? It was something about the longest journey starting with the first step. I'm sure he's right Jack if you just keep chipping away at it eventually you'll find the answers."

"I hope you're right George, it's just that at this present moment I'm not sure whether I should continue trying to find out what exactly happened to Paul Blanchard, or throw all of my efforts into finding Amelia."

"From what you've said, and reading between the lines old boy, I think you're right about all of this being linked. This electrical message thing that was delivered in the post confirms it."

"You mean the flash drive, yes it's true enough. Whoever's taken Amelia knows that Paul Blanchard most probably *is* alive and in hiding somewhere. Why they want him God only knows but it's got to be pretty damned serious." Jack got to his feet, picked up the two mugs and plates and took them into the small kitchen where he proceeded to wash them up. "In terms of priorities George, I have to start by finding what's happened to Amelia. The police can only really act on information they receive and by that time its history. They're not exactly proactive!" Jack finished drying the mugs and plates.

"You said Jack, that the letter didn't have a stamp. Evil bastards couldn't even post it properly."

"I pretty damned sure it was done for a reason George, and I'm now beginning to think I know *how* it was done. If what I'm thinking is correct then I need to move quickly."

* * *

He felt the vibration in his pocket before he heard the phone ringing. Paul quickly took the phone out and answered realising it was Maria. For half a minute he said nothing, holding the phone away from his ear while Maria was in full flow. She was asking questions, accusing him of being with another woman, wanting to know where he was, asking him when he'd be back and eventually blaming him for spoiling the dinner and the whole evening. Paul sat down again on the kerb unable to get a word in and unwilling to open a can of worms and explain the reasons for his absence. Eventually, Maria fell silent; her tirade had run its course. Paul could hear her heavy breathing and in the background, the radio station was playing jazz. He thought it sounded like Django Reinhart and the quintet du hot club Paris. Paul took a deep breath, closed his eyes and thought quickly about how and what he was going to say to her. The seconds ticked by while he composed himself.

"Maria, will you listen? Please don't talk or ask questions just listen. I assume you're alone." Her voice had lost some of its venom when she answered in the affirmative. "I want you to pack a small bag, just a few things enough to last a few days. I want you to bring your passport with you." She started to interrupt. "No, listen to me this is important. Knock next door, and ask Didier if he'll take you down to the train station. If he can't do so then you'll have to get a cab. You need to do this quickly Maria, it's important that you don't hang about, or talk to anybody. Don't answer the door, turn the radio off." Maria tried to interrupt but Paul continued. "Call me when you are at the station. Call me on *this* number. I've changed my mobile number. *This* is my new number, OK?" She started again to protest, asking why, but Paul silenced her with his final sentence. "It's most important that you do this, not only for your safety but also for that of your baby." He paused momentarily. "I mean *our* baby."

He could hear the sound of a vehicle approaching from behind. It was a small van and as it drew near it began to slow down. The driver leaned out of the open window and pointing back along the road asked Paul if the Citroen sitting in a puddle of oil and water was his. Paul smiled and asked if he was going near a town where he could catch a train.

"Oui Vivonne, s'il vous plaît, prenez le fourgon." The driver smiled and beckoned Paul to get in which he did. He was relieved at last being able to take the weight off his throbbing foot.

After a period of small talk, the two men sat in silence each in their own worlds. The minutes passed and Paul became more and more concerned about Maria. He knew she'd phone him when she arrived at the train station. He hoped that Didier had been able to drive her there and that she'd not had to wait for a taxi to arrive. He sat holding the phone praying for it to ring and when it did the shock made him physically jump. Maria had had time to digest the strange conversation with Paul. Her voice had lost its venomous tone and in place had become quietly cautious. Paul told her to buy a single one-way ticket to Vivonne and that he'd be waiting at the station for her. He told her to take great care, not to talk to anyone and to be sure she was not being followed.

Paul settled back in the seat and watched the countryside pass by while his driver chain-smoked cigarettes. Fortunately due to the heat the van windows were wide open allowing the acrid smoke to dissipate fairly quickly. Reading the signposts on his way Paul estimated he'd be at the station within the hour. He relaxed as best he could, the smoke and the bouncy ride of the old van a combination that was not conducive to making the ride enjoyable, but at least took his mind off his toe!

* * *

Jack had left George to enjoy the remaining two pastries in the bag. He headed towards the town of Newport and the main post office, where he hoped he might catch the postie he'd met earlier, finishing her shift. The town was busy and Jack had to park in the centre of the town in the carpark and then thread his way back to the post office. It seemed as if the entire population of the small island had decided to walk the streets of the town, and in Jack's view, most of them walking in the opposite direction to him! Eventually, he arrived at his destination and entered the building realising as he did so that he had absolutely no idea how he was going to find *his* postie! The place was busy with queues eight to ten deep at each of the three open counters, mainly locals going about their daily business but with a smattering of holiday-makers intent upon buying stamps for postcards. Jack smiled to himself, remembering when he was about eight years old and buying postcards to send to his grandparents. For some reason, his parents had decided that Scotland would be nice to visit for a holiday. Two weeks of cold rain and high winds in a flimsy tent seemed to Jack the longest fourteen days of his life!

"Can I help you?" She sounded both tired and bored, sighing loudly when Jack didn't immediately respond. "What do you want?"

Jack was catapulted back to the present. "Oh, sorry I was miles away." The apology did nothing to ingratiate him and she repeated her question while raising her eyebrows and looking towards the high ceiling. The people in the queue, now five deep behind Jack began to make noises, indicating their irritation. "Where do the posties have their office?"

"Are you having a laugh? This *is* the post office."

"No sorry I didn't make myself clear. The postmen and postwomen, when they go out or come back from doing their rounds, do they have an office?"

"Yeah, just go down the side of the building." She rotated slightly on her swivel chair which groaned under her weight. "You'll find a door, just ring the bell." She let out another big sigh. "Is that it?"

"Yes, thanks very much." Jack moved to the left allowing the next person in line access to the counter only to be greeted with *'Can I help you... What do you want?'* and a sigh.

He shuffled his way through the crowded post office and out through the main door. Looking both to the left and the right he saw a narrow passageway leading down the left of the building. Reaching the door he realised there was no door handle, just a touch pad. To the right of the doorway was a small speaker and button. Unsure of what he was going to ask, Jack's hand hovered over the button.

"I hope you're looking for me." The voice came from behind. Jack turned quickly to find not one, but two identically clad women, one he recognised as *his* postie and behind her another considerably older woman who eyed him up and down as if considering him as a side order.

Jack looked the younger woman directly in the eyes and in a carefully measured voice, trying not to sound like a sad pick-up line, spoke. "I wondered if I could talk to you a little more about.........."

"Leave off, you pervert, you're old enough to be her father!" It was the older woman now speaking. She stepped in front of Jack's postie, placing herself between them. He wasn't sure whether as a form of protection or because she wanted the opportunity to put herself forward for whatever Jack was suggesting. "But I'll take you on." She smiled revealing a chipped tooth and breathing nicotine in Jack's direction. "...... and I'm free *all* afternoon!" She looked probably ten to fifteen years older than Jack's postie. She wore her hair shoulder length and cut in a style more suited to someone in their twenties! It was clearly bleached and coloured a strange apricot shade but with half an inch of brown and grey roots also on display.

"Look, all I want is a few minutes more of your time........ Please?" Jack said now looking past the older woman who was standing defiantly between them and edging ever closer to Jack.

"Give me time to clock off. There's a café across and along the road." Jack's postie pointed in the direction from which he had walked a few minutes earlier. "I'll see you there in about fifteen minutes."

"OK." Jack smiled and turned to walk back down the passageway

"I could see you there in five minutes darling!" The somewhat strident voice belonged to the older woman. "..... And I'm *still* free!" She gave another of her toxic smiles.

Jack cringed inwardly, a nightmare scenario forming

in his brain of being trapped by this woman, *free* in *all* respects for the entire afternoon. He quickly tried to dismiss all thoughts and continued walking not daring to turn his face and see her watching and leering after him.

* * *

He'd been waiting for the best part of an hour. Trains had come and gone from both directions. The station wasn't overly busy, hardly what might be referred to as a rush hour, but there'd been a constant hum of activity all the same. Now it was quiet, lights on the platform beginning to fend off the darkening evening. Paul looked again at his watch, concerned because she'd been longer than he'd anticipated. He'd tried to phone her again but without any success. The battery level on his phone was low. He cursed not having the car to wait in and charge his phone at the same time. He hadn't been able to find a garage when the van driver had dropped him off and his priority had been meeting Maria. The next train was due in about twenty minutes so he decided to get a coffee; sitting still had made him feel cold. It had been a warm day but now that the sun had set there was a cool breeze blowing over the adjacent fields and straight onto the platform. Paul cursed his luck on finding the drinks machine out of order and ambled slowly back to the seat he'd been occupying. He looked again at his watch. The train was due in just over ten minutes!

She'd followed his instructions to the letter but missed the train by just a few minutes. Didier had offered to wait with her but she'd said no, he'd been kind enough to take her at such short notice and his meal was waiting for him at home. She had suddenly felt very alone and scared. She wasn't sure what she was scared of, but it had been the way Michael, whom she now knew was Paul, had been acting, both at their flat, and also when he'd spoken to her on the phone. She could tell something had happened but she had no idea what. The train's speed started to fall away and Maria could see that they were approaching the town. A few houses then more, eventually a small industrial estate and finally the train slowed to a stop whereupon a few of the passengers in her carriage started to get to their feet and shuffle towards the door. Maria picked up her small wheeled case and followed the small procession out onto the platform.

At first, she saw nobody. The air struck chill and she shivered. There was a noise behind her as the doors of the train slid and closed shut, their pneumatic hissing and whooshing loud and out of all proportion to the door's movements! The train began to move off and she was worried again that she was alone. She began to wish she was still on that train sitting on the warm seat, safe in the carriage. She looked up and down the platform; the other passengers now moving towards the exit gave her an increasingly clearer view along the platform.

Maria spun quickly around upon hearing her name. "Michael!" She flung her arms around his neck, dropping the handle of the case and letting it topple over. He held her close, smelling her perfume and kissing her gently on her cheek. "You have to tell me all the things that have been going on!" She kissed him back. "No secrets Michael. You tell to me all the truths, you understand?"

"OK, but let's not stand here, we need to find somewhere to stay." He picked up the handle of her case and with his bag over his shoulder they made their way out of the station and into the town. It was now quite dark and most of the shops and houses were in darkness, their shutters closed for the night. They turned left out of the station and crossed the road heading for the town centre. They then turned right into a tree-lined avenue and left into the main street. A few short steps led them to a small Italian pizza restaurant which was still open although devoid of customers. To call it a restaurant was probably an exaggeration as the place was no more than three metres wide and five deep. It was clean and the plastic chairs were more comfortable than they looked. They ordered drinks, Maria wanted only a soft drink but Paul chose to have a beer. They chose pizza to share which arrived within a few minutes. They were both hungry and for a few minutes just ate.

"Well.............? So start telling me everything please!" Maria took her glass of fruit juice, cradling it in her hands while resting her elbows on the pine-topped table at which they sat. "I'm waiting.........."

* * *

Katrina copied the sheet of paper using the scanner in the small office area at the rear of the café and placed the copy in her bag. The original she decided had to go to the gendarmerie. A day had passed since the accident had occurred and it was her lunch break. She informed her mother that she may be back a little late and before waiting for a reply closed the door to the café a little too energetically making the glass panel rattle in its old wooden frame.

It was another fine day although now that September was coming to an end the temperature was lowered somewhat by the slight breeze. She wished she'd taken her cardigan from the hook and slipped it on but she decided not to go back and get it now. The walk would warm her and if she kept up a good pace she'd be there in twenty minutes. As she walked along she allowed her mind to ponder over the tragedy that had occurred less than twenty-four hours earlier. She thought it strange that since then she'd not seen Michael, especially as the accident had happened so close to the café and he normally called in at least once a day.

With her head still swimming, full of the terrible death of Jason, she found herself at the main entrance and walked up the few steps to the door into the police station. She waited at the counter there being nobody else in the small lobby area. She could hear voices coming through the open door from an inner office and eventually a somewhat rotund police officer waddled through, carrying a coffee and patisserie.

"Mademoiselle ...." Quickly he placed both items to one side and after shuffling a number of pieces of paper around in front of him he attended to her.

Katrina explained the reason for her visit, having witnessed the terrible accident the previous day. She was a little elastic with the truth about the piece of paper, saying that she'd found it alongside the poor victim and hadn't realised that she was still holding it when she was helped back to the café. The officer bent down and she could hear him rummaging through a box. When he stood up he held open a plastic evidence bag and asked her to place the paper carefully inside. He then sealed, dated and signed the bag, placing it into an 'in-tray' as evidence for further investigation. He thanked her for bringing the item in but seemed unconvinced that it was of any real importance with regard to the case. "L'accident du voiture? Oui, très bien!" He shrugged.

Back in the sunlight again Katrina was relieved at having done her civic duty and slowly made her way back to the café. No doubt her mother would be ready to question her when she got back but for now, she walked along the street listening to the hum of the traffic, voices, and birds, all going about their business.

* * *

When just one woman entered the café and sat down at the table next to him he inwardly breathed a sigh of relief.

"My name is Jack, Jack Ramsey." He handed her one of his slightly 'dog-eared' cards thinking he must get round to getting some new ones! "Please let me get you a drink." He got to his feet. She was reading the card and looked up wide eyed.

"Shit! You're a detective!" Placing the card on the table she looked nervously around. The other people sitting at tables nearby were taking no notice. "I'll have a skinny latte please Mr. Ramsey." She said a little more quietly.

"No, call me Jack...... and you are? Your name I mean."

"Mireille, I hate it but my mum was French so that was that. I'm stuck with it!"

"I think it's a lovely name." He smiled and she blushed slightly. "OK, then one skinny latte coming up!" Jack made his way over to the counter and ordered for them both. Two minutes later he was back with their drinks and sitting down at the table.

"So am I in some kind of trouble? I mean is it something to do with my job?" She looked at Jack, her stare both questioning and more than a little alarmed.

"No, it's not anything like that. You're not in any trouble at all. I'm trying....... I mean I'm working on behalf of the lady in the big house, just down the road from where I spoke with you this morning." Jack didn't want to give too much away, it was bound to hit the news at some point but he didn't want to be the one responsible for the leak, especially with a child involved.

"You mean the Blanchard's place, *that* big house." Mireille sipped at her latte and realising it was still very hot placed the cup back down again quickly.

"I can't say too much but I'm trying to discover whether a small letter could have been slipped into your post for you to put through her, I mean the Blanchard's letterbox this morning." She was listening intently so he continued. "You mentioned when I spoke to you this morning that the chance of a letter getting delivered without a stamp was pretty small. I'm fairly certain the letter I'm talking about was placed in your trolley unbeknown to you *after* you started your rounds."

"So I am in the shit then!" She took a serviette from the table to wipe some latte from her lip. "Like I said to you this morning, I have to keep an eye on the trolley at all times and if someone is slipping letters in and out then it's my head for the chop!"

"There's a strong possibility that the police may want to talk to you about your delivery round. A serious incident has occurred, I'm sorry but I can't tell you anything more."

"Fucking hell, it's getting worse by the second..... I'm definitely going to lose my job!" Suddenly tears were welling up in her eyes. She started to get to her feet. "I've got to get back and tell them it was nothing to do with me."

"Wait!" Jack grabbed her hands and gently eased her back into her seat. "The Post Office isn't aware of anything at the moment and I want to keep it that way. I don't think the police have contacted them. And as for your situation Mireille, you're *not* in any trouble!"

"But I let it happen. I'm supposed to be looking after that trolley! They'll say it was my fault!" She was almost hissing at him through her teeth.

He smiled trying to calm the situation. "I can understand this is all very scary and sudden but you're not at fault Mireille, believe me." Jack held on to her hands but easing his grip slightly. She didn't pull away. He lowered his voice. "There's a way, however, I think you can help."

* * *

CHAPTER ELEVEN

Catherine's mobile rang. She was having a shower and didn't hear it but when she looked she noticed there'd been a missed call. It was a number withheld. She cursed and threw the phone onto the chair.

* * *

Maria was silent as Michael, or Paul as she now knew him, explained to her the full story and the circumstances that had brought him, and her, to this small pizza restaurant in Vivonne. She listened without interrupting but with tears welling in her eyes. He held her hands as he told her he knew she was pregnant and he was happy they were going to have a child. She was shaking, trembling with a full palette of emotions swirling around in her head. She was thinking of so many things at once she felt her head would explode or that she'd wake up and realise it was all some terrible nightmare. But she knew it was real, that it *was* happening, and that nothing would ever be the same again. She felt sick inside, the pizza she'd eaten felt like lead in her stomach. Somehow she resisted the urge to go and throw up.

Eventually, he fell silent, he'd told her everything. For him, there was some kind of relief at being able to share his plight. He realised, however, that in doing so Maria would have to judge him. He was now at her mercy. He didn't know whether she'd stay with him or whether she'd run, perhaps back to the flat or even back to her family, her mother. She pulled her hands away from him suddenly and reached into her bag for a tissue. She wiped her eyes and blew her nose before placing tissue back in her bag. While doing so she pulled out a folded sheet of paper and placed it on the table between them.

"What's this?" Paul unfolded the sheet and for the first time saw his baby. His hands started to shake uncontrollably as he stared at the ultrasound image. "Is this *my* baby?"

"Oh, mon dieu!" Maria jumped to her feet. "Of course it's yours! What kind of woman do you think I am?" She started to pick up her bag and case. "I thought that we....... Oh never mind. You have a saying that the water has already passed under the bridge, am I right?" She snatched up the paper from the table. "So I am now going."

"No, Maria, don't go. We'll sort this out, please let me try to put things right." Paul was on his feet and leaning across the small table was holding on to the hand that held the image of their baby.

"It's all too much mess of things." She did not pull her hand away. "I thought that we had a future together, but now that I hear all of this then it cannot be." She looked him in the eyes. "You have a wife, and you have a daughter and you didn't think to tell me all those things!" She started to sob. "You don't want me and now you find out that I am going to have a baby I will be a burden, like the milling stone, around your neck. You are better off being without me. You must go back to your wife!"

"It's *you* I want Maria." Paul stepped around the table to get closer to her. "You have to understand, I left my wife, and now I am with you and I want to stay with you, you *must* understand that. I want to be with you and our baby!"

* * *

"You think that they are going to try and put something in my bag again?" She let out a long breath. "How will they do it?"

"Probably the same way they did it this morning I expect. That's why I'd like to follow you when you do your round tomorrow morning......... But only if that's OK with you."

"I suppose so but how will I know if they do put something in the bag?" Mireille leaned back in the chair pouting slightly and drumming the fingers of her right hand on the table top. Her long, painted multi-coloured nails mesmerising Jack as they reflected brightly in the sunlight.

"I'm really hoping you won't notice Mireille! I want them to do it again. I want to see who does it! After all, it would appear they managed it this morning. I'm not saying that you were lax in any way but we are dealing with a clever and devious person. It could well be more than one person, I just don't know. You won't be in any danger; I will be watching and will be close by."

"OK, I'll do it. The van drops me at about six thirty so you'll need to get up early!" She took a pen and paper from her bag and wrote down the street name handing it to Jack. "So I'll see you then. Oh, and thanks for the drink."

* * *

She'd looked at the sheet of paper a number of times but much of what was written was meaningless. Place names, dates and times which all seem to be listed randomly. There were some names which she didn't recognise and a couple of mobile telephone numbers. She knew the police would take ages finding next of kin. She felt she needed to do something herself, something to try and speed up the process. She was sure there'd be family, friends or somebody who'd want to know what had happened to Jason. She'd tried phoning one of the mobile numbers, she'd let it ring but nobody answered. She wondered perhaps whether she should have left a message but the news she was delivering was not the sort of thing to be left as a voicemail message. She'd tried the other mobile number but it didn't connect and just gave an unobtainable sound.

Katrina cleared the coffee cups and plates from the table outside and flicked the crumbs to the ground. A small pair of finches flew down from a nearby tree to investigate. A couple of days had passed since the terrible accident and yet both the image and sound haunted her. She'd watch the traffic passing up and down the street looking to see if she recognised the car but to no avail. She'd physically jump upon hearing the sound of a car horn or a squeal of brakes. The regular customers came and went and she wished them a good day but her sparkle had diminished, a few of the regulars had said as much. She knew she'd never see him again but she was sad at the thought that she'd soon begin to forget what he looked like. In just those few days she'd already begun to forget little aspects of the way he was, how he looked. She had to concentrate really hard to remember his face and the way he spoke, his smile. It was as if he was fading away in her memory and it upset her deeply.

She decided she'd try the numbers again but not today. She needed time to think about what she was going to say and she needed also to practice her English. Although she'd done well in her English at school she'd found it difficult to understand the different dialects she'd been confronted with when she had travelled to London and stayed with her pen-pal in Sutton. She looked up at the clock, it was fast approaching mid-day and still there was no sign of the café owner Michael.

"Do you think it not strange that Michael has not been in today again? It's three days in a row mother, should you call him?" Katrina flicked the towel she was holding over her shoulder to leave both hands free at the sink.

"I will do it, not now but later. He may come by this afternoon. Leave it for now." Yvette placed more dirty cups and saucers she'd been carrying through down next to the sink.

"I'll do it... I'll do it when I've finished this."

"Why are you so interested in Michael all of a sudden? He has probably gone away for a few days........... To have a rest from you I expect! Anyway,

I have his mobile number, not you!" She sighed and looked at Katrina who was staring back at her pleadingly. "OK Katrina, I'll do it now..... Oh, you are so stubborn, just like your father!" Yvette looked in her bag for her phone and called his mobile while Katrina finished the rest of the crockery with more haste than attention to cleanliness. "That is strange, it's not ringing.......... number is unobtainable!"

"Are you sure mother?" Katrina asked coming over to where her mother was standing. "What's the number? Perhaps you dialled it wrong!"

"I didn't dial it, it's stored, see?" She held the phone out for her daughter to see.

When Katrina looked at the number on the display she didn't immediately realise the significance of what she was looking at. She'd never seen Michael's mobile phone details, but she immediately recognised the number! A wave of heat passed through her making her feel slightly nauseous as she remembered dialling that exact number earlier in the day. The number she had seen next to the name Paul on the photocopied paper which had been written by Jason.

* * *

He knew she'd be angry and he knew also that he'd been wrong to just run off as he did. Maria had found it difficult to forgive him for that and she told him so in no uncertain terms. She told him also about how she cared about him very much. Paul felt angry and annoyed with himself for causing so much extra pain and suffering for her to endure and he knew he couldn't just fix that in an instant.

They left the small restaurant and, turning right, walked on round the corner into the old part of the town. In silence, they continued passing by a small memorial garden to the fallen dead of two world wars. A few yards further on they found a hotel which nestled alongside the town's only church. The building was of local stone and dated back some two hundred years. The road was very narrow and steep at this point and the door opened directly onto a pavement barely wide enough to walk upon without risk of being hit by passing traffic. It was, they were told, the only one in the town and fortunately they had vacancies. Paul and Maria were shown up the stairs to a double room on the second floor. The shutters were closed but they accepted being told it had a view over the river which skirted the town. They unpacked the few clothes they had between them and having done so sat on the bed leaning back on the pillows.

"What's to happen with the café?" Maria broke the silence turning her head towards Paul who was staring blankly into space. "How will they know where you are?"

"They'll just carry on, don't worry." Paul rubbed at his temples. "Yvette will just assume we've gone off for a few days and forgotten to tell her. It'll be alright."

"But what if they have to speak to you and you have changed your telephone number. How can they tell you if there is a problem at the café? You haven't thought all the things out properly Michael................ Sorry, I mean Paul!" She punched his arm. "I *cannot* get used to you having a different name!"

"We can always phone Yvette in a day or two on your phone Maria. Don't complicate things please!

They're complex enough as it is!" Paul put his arm around her. She didn't move away but rested her head against his shoulder and within minutes she was soundly asleep.

Gently, Paul eased his arm out from under her and climbed off the bed. In his bag, he found the half bottle of cognac he'd taken from the cupboard when he was hurriedly packing his clothes. He filled the glass that he'd fetched from the bathroom and quietly repositioned himself on the bed. He made the drink last half an hour and contemplated refilling it but in the end decided he needed a clear head in the morning. Paul pulled the duvet over them both and lay there next to her. The traffic in the street outside had reduced considerably and just the occasional vehicle could be heard negotiating the steep hill upon which the town stood. Paul tried to clear his head of all the scenarios whirling around, fighting for precedence. He began to wish he'd not succumbed to the cognac. It was blurring his thoughts. Thinking about, and trying to plan, his next move was becoming impossible. Eventually, he too drifted off, the glass virtually empty, falling from his grip to nestle between them on the bed.

* * *

CHAPTER TWELVE

Jack was back at the hotel. He called Cleo and she picked up almost immediately. He told her of his thoughts with regards to the letter and how it may have been placed in the post trolley while out on the rounds. Cleo thought it was rather a long shot but went along with the theory. Jack explained how, upon meeting the postie, he'd arranged to follow her the following morning. He added he'd have to be very careful not to arouse suspicion, and certainly not to scare off anybody intending to use the same method again to send information to Catherine. She filled Jack in regarding the goings on at the Blanchard's house. The various comings and goings, the police visit to tell Catherine there'd been no further developments and that they were still waiting for the results from the memory stick. There being nothing else to say Jack told her he'd call by tomorrow after the post round.

George called him just a few minutes later. Jack asked if he was feeling any better and was glad to hear that he'd even been out for a 'constitutional' during the afternoon. He told him he was thinking that a walk in the evening air would be just the thing for him as well after he'd eaten.

Jack showered, changed and went down to the restaurant. It was fairly quiet and he sat at a small table in the corner of the room. Forgoing a starter, he chose the sea bass followed by a small portion of clafoutis for dessert. Jack accepted a coffee when the waiter cleared his plate and sat drinking the hot liquid while contemplating what the following day may bring. It was still early in the evening and, although he had an early start the following day, he needed some time to unwind. He knew if he went to bed now he'd not be able to get to sleep. Jack got up from the table and went up to his room to collect his jacket and car keys thinking that a walk in the fresh air would be beneficial in all respects.

It was a fairly short drive down into the town of Yarmouth where Jack parked the Astra in the main car park. He crossed River Road and walked along Saint James's Street on into the town. He walked on passing the pubs until he reached the yacht club where he stood watching the ferry making its way slowly out into the Solent. As he looked out to sea, the lights of the sister ship could be seen holding station and awaiting clear passage in. Jack closed his eyes and breathed deeply, or as much as he could with the pain in his side but feeling the cool air refreshing his lungs.

Suddenly he felt a hand on his shoulder pulling him round. It happened so quickly he didn't have time to resist. His cracked ribs were still giving him pain and restricting his movement. His head spun 180° and when he stopped moving and focused his eyes he was confronted with a vision. It sent a cold chill down his spine. It was Mireille's work colleague, the 'lady' by whom he'd only earlier that day managed by the skin of his teeth to avoid being propositioned!

"Hello, darling...... so what brings you down to my manor? Fancied a night out did you?" The evening was drawing in and the breeze coming in off the sea had a definite chill to it. The woman standing before him was sporting a thin blue cotton dress, so short it was hardly more than a tee shirt. It was nonchalantly off the shoulder and in danger due to the wide neckline of being off completely! She held up the empty glass she was holding. "I'm having a drink! Want to join me?" She moved closer and ran her arm round his waist. He flinched with pain as she pulled him towards her, his ribs protesting. "Come on just one! I'm all on my own with nobody to talk to."

He felt beaten and he couldn't see an easy way out of this situation. Before he'd had a chance to think of a polite refusal he was being pulled in the direction of the pub he had passed earlier. "Look, this is very nice and normally I'd be happy to sit and have a drink but I really do have to get back to my hotel. I'd quite like to have an early night!"

"We could do that.......... You can take me back to your hotel for a drink!" She stopped pulling him and the pain in his side abated slightly. "Mireille told me all about you........ Mr. Detective Jack Ramsey!" She tried to focus on his face. "By the way, I don't expect Mireille told you *my* name."

"No... No, she didn't." Jack was desperately trying to be polite.

"Allene... It means 'little Eve'. I can show you my fig leaf later!" She laughed, toppled backward and her high heels went off the edge of the pavement. Jack threw himself forwards and grabbed her around the waist before she fell. The sudden pain in his side caused him to wince. "Oh.... That's nice! Come on then, where's your hotel?"

Jack inwardly groaned to himself wondering why it was that he always seemed to get himself into difficult and embarrassing situations like this. His mind flashed back to a time when he was on his first and only date with a girl he'd met while travelling on the bus to college. They had gone out for a drink and unbeknown to Jack, before he had called to collect her she'd drunk virtually the entire contents of a bottle of her father's favourite Irish malt. She'd ended up dancing naked in the fountain of the park. He'd had to dress her and carry her, singing and vomiting, back to her house and explain the story to her father!

"Look Allene........ Let me see you safely home." She was leaning heavily against him and with a couple of broken ribs Jack wasn't sure he'd be able to carry her if it became necessary.

"I'd rather come with you." She placed the glass down heavily on the centre of a table outside the pub interrupting the four young men sitting quietly drinking pints of beer. "It's quite a way. You see I came on the bus." She tried again. "Couldn't I just come back with you? I'd be very quiet!" The four seated men were watching both her and Jack as if it were some arranged entertainment put on especially for their amusement. Jack was aware they were nudging each other and enjoying his embarrassment.

"Let's go and get my car and you can direct me. Is that OK Allene?" Jack placed his hands on her arms both in an attempt to steady her, but also to try and move her dress back over her shoulder and cover up her right breast which was in imminent danger of display to the four beer drinkers!

She was able to walk, albeit a little unsteadily on her high heels, with Jack's arm for support. They crossed the road and walked back to the car park. The cool air was having a beneficial effect upon Allene and as they approached the Astra she began to speed up slightly. He unlocked the car and opened the passenger side for her to get in. With his keys in his right hand and holding the door with his left Allene was now both unsupported and out of his control. She fell towards him throwing her arms around his neck and planting her lips on his. He could not step back as the open door was behind him and he only had one free hand with which to try and regain physical separation. He could hear himself groaning with the pain from his cracked ribs.

"There see? I *knew* you wanted it." Allene had mistakenly assumed the groan was one of pleasure. "There's plenty more where that came from!" She stepped quickly into the passenger seat and Jack tried to wipe the sticky lipstick from around his mouth with the back of his hand as he rounded the rear of the car and opened the driver's door. He got in and helped her with her seatbelt before attending to his. Jack started the engine and backed the car out of the space. "Right just follow my directions OK?" Allene said as she slipped her shoes off and pressed her bare feet into the carpet. Jack nodded but said nothing. He just wanted to get her home. The gentleman in him could not just walk away and leave her drunk in the town. He had to make sure she was home and safe. He was quietly reprimanding himself for feeling animosity towards her but he just wished this had not happened!

They turned eastwards and she directed him up the hill out of the town. Jack listened for the next direction while Allene was rummaging through the contents of her handbag. "Oh, take the next on the right!" Jack quickly indicated and turned off the main road. He tried to see the number but with a little time and it being quite dark he just noted it was the B34 something!

On they drove and Jack could see only dark hedges or trees to both sides with just the occasional property. The road ahead bending gently to the left and then right, illuminated just by the car's headlights. Just as they were approaching two houses on the left she shouted out making him jump. "Turn right now .... right here!" He spun the wheel and found that he'd left the tarmac and was bumping along a narrow lane down beside a barn. He slipped the car into a low gear. "Not far now, just a few hundred yards."

"You live down here?" Jack gesticulated with his hand but she couldn't see because by now it was quite dark.

Allene giggled and quietly said something which Jack missed. They passed a small property on the left, a dog barked but there were no lights other than the glimmer of a television reflected in one of the front rooms. Jack was driving slowly now the lane was becoming little more than a track. He could see that the hedges to either side were low and fields stretched out beyond. They passed a small junction with another lane off to the right. "Right, turn in here!" Allene said as she un-clicked her seatbelt. Jack could just make out a small entrance through an open five bar gate to a flat chalk covered area surrounded by thick gorse. He manoeuvred the Astra carefully into the area watching the headlights pick out the edges of the turning space. He could hear Allene moving about while he positioned the car and assumed she was looking for keys and searching in the foot-well for her handbag. Jack couldn't see a house just the dark shadows of gorse bushes around the perimeter of the area.

"Come on then. I'll see you to your door." He took the key out of the ignition and unbuckled his seatbelt.

Allene giggled again. "Don't you get it, Jack? This isn't where I live! We're in the middle of nowhere!" Jack turned to face her and although now dark he became aware that she was holding something in her left hand. It happened so quickly that Jack didn't have time to stop it. She threw the bundle at him covering his face. Jack could smell cheap perfume and nicotine and realised it was her dress. She'd slipped it off as he was concentrating on parking the car. "Chase me Jack! Mr. Detective..... Chase me and catch me!" As she opened the car door the interior was flooded with light and Jack realised she was naked!

"Allene!" He tried to stop her but she was out of the car before he'd time to grab her arm. "Get back in and put this on!" He held the dress towards the open door the interior light shining brightly and illuminating her body as she stood alongside the car.

She turned and ran. "Come on........ *Chase* me!!" She vanished from sight. Jack's view was of her plump buttocks receding into the night.

Jack's blood ran cold *'fucking hell'* he groaned inwardly. "Stop, Allene, for god's sake..... Please!" For two pins he'd have just driven off back to the hotel but

Jack being Jack, he jumped out of the car slammed the door shut and ran to the passenger side of the car. She was nowhere to be seen. "Allene where are you?" He reached in and picked up her dress from between the seats noting that her handbag and shoes were in the passenger foot-well. He closed the door and locked the car. "For goodness sake Allene, come back here!" He didn't know what to do. He'd no idea in which direction she'd gone, whether she knew the area, or even if there was a house nearby!

"This way Jack, I'm over here!" The voice seemed a long way off over his right shoulder. Jack turned and started walking in the direction he imagined the voice had come. He found himself back on the track but still headed away from the road. In the distance and silhouetted against the slightly lighter sky to the west he caught sight of her. She was waving her arms at him.

Jack estimated that if he could run and get to her before she moved, he could get her back to the car without too much more time being wasted. He was sure that she was bound to have something in her bag to indicate where she lived and he could then get her home. He moved forward quickly, and as quietly as he could, keeping her in his view but at the same time wary of where he was treading. The track was rough and overgrown. He was within twenty feet and just seconds away when it happened! He caught his foot on a large piece of wood where a tree had shed a branch and it had fallen just on to the edge of the track. He fell forward his arms outstretched to protect his body from imminent impact with the ground. What he did contact, however, was Allene's naked body as together they fell in a heap on the soft long grass in the middle of the track. She ended up on her back while he landed with his face nestling her ample breasts. He pushed himself off her and rolled onto his back desperately trying to catch a lung full of air. "My ribs... Oh shit, they hurt!"

"Oh, Jack you caught me! You know what that means don't you?" She grabbed at his belt trying quickly to unbuckle it. Jack groaned, the searing pain in his ribs exploding again. He was clutching at his ribs trying to breathe deep and slow but instead found he was gasping and groaning. She was giggling again, pulling at the zip of his chinos while kneeling over him. "Ooh Jack..." She said as her hands pulled and tugged them down. "Now I've *got* you!" And with that she gripped him.

Jack tried to take her arm. "Please, Allene.........Don't! This is not what I......" She was still holding him but suddenly she started to make a sound, a noise that came from deep inside her. Jack was aware of a sudden rush of warmth on his stomach. Then it came again as she vomited a second time. Together they lay there for what seemed an age before Jack was able to move. With one hand still clutching his ribs as if holding them in place, Jack forced himself into a sitting position and grabbed his phone so he could use the minimal light output to survey the carnage. Much of Allene's stomach contents had, in fact, missed him and with a pack of tissues he had in his pocket he was able to clean himself up. Allene was curled up alongside him in a foetal position crying softly. He placed his hand on her bare shoulder, she was cold and shivering. He looked around and found the dress he'd been carrying just a couple of feet away. Pulling her into a sitting position Jack placed the dress over her head and eased her arms into it. "Come on let's see if you can stand up." She did so without a word and he carefully pulled the hem of the dress down to cover her modesty.

She looked up at him questioningly. "Have you hurt yourself? Did you do it when you fell?" She turned suddenly and heaved again, fortunately, missing both of them this time.

"It's a long story but I have a couple of broken ribs... Come on, let's get you home.... properly home!"

He placed an arm around her waist, she placed one of hers around his neck and they carefully retraced the track back to the Astra. Her head rested against his shoulder and he became aware of her constant sobbing.

"I'm sorry... I'm sorry!" She kept whispering at him.

* * *

CHAPTER THIRTEEN

He'd not been wrong, and the view as described by the boy who'd shown them to the room the evening before did not disappoint. Paul pushed open the shutters on the two windows which looked out on the streets further down the hill. Beyond was the river, the sun catching and reflecting like small diamonds on the rippling surface.

"What time is it?" Maria turned her head towards the open window. "I feel........" She moved quickly, throwing off the duvet and running across the room to the bathroom and to the basin where she heaved loudly! Paul took a white robe from behind the door of the en-suite placing it over the shoulders of her naked body.

"Are you OK?"

"Of course not, it's the sickness I'm getting now in the mornings!" She heaved again and Paul gently rubbed her back with his hand, not sure whether it would do any good but he remembered when Catherine was pregnant with Amelia she'd said it did. Eventually, Maria moved away from the basin. "I need to take a shower. The hot water will help." She slipped her shoulders out of the robe and let it fall. Stepping past him she turned on the tap to the shower head. "You come in with me, yes?" She smiled at him but he knew he had a long way to go in order to repay the upset he'd caused.

Later they dressed and went down to breakfast. There were a few others, mainly couples sitting at the tables when they entered the room. Paul guided Maria towards the corner where there was a vacant table set for two. Music was being piped through the room but the volume was set so low it was difficult to make it out above the gentle hum of the street outside and the various conversations around them. Paul felt more relaxed and reached across the table to take hold of Maria's hand with his own.

"What are we now going to do?" She spoke uncharacteristically quietly her eyes focused on Paul. Maria took the napkin and placed it on her lap. "I'm not sure I want to eat anything. I am uneasy in the stomach still....... I may just have coffee."

"After we've had breakfast we will make plans. If we're going to stay here for a while or move on, I don't know at the moment, Maria." They fell silent as the coffee was poured and croissants arrived. "I think it best we wait until after we've eaten and we'll go back up to our room." Paul nodded towards the other people in the room who could hear them if they so desired, but appeared blissfully unaware of their existence. Maria sipped the coffee and ate half a croissant while Paul tucked in. The room filled with more guests, tourists in the main and mostly couples. They didn't feel out of place or that they were conspicuous in any particular way and so they both began to relax a little until Maria's phone began to ring!

* * *

She was at least honest about her address the second time and Jack eased the Astra into a vacant space in the street. Apart from continuing to apologise to him, she'd not said much more. The journey back towards Yarmouth had been somewhat subdued. It was now almost midnight and Allene's house, like most in the street was in darkness. Jack helped her to the door and she fumbled fruitlessly in her bag for the key. In the end, she tapped at the door the sound seeming to echo around the quiet street. After about a minute the door creaked open just a few inches and a hushed conversation between Allene and the person inside resulted in the door being opened fully. The light in the small hallway illuminated the step.

Jack started to say his 'goodbyes' but Allene pulled his arm. "Come in and say hello to Harry."

Jack didn't relish the thought of meeting her partner, husband or whatever and started to make excuses. "Look Allene, I really can't........" His apology was cut short when he heard a softly spoken and a cultured male voice emanating from the man in the doorway.

"It's so kind of you to escort my sister home. Please do come in so that I may thank you." Jack was taken aback and followed her into the hallway. Allene quietly excused herself and headed up the stairs. Jack watched but remembered she was wearing nothing under the dress and quickly averted his gaze. "I'm Harold Jenkins-Smyth." The man held out his hand. "I'm Allene's brother." Jack introduced himself and shook hands with Harold. "Please come through to the sitting room. May I offer you a drink tea, coffee? I can't offer you anything stronger I'm afraid."

"Nothing for me, thank you very much." Jack was feeling somewhat awkward, looking dishevelled and also arriving with his sister in clearly a similar state! He tried to form a coherent explanation in his head but before he was able to deliver his defence Harold spoke.

"I have to say that very seldom do the people with whom Allene socialises, have the courtesy to escort her safely home." He looked back towards the door to make sure she was still upstairs. He lowered his voice until it became little more than a whisper. "Please accept my sincere thanks. I do worry when she goes out drinking! She seems to become a different person. I suppose she turns from Jekyll to Hyde or is it the other way round, I can never remember."

Jack could certainly vouch for her change of personality. In just an hour or so he'd witnessed first-hand Allene as a drunk, a drugged-up nymphomaniac and finally as a quiet, sobbing and very unhappy individual.

"She's not had much in the way of luck in recent times. Her partner Derek walked out on her a few years back. I have to say he was a bit of a waster but she was very fond of him and was devastated when he left. She couldn't keep up the mortgage and so the house was sold. I live here on my own, always have done, and it seemed logical for her to come and live with me. She's managed to hold down a job as a postie for nearly two years now. It gives her spending money which unfortunately she squanders on alcohol and goodness knows what else! I know I shouldn't have looked but I've found tablets hidden in her room." Harold moved to the door and listened again. He continued in a low voice. "My father, sorry I mean *our* father, is now living in a home. He's been diagnosed with Alzheimer's disease and this upsets Allene. He no longer remembers her. He always used to call her his special little angel but now she's a stranger to him!"

There were soft, slipper-shod footsteps on the stairs, the door opened and Allene came quietly into the room. She'd washed her face and combed her hair. She was wearing a long white towelling robe. She looked at her brother and then to Jack, her eyes questioningly looking for approval. "I just want to thank you for driving me home tonight. I apologise, Jack, if I've spoiled your evening and kept you later than you'd intended." She looked at Jack with a pleading expression and hoping the events of the evening would remain undisclosed. "Sometimes I'm not me and I do things." She swayed slightly and Jack thought she was going to fall. "And the rest of the time I wish I wasn't me! I'm not sure you understand, I don't think I do really."

Jack smiled and nodded his head almost imperceptibly, but sufficient for her to understand its significance. "It's fine, really, but now I really must be going." Jack shook hands with Harold and handed him one of his cards almost as a subconscious gesture. Harold took it and studied it intently. Jack made his way to the door and she reached out and lightly touched his arm.

"I'm so sorry Jack….. Please don't think too badly of me!" She whispered.

* * *

Telling Yvette that they'd come away for a few days holiday seemed to satisfy her curiosity when she phoned. Maria explained it had been a surprise for *Michael* and that *he* knew nothing about it until they were about to go, as a result, they'd forgotten to let them know. After a few pleasantries had been exchanged she finished her call and placed the phone on the bed next to where she was sitting.

"Good, that should keep everyone happy for a while." Paul came over to the bed and sat down beside her. "The next thing, what shall we do about the car?"

"You said it was broken!" Maria's view was that either it worked and therefore was OK, or it was not working and thus broken.

"We'll have to get it moved, it can't stay sitting at the side of the road! If there's a garage in the town they may be able to tow it. What I think they will say is that it's probably beyond economical repair." While he was talking she'd eased herself back on the bed and was resting her head on the pillow. "Do you want to stay here? I'll go and find a garage. Yes?"

"Mmm….. OK." She closed her eyes. "But let me know where you are and don't be taking too long."

Paul went down to the reception and booked them in for a further night's stay. Taking one of the free tourist maps from the stand on the table, he set off down the road to the bridge where he crossed the river. About a quarter of a mile down the road on the right was a garage and upon enquiring was pleased to find they'd be able to tow the car immediately if he so wished!

Twenty minutes later and Paul was sitting in the passenger seat of the tow truck's cab bumping along the road towards town and back the way he had come the previous day. He phoned Maria to keep her up to date, but whether the signal was poor or she had her phone switched off he didn't know. It went directly to answerphone so he left her a short message before placing his phone back in his pocket.

* * *

The following morning Jack was woken by the alarm on his phone. Knowing that he'd arranged to meet Mireille at the start of her round he'd at least remembered to set it after getting back to the hotel. It had been nearly a quarter to one in the morning when he'd got to his room, showered and crawled straight into bed. Having decided that his chinos were beyond cleaning, with grass stained knees and his shirt smelt of vomit, he placed them both in a plastic bag to be thrown away. He dressed in a similar, but clean, shirt and light tan chino trousers. Luckily his jacket had survived the previous evening's excitement unscathed, for which he was grateful.

After a coffee in his room, he walked out to the Astra parked in the hotel's car park and upon opening the driver's door was given a sensory reminder of the previous evening. The smell inside the car was still strong, a mixture of cheap perfume and vomit in about equal measures! With the windows all opened, and the fan on full, Jack decided he'd be able to tolerate it for a short while until he had a little time in hand. He found a small shop which seemed to sell everything and purchased cleaning wipes, a scented fabric spray, and two car air fresheners! There and then he set to work on the upholstery, cleaning and spraying as he went. The source of the perfume smell was located when he discovered Allene's bottle. Something which was certainly not a perfume he recognised and was clearly some cheap imitation. It had fallen out of her bag when in the foot well of the car. Jack checked all around and under the seats in case anything else had fallen out. He almost dreaded what he might find as he tentatively ran his hand over the carpet but fortunately there was nothing else. He hung one of the air fresheners on the mirror and started the engine. The smell of the combined fragrances was quite strong, almost overpowering but highly preferably to the fragrance it had replaced!

The drive to the rendezvous was completed without any holdups. It was still early and he parked on the side of the road. Jack sat in the car listening to the radio while waiting for his postie to arrive. The van passed close by at speed causing the Astra to rock and stopped about fifty yards further down the road. She jumped down from the passenger side door as it opened onto the pavement. The rear doors of the van were opened by the driver who in Jack's opinion didn't even look old enough to have a licence! The trolley, loaded with letters and small parcels, was manoeuvred somewhat unceremoniously with a bump down and on the road. Within seconds the van sped off to drop the next trolley. She eased the trolley onto the pavement and waved when she saw Jack emerge from the Astra.

"I have to do a double shift today... Allene's only gone and called in sick!" She reached into her pocket for a piece of paper and handed it to Jack.

"Sorry to hear that." Jack swallowed trying not to look like a guilty schoolboy who was about to be found out!

"Actually it was her brother called in for her. He gave them some lame excuse." Mireille ran her fingers through her hair and placed the cap on her head. "Probably another of her wild evenings out…….. She's a girl that one!" She smiled at Jack. "The trouble is she's taken so many 'sickies' in the last few months she'll end up getting the sack!" Mireille paused momentarily and looked at him. "You OK?"

"Yeah….. No, I'm fine. I just had a very late night. I think I overdid it."

"You weren't out partying with Allene then?" She said jokingly, not realising the accuracy of her comment. "Still if you were you'd probably not have made it this morning either!" She paused and looked at him. "Are you blushing? Christ, you don't fancy her, do you? Wait 'til I tell her. She'll chase you all over the Island she will!" She laughed but Jack just smiled, a technicolour flashback causing him considerable internal turmoil. He wasn't sure whether she knew he'd seen her and was playing a game with him, and if so, he should come clean. In the end, he stood in silence until she spoke again. "Anyway, that piece of paper!" She pointed to his hand. He was still holding the folded sheet.

"Oh good, it's a route!" He said upon opening it out.

"You really are 'on the ball' this morning aren't you?" She giggled. "Anyway I have to get on with two rounds to do!" Mireille opened the trolley bag and took out a bunch of letters held with an elastic band. "So you're going to just follow me….. Yeah?"

"Yes from a distance and in my car. I just want to watch your trolley as and when you're delivering at the door."

"There, and I thought it was me you were interested in." She laughed again and with that turned and walked up the path to the door of the first house.

Jack turned and walked back to the Astra unlocked it and climbed in. He could clearly see as she made her way down the short road to the corner. Timing his move Jack started the engine and double checked the piece of paper sitting on the passenger seat. He signalled and pulled out of the space. Staying in second gear, and occasionally pulling in to allow other vehicles to pass coming the other way, he arrived at the corner and turned left. It was another fairly short road and the only space appeared to be about three-quarters of the way down on the other side. He drove slowly, signalled and pulled into the space trying at the same time to keep Mireille and the trolley in view. This, he soon discovered was decidedly more difficult in practice than it had seemed to him, in theory, the previous day!

He sat and watched as she made her way towards him. At no time was the trolley left unattended for more than a few seconds. Jack began to wonder whether he was wasting his time and decided to turn the car radio back on for company. She passed by the car and blew him a kiss which he tried to ignore. He remembered Allene's mocking words the previous day regarding him being old enough to be her father.

This continued for about half an hour. Jack would move the car and wait until she was just about out of sight and then move the car again. They were now in what could be described as a slightly upmarket part of Mireille's route. The houses being nearly all detached and with drives to garages. Island Radio was playing 'Sunny Afternoon' but the weather was decidedly undecided! Dark clouds were gathering and it was threatening rain. The wind was beginning to freshen and the temperature dropping. A small scooter, an 'L' plate hanging off at the back, weaved down the road. The lad appeared nondescript. He was wearing typical 'off the arse' jeans, a grey hooded tracksuit top unzipped and flapping over a green tee shirt, white trainer type boots and a red crash helmet. Jack congratulated himself on his attentive and complete description having only such a short glimpse and turned to watch his postie. He could see the trolley in his rear view mirror but Mireille was temporarily out of sight. Jack turned in his seat to look down the other side of the road but she was nowhere to be seen. He looked again in the mirror and caught a brief glimpse of someone next to the trolley. It was the scooter-lad!

Jack jumped out of the car a stab of pain reminding him to take it easy! He looked back up the street to see the scooter-lad heading off in the opposite direction and Mireille just emerging from the front garden of a house on the other side of the road. He got back in the car and started the engine. As quickly as was safe he turned the car around and headed up the road in pursuit easing slightly to call to Mireille as he went past. "I'll catch you later!"

Scooter-lad turned left and then left again. Jack was keeping him in view but trying not to get too close! He was weaving between the cars while Jack was constantly having to stop and let vehicles through. This meant keeping him in sight was becoming difficult. The parked cars were causing countless chicanes. At one point Jack lost him, the road was fairly straight and yet he was nowhere to be seen. He drove as quickly as he dared, peering down side roads as he passed them. He was beginning to think all was lost when he looked down a road to the right and caught just a glimpse of a red helmet as scooter-lad vanished round a bend in the road. Jack stood on the brakes and quickly reversed in order to turn the Astra up the road. As he reached the bend he looked desperately on in the hope of seeing him in the distance but to no avail! He floored the accelerator and the Astra leapt forward shortening the gap to the visible distant point on the road ahead.

Then he saw him! Or at least his crash helmet! The scooter was parked outside a newsagents shop on the corner of a parade. There were other scooters and motorbikes parked but it was the red helmet perched on the seat that caught Jack's eye. He slowed the car and pulled into a vacant space. He was feeling slight relief but wondering what may happen next. He waited. A couple of minutes slowly went by and a few people came out of the shop, none matching the description of scooter lad. Jack was contemplating walking over to the shop. He weighed the pros and cons and opened the door to get out but as he did so scooter lad appeared and placed a plastic carrier bag in the box on the back of the bike.

In no time he was off again. He was weaving his way through the residential roads with little or no regard for other vehicles, his hoodie flapping out behind him and the top two inches of his underpants also on show. He was headed east out of town and Jack felt a moment of déjà vu when scooter-lad turned right onto the road Jack had travelled less than twelve hours earlier! Keeping a safe distance Jack followed him as he turned right and left eventually approaching the outskirts of

Newport where he did a sudden left turn into a housing estate. It was not a particularly large estate, built in the early sixties. Many of the houses had clearly been bought by their tenants. They stood out from the rest, their brightly coloured doors and replacement windows, clean net curtains and manicured front gardens all indicating a sense of pride and achievement. Others were at the opposite end of the social spectrum. Jack noted an old Toyota minus its wheels sitting up on bricks on the front grassed area of one property. The grass so tall and weeds even taller almost hid the vehicle from sight! England flags hung in the windows of another property. The flank wall adorned with a selection of graffiti tags in lurid colours. Two girls were walking towards him as he drove slowly on. They were both identically dressed. Denim shorts, a white jacket over a pink tee shirt, enormous gold-plated hoop earrings and hair tied in a ponytail so tight and high it was almost pulling their dyed blond hair out by the roots! One was walking, head down and fixated on her phone while the other stared at Jack as he drove slowly past yelling 'Not working….. Fuck off!' into his open window.

Scooter-lad turned down the side alleyway of a particularly squalid looking residence and leaned the scooter against the wall. He took his helmet off and placed it on the ground while appearing to look for his key. He took no notice of Jack as he parked the Astra across the road. He opened the door and holding it open with his foot picked up the helmet with his spare hand.

Jack's phone started to ring making him physically jump with surprise.

"Jack, it's me!" Cleo was trying to contain her composure. "There's been another letter delivered! They're demanding money now. They want half a million cash or Amelia........." She couldn't bring herself to continue. "Oh Jack, Catherine's been going mad, she's smashing glasses and stuff. The doctor turned up five minutes ago and has given her a sedative. I've had to literally hold her in a bear hug to keep her from doing herself harm until he arrived."

"OK, stay with her. You're doing a brilliant job, Cleo. It's difficult just waiting but I'll be over as soon as I can. Love you......." He rang off and climbed out of the car.

* * *

CHAPTER FOURTEEN

Waving his Gauloise around and pointing at various parts of the engine while sucking at his teeth, he made it clear to Paul that the engine was shot. He'd thought as much and as far as a repair was concerned it was uneconomic according to the mechanic. He couldn't leave the car where is stood at the side of the road so agreed for it to be towed to the garage while he considered his options. He didn't have the car's paperwork but Didier had a key to the flat, he could ask him to post it to the garage. It was looking like the easiest way out would be to buy one of their second-hand cars.

The car was pushed to the back of the garage parking area in an out of the way corner. Jack accepted the one hundred euros offered and signed the vehicle over to the garage, agreeing to get the paperwork posted soon as. There were three of four very new looking Renaults parked at the front and even more expensive ones in the small showroom. The dealer did have two cars that had been taken in part exchange and Paul was shown each in turn. He settled on a Volkswagen hatchback. It was fairly old but in good overall condition and the service history looked genuine. A service and full valeting promised and Paul could collect the car at the end of the day.

Paul started to walk back to the hotel and as he crossed the bridge he called Maria to let her know what he'd arranged. He cursed to himself and looked at his phone to check the signal strength as the number he'd dialled went directly to voicemail. Leaving an even shorter message to the one he'd previously left her from the tow truck he hurried back to the hotel. When he arrived he was puffing slightly from the exertion of walking quickly up the hill from the bridge. He entered the reception area and was just making his way to the stairs when the receptionist called him over and spoke quietly to him.

"What do you mean? .... Checked out?" Paul could not believe what he was hearing. "She hasn't got a brother!" He started to panic and looked around as if expecting to see her. "...........and she didn't leave me a message, a note or something?"

The receptionist shook her head slowly and looked at him. "Non Monsieur, I am afraid not. They just left without saying anything more." Another hotel customer had walked over to ask directions to the station and she turned her attentions to dealing with her. Paul stood fixed to the spot, unable to think, to move or assemble any rational thought. His head began to spin as he contemplated the possibilities!

* * *

Jack stood and looked around. The estate appeared quiet although he was aware of a curtain twitching and a woman watching him. He'd obviously parked the Astra in a space normally used by one of the residents and this woman was clearly upset by a strange car in its place. Jack looked back but she'd vanished from sight, at least for the time being. He considered his options. Going and knocking on the door of scooter lad's house seemed too risky. He had no real plan of what he'd say let alone what he may find. He took a deep breath and his chest reminded him of the cracked ribs by sending a searing pain shooting around his side. Jack eased himself back into the seat of the Astra taking short and shallow intakes of air in an attempt to ease the discomfort.

Ten minutes passed while he thought about what to do. He considered calling the police, but he couldn't be sure Amelia was actually in there. All he'd achieved was discovering the address of scooter lad and he may only be being paid to act as a delivery boy. If the police turned up 'mob handed' the upper hand could be lost.

The door opened and out came scooter lad wearing his helmet. He jumped on the bike and shot off up the road before Jack had a chance to start the engine. Jack had a sudden change of mind and switched the engine off. This was his chance, an opportunity to check out scooter lad's abode. Jack locked the car and walked across to the house. As he got closer the neglect and poor state of repair became more apparent. The original wooden window frames had been melded with aluminium frame inserts, probably in the late seventies and many of the glazed panels had cracks. The water down pipe had become dislocated from its gutter fixing and the resultant water damage was clear to see down the corner of the pebble-dashed wall, areas of which were missing, having fallen out to expose the cheap and shoddy brickwork. What woodwork there was to be seen was almost devoid of paint and the house appeared to be at the end of its useful life.

The main door was situated at the side of the property and Jack walked up the concrete path littered with cigarette ends and chewing gum deposits. Empty lager cans nestled in the weed-ridden border and the waste bin made itself known by emitting an evil aroma.

Jack knocked at the door. There was no bell push, no door knocker. He just tapped his knuckles on the dark green paint peeled surface. There was no sound from inside. There was no radio or TV playing, he knocked again. There was no answer. Jack looked around and edged closer to the waste bin, the smell causing him to hold his breath. There was a plastic ice cream container, fortunately, rinsed out sitting at the top of the rubbish. With a small knife he'd taken from his pocket Jack cut a flat strip of the material about 15cm by 6cm. He approached the door and, looking to make sure nobody was passing by, edged the plastic between the door frame and the door. As he pushed the plastic deeper it came up against the latch. With a careful sliding motion, he eased and pushed. Eventually, the latch moved and he was in!

The hallway was cluttered with a multitude of items none of which belonged in a hall and most probably stolen. There was a laptop on the stairs and two mobile phones piled on top, one with a smashed screen. A camera, an expensive digital SLR adorned the next stair. The floor was decorated with pizza boxes with a sprinkling of burger and kebab containers. The smell coming from the kitchen was sufficient to persuade Jack not to investigate further. He looked into the room at the front of the house. The curtains were drawn and it was dark but Jack was able to make out a large television and game console taking pride of place amongst the squalor. He looked around the room. His nose twitched at the smell of stale lager and cigarettes. There were crushed cans everywhere and saucers filled to overflowing with ash and butts rested precariously on the arms of the stained, threadbare sofa and armchairs.

Jack wasn't quite sure what he was expecting to find but stood and looked at the room for a full minute taking a mental snapshot. Stepping carefully back into the hall he looked up the stairs and at the array of electrical spoil. He listened but could hear nothing so ventured the first step. The carpet had long since shed its pile and the remnants were so thin in places the wooden boards clearly visible. Jack continued slowly one step at a time and eventually found himself standing on the narrow landing. Like the rest of the house, horizontal surfaces were all fair game for the detritus of life and a myriad of unrelated items fought for space. The door to the bathroom was open and without a closer examination it was clear it had not been singled out for special treatment. The stench was wafting onto the landing area courtesy of a broken bathroom window and a westerly breeze. Jack turned to look at the two rooms at the front of the house. Both doors were open and there were signs that one of the rooms was used for sleeping. A crumpled and stained duvet was thrown in a heap at the foot of the bed. There was little in the way of furniture, but what there was, appeared old and battle-scarred. The room at the front was no more than a box room. It was filled with boxed televisions, toasters, electric kettles and other domestic items clearly having made their way to this room via uncertain and illegal means. Jack moved with caution to the next door at the back of the house and situated next to the overpowering bathroom. This door was different; it was substantially reinforced with thick plywood and had a spy hole. Jack put his eye to the small lens but could make out nothing; the room looked to be in darkness. To the side of the door was a light switch which he'd assumed was for the landing light but realised that one was on the other wall near the stairs. He flicked it on and peered through the spy hole again. There appeared to be very little in the room, he could just about make out a small table and a chair but the view somewhat limited. There were heavy bolts top and bottom, Jack slid them across. He placed his hand on the handle and slowly turned the lever. The door didn't move it was locked.

* * *

Paul ran quickly up the stairs and opened the door to the room. Closing it behind him he looked and found her small case still on the chair in the corner. It was open and he could clearly see that she'd been in the early stages of packing. He studied the room; her handbag was nowhere to be seen, nor her phone. He phoned her number but she didn't answer. A chilling thought ran down his spine and he desperately tried to think of what to do.

He sat down heavily on the bed and put his head in his hands. After a while, his breathing began to slow. He concentrated on taking slow deep breaths while considering his next step. Paul dialled Maria's mobile again and waited for the sound of the phone ringing.

It seemed ages before a voice cut in, informing him that the phone was not responding, and to try again later. After a few long minutes, Paul slowly got to his feet and retraced his route to the reception area.

"Explain to me what exactly happened..... Please!"

"The man came into the reception. He said he was the brother of your partner. He knew you were on a holiday here. He said he wanted to surprise you."

"What did you do?"

"I telephoned your room, he asked me to do so and to say to come down to reception."

"Did Maria; my partner. Did she come down?"

"Yes." The woman lowered her voice. "He whispered something in her ear. I didn't hear what he said. And then she just left with him. He held her arm and they just left."

"And she didn't leave any note or message for me?"

"No, I'm sorry I didn't think to ask. It all happened so very quickly". The receptionist was looking at Paul, concerned she'd done wrong.

"Did you see which way they went? Were they walking or did they get into a car?"

"They walked around to the side of the building. I think they got into a car because I heard one drive off. It went up the hill. It must have done because I'd have seen had It turned down the hill."

"How did she appear, was she worried?"

"I'm sorry, as I said it happened so quickly and there was another man asking directions and he was leaving as well. So it was all rather rushed you see."

"Another man? Someone else was in here as well?"

"Yes, he came in just before and asked directions to the railway station. So I was talking to him as well."

"Describe both the men. Do you think they were together?"

"They were both about 40 years old and dressed in jeans and light coloured polo shirts, casual. The one who asked for your partner had short dark hair and the other man wore a blue or it may have been black baseball hat. That's all I know, I'm sorry I can't tell you anything more."

"That's fine, thanks." Paul rubbed at his chin. "Look, I'll settle the bill but add one more night. I may need to vacate the room very late tonight or early tomorrow morning so I'll pay now." Paul sighed and drummed his fingers on the counter while she made out the bill, his mind racing, wondering what on earth could have made her leave. He tried to think of logical explanations but he knew deep down what was really happening. *They'd found him! .... But they'd got to her first!*

* * *

Jack searched around the landing and found a key hanging from a bent nail in the woodwork. He quietly unlocked the door the mechanism making next to no noise as it released. All was quiet as Jack decided what to do next. He flicked the switch and peered again through the spy hole. It was difficult to make out any real detail. The glow from the ceiling light had hardly sufficient power to do more than raise the gloom by a factor of one. He opened the door just a little and waited. Nothing, no sounds came from within. He opened it further and peered into the room. Scanning round he saw the small table, the chair and in the corner a portable toilet like the one he remembered from his grandparent's caravan. The window was boarded up. Thick plywood was securely screwed into the wooden frame. The carpet was worn and heavily stained and in the corner Jack could see a bundle of rags. He stood there while his breathing slowed and the ache in his ribs subsided. His eyes began to acclimatise to the dim light and as he looked around he was able to make out empty sandwich cartons and water bottles piled next to the rags.

Jack was suddenly aware of two things. The rags began to sob and move and there was a crash from downstairs as the front door was slammed shut!

* * *

Paul retraced his steps back to the garage. He needed the car, it was ready for him and after some hasty paperwork he filled it with fuel and headed back to the hotel. He parked the car in the small car park at the rear of the building. He'd tried to phone Maria countless times and the request to leave a message mocked him on each and every occasion. It was somewhat of a shock when the call was answered. He unclipped his seatbelt.

"Maria, where are you? Tell me where you are, I'm coming to get you." Paul took a breath. "Are you OK?"

"She's a bit tied up at the moment she can't come to the phone." The man's voice was cold and threatening.

"Who are you? What do you want?" Paul was out of the car looking around expecting to see the person on the phone.

"I think you know exactly what I want........."

Paul's blood started to run cold. "Don't you hurt her she's done nothing."

"Do you mean Maria? As I said she can't come to the phone." There was a pause and he spoke again. "Or do you mean Amelia?" There was another pause, sufficient to let the words sink in. "We have her as well. She's a pretty little thing. We borrowed her to use as leverage on your wife just in case she knew where you were. She didn't, did she? But we don't need her anymore. We're hanging on to her as she may just urge you to cooperate!" There was a chuckle down the line. "Jason, now he came up trumps, found you for us. Pity he couldn't stay for the reunion, he's gone now."

Paul fell to his knees. He'd been crushed. "Please, oh god, please don't do anything......"

* * *

Scooter-lad was back! Jack considered the situation quickly and quietly closing the door and sliding home the bolts. He locked the door and placed the key in his pocket thinking she'd be safer locked in the room if he had the means to unlock it! Jack realised he was in no state to take on someone ten to fifteen years younger. His recent injuries had rendered him easy prey. The only advantage he had was that of surprise, and that could evaporate the moment scooter-lad came up the stairs! Jack listened. He could hear cupboard doors being opened and slammed shut, the sounds of tins and wrappings being opened. Scooter lad had been shopping and it sounded as if he were making himself something for a meal. A radio started to belch indescribable music at full volume and a microwave buzzed into life. Jack had no idea how much time he had and, more importantly, what to do.

He crept as silently as he could and looked again into the larger of the other bedrooms. Scanning the room quickly he noticed a baseball bat propped against the wall near the bed. Clearly, this was scooter-lad's own personal protection equipment. Jack picked it up calculating that the odds were slowly improving. He realised he'd never actually hit anyone with a baseball bat and wondered where he should hit him and how hard! It was a difficult calculation to make as he only wanted him incapacitated, not dead!

The noise from the kitchen continued and Jack considered he'd a few minutes in hand. He took his phone and prepared a text message. DI Hill had given him her mobile number should he need to contact her with anything more that he might remember about the recent events that had resulted in his injuries. He realised he couldn't call her his voice would immediately be heard by scooter lad.

URGENT Amelia Blanchard found! I am secreted in the front bedroom of the house she is safe at present locked in a back bedroom. The abductor is in the house at present in the kitchen. Please send help to secure the situation and arrest abductor. Suggest SILENT arrival! I will intervene as last resort! 38 Blackberry Way Newport. Jack Ramsay

Jack sent the message praying that Janet Hill was near her phone, not in some meeting or other. Jack suddenly remembered and muted his phone just in time as it vibrated to indicate a message.

Do nothing. Help is on way, ETA in fifteen minutes.

Jack looked at the phone message. Fifteen minutes was a hell of a wait, he had no idea what scooter-lad may do. Music or what passed for it still could be heard from the kitchen. Jack moved across the room and looked in a cardboard box that was pushed into the corner. It was open and Jack could see a variety of items, clearly stolen goods taken from a local DIY store. Pliers, spanners, screwdrivers and other assorted tools all still with their cardboard backings and price labels. Jack's eye was caught by a bundle of cable-ties. He picked one up; it was about 45 cm long. He took half a dozen and carefully put them into his back pocket. He looked at his watch. About five minutes had elapsed since he'd received the message from DI Hill.

Suddenly somebody was banging on the front door! The noise echoed through the house shaking the very fabric of the building. Jack tensed and waited. Scooter-lad opened the door and Jack could hear a heated discharge of expletives from scooter-lad before the door slammed shut again. He could now hear voices in the kitchen. Jack strained to listen and immediately could tell it wasn't the police. It was a female voice and she was clearly giving back as good as she received, with additional colourful and foul language thrown in for good measure. The exchange continued for about a minute and then all of a sudden scooter lad ran up the stairs and into the small bedroom. Jack froze, hardly breathing and baseball bat held tightly as he stood behind the half-open door. He could hear boxes being torn open and then he was running back down the stairs. Another exchange, this time with fewer expletives and again the front door slammed shut. Jack dared not move but stood listening while glancing at his watch. Ten minutes!

* * *

"We need to have a little chat, Paul, sometime soon." The voice could not hide the underlying menace with which it was delivered. "Stay happy... Oh, and don't go anywhere. That hotel can put you up for a while longer I'm sure."

The line went dead. Paul could see the number had indeed been Maria's. He tried to call it back but it was already switched off. He was shaking, tears running down his face. They had him exactly where they wanted. He was helpless, they had the upper hand and all he could do was wait to be contacted again. They were going to make him sweat! Paul made his way back to his hotel room. It seemed quiet and lonely as he sat on the edge of the bed. Only this morning they'd been planning their next steps. He collected the remaining items of Maria's, some toiletries and items of clothing that had been discarded on the chair and placed them in the small case. He couldn't bear to sit and look at them. Then he placed everything of his except essentials in his case so if needed he could move quickly.

* * *

Scooter-lad was finished. The radio was switched off and the silence seemed suddenly deafeningly loud. Jack was convinced scooter-lad would hear his breathing and the game would be up. He came up the stairs at a walk this time and clearly carrying something heavy.

Jack could hear his laboured breathing as he kicked open the door and walked into the room. With his hood over his head, Jack had the advantage as he stood behind the door. Scooter-lad started to bend down to place the box on the floor by the bed. Jack acted on instinct and swung the bat at the hood. It was a glancing blow and not too hard but the result was an almost textbook execution of laying out an assailant. Scooter-lad fell forward and crumpled in a heap next to the bed. Jack looked at the bat and decided he didn't need it anymore. Quickly he took a cable-tie and secured his wrists behind his back. With another, he did likewise with his ankles. The third he used to pull his wrists towards his ankles. By now scooter-lad was coming round. Jack was somewhat relieved he hadn't killed him.

"Fucking wanker....... I'll 'ave you!"

Jack decided to use the other three cable-ties as well and proceeded to attach them to the squirming and blaspheming heap on the floor. He stood and watched as the figure tried unsuccessfully to free himself. When Jack was happy with the situation he left him and made his way to the bedroom where Amelia could be faintly heard sobbing. He unlocked the door and slid the bolts. Flicking the light switch he entered the room and crossed to where she lay.

"Amelia, It's Jack. I've come to take you home."

The pain in his side was almost unbearable but he managed to lift her in his arms and make his way down the stairs whilst listening to a catalogue of the fate which awaited him once scooter-lad had managed to free himself from his impromptu shackles. As he reached the bottom step the front door exploded as three heavily padded police officers cascaded over the threshold.

"Spot on timing lads...............fifteen minutes exactly!"

* * *

Chapter Fifteen

Detective Inspector Janet Hill sat in the deeply padded leather armchair and sipped at the coffee. Amelia cuddled into her mother's side, squashed into the other chair while Jack and Cleo sat on the sofa. Catherine looked drawn but she was smiling, her arms wrapped tightly around her daughter who was drinking an almost florescent pink fizzy drink.

"We'll be talking some more as there are still many unanswered questions, but for now try and get some rest." Janet Hill looked across at Jack. "I'd thought you'd have had enough excitement for now." She turned back again to face Catherine. "We think the two communications were ….. How shall I put it?" She placed the coffee cup on the tray. "The first was a demand to know where your husband was, or possibly is. Clearly, somebody's convinced he's still alive. But the second demand was purely for financial gain. The same MO but we think that the male we have in custody was working for a person or persons unknown.

"He hasn't talked then?" Jack eased himself forward and placed his empty coffee cup on the tray sitting on the table in front of him.

"He denies everything. But with your statement, Jack, and what Amelia has managed to remember of her experience there, we have enough to make a charge stick. Plus his little sidelines. Handling stolen goods and dealing a range of drugs to kids at the local secondary school. We have him on CCTV." She smiled. "He'll be going away for a while."

"But you don't think he was behind Amelia's abduction." Amelia by this time had wandered back to the kitchen and was busy opening a packet of chocolate biscuits. Jack looked at Catherine who was staring unfocused at her cup.

"So he *is* still alive! Somebody thinks so, somebody wants to find him. I want you to find him, Jack."

"For the time being don't let Amelia out of your sight. Don't fall into a pattern, vary your routines and let us know if anything, however, trivial it may seem, causes you any concern." Janet Hill got to her feet. "We'll be keeping the house under surveillance for a while just in case. Thanks for the coffee, I'll see myself out."

The three sat in silence while she made her departure, and when the front door closed Catherine spoke. "Jack, I'm serious, I want you to find Paul. He didn't die as a result of that plane crash. He's alive somewhere."

"Catherine, you have to ask yourself the question. Why hasn't he contacted you?" Jack shuffled on the sofa trying to breathe slowly in order to allow the pain in his side to ease. "*If* he was alive and wanted to get in touch surely he'd have done so." Cleo held Jack's arm and he could feel her grip tighten when he'd spoken. He realised that perhaps he was being unthinking. "I'm sorry Catherine, I'm not trying to be cruel, but think about it. It's been so long since he vanished the trails have gone cold. Everything seems so vague; people forget details and their lives move on. I've nothing of any substance to go on. The leads I've had have all come to dead ends. It's like chasing a ghost. You could be wasting your money. Sorry, but at the moment that's how I see it."

"One more week Jack, work on this for one more week. Just to pacify me. I know you you're not one to give up that easily. Will you do that for me, Jack?"

"I think you could dig a little more Jack, just for Catherine's peace of mind." Cleo's eyes met his and he melted. He knew he'd have to agree to another week.

"OK, I can see I'm being ganged up on here. Another week and we'll see where it gets us." Cleo squeezed Jack's arm as if to let him know he was doing the right thing. "I'd better get started then."

* * *

George was already on his second pint when Jack and Cleo entered the pub. Cleo went over to where George was sitting and Jack joined them a few minutes later with drinks and a menu.

"So old boy, we've got another week on this job." George took a gulp of beer. "What do you want me to do?"

"I don't want you to do anything George." Jack felt a kick on his leg as Cleo looked at him.

"George wants to help. You know what they say, Jack. One volunteer is worth ten pressed men!" She pleaded with her eyes and Jack turned to George.

"OK then, let's get a plan of action written down."

"Good show what?" George beamed, and Cleo placed her hand on Jack's knee, squeezing gently.

Over their lunch, they talked about the events that had lead up to Amelia's return. George had many questions and Jack did his best to answer them all. Cleo was pleased to be out of the house where she'd felt almost trapped herself. The strain of looking out for Catherine had been more than she'd expected.

"So the police think that this little scumbag wasn't the one who'd abducted her?" George looked puzzled.

"I'm sure he was the one who abducted her, George. But the police, and I have to say I'm inclined to think they're right, seem to think somebody paid him to take Amelia and deliver the flash drive. But then he got greedy and decided to add his request for half a million." Jack finished his pint and gestured for another. George and Cleo both declined. "I don't think the person, or persons, who initiated this abduction, know what's happened. They probably still think scooter lad has Amelia locked away. They're not going to be too amused when they find out. And unless the police can get a name I can't see them moving this investigation forward."

"So what'll they do? The police I mean." George queried.

"Sit on it I expect. Wait for something to turn up. Anyway, they've enough to be getting on with dealing with scooter-lad and all his petty mischief."

"So what's the plan old chap?"

"I think we need to find the other two partners who shared the plane. They can't have just accepted Paul's death as an accident. There has to be more to it and I think that's where we need to focus."

He sat in his room for hours waiting, willing the phone to ring. At the same time terrified it might. He paced the room, decided to go for a walk but was unable to clear his mind. *'They had Maria and Amelia.'* He couldn't bear to think about what they might be suffering. All of this was his fault and he was waiting helpless, unable to do anything. He was angry. He walked aimlessly, watching people around him going about their lives. *'Was anybody watching him?'* He kept trying to see if he were being followed. He'd stop turn around and double back to see if he recognised anyone he'd seen earlier. He was becoming paranoid. *'They're too clever to be caught out like that!'*

Paul returned to the hotel and asked if there'd been any messages. Upon being told there were not, he wearily climbed the stairs back to his room. The room was hot. He walked to the window and felt just a hint of a warm breeze. He looked out over the town and river below with the world going about its business, the sounds of distant traffic, and a train making its way south out of the station and crossing the river. The whole scene like some miniature landscape reminded him of the train set that his cousins had built for them by their father, his uncle. It occupied the entire loft space of the house where they lived. He had envied them the hours of fun, the closeness they'd had with their father. It was a closeness he'd not had with his. He began to daydream, imagining that the scene below was his big train set. He watched as the northbound train appeared from way off in the distance. He watched as the two trains passed each other. They were too far away for him to hear the sounds, the rattles of wheels on rails and the whoosh of the air as it was compressed between the carriages. One of the train's horns was sounding. Paul could hear it clearly. He listened and then an icy cold finger ran down his spine. It wasn't the train! He turned to the bed where he'd thrown his mobile. It was vibrating!

* * *

The mobile was ringing. It didn't get answered because Catherine was not in the kitchen. She was at the bottom of the garden with Amelia. They were both mucking out Gypsy's stable. It was twenty minutes later when they returned for a drink. She made a coffee and a squash for Amelia. It was only then she noticed she'd missed a call. This time there was a number. She didn't recognise it so ignored it, placing the phone in her bag. They were just finishing their drinks when the house phone rang making them both jump. Catherine snatched the receiver from the wall in the kitchen.

"Oh Jack, sorry I thought it might have been…… No, it's alright." She swallowed and cleared her throat. "Is there any news yet?"

"No, I was just checking in to make sure you were both OK." He paused. "You are OK aren't you?"

"Yes, we're both good. Listen I had a call, well a missed call on my mobile, we were both down at Gypsy's stable. They left a number but I don't want to call it Jack, I'm scared of what it may be. Can I give you the number to check out for me?" She read the number and Jack copied it to his phone with a note added to call it.

"I'll call the number and let you know what it is soon as. Is there anything else?"

"No Jack but thanks. We're having an 'at home' day today. Feel free to call by later if you like. Bye for now."

"Jack, are they OK?" Cleo was sitting across the breakfast table, her foot resting against his ankle. They'd finished eating, Jack having managed 'full English' while Cleo had chosen a natural yogurt over muesli. They were just finishing their coffees.

"Yeah, seems like they're trying to get back to normal." He pushed the cup and saucer to the middle of the table. "Catherine had a missed call. She didn't know the caller. I mean she didn't recognise the number. She's asked me to phone back for her. She's worried it might be …. You know; something to do with Amelia's abduction." Jack made to get up. "Shall we go back up to our room? I'll make the call."

"Gosh Jack, when you said shall we go back up to our room I thought you meant something quite different!" She melted him with her smile, rubbing her foot again on his ankle.

The room overlooked the sea in the distance and while Cleo sat at the open window admiring the view Jack dialled the number Catherine had given him. It rang for what seemed like ages and Jack was set to end the call when it was answered.

"Hello?" It was a young woman's voice and Jack assumed by her accent, she was French.

"Hi. I'm calling this number because someone made a call about an hour ago from it to a mobile number and the call was missed." Jack was finding it difficult to explain clearly why he was calling back from yet another mobile number albeit withheld.

"I'm sorry I wanted to speak to somebody called Catherine who knew Jason. He had an accident you see and I knew him." Jack could hear music and voices in the background and it was clear the woman was somewhere very busy. He suddenly heard another woman shouting a name and scolding her for slacking when there was work to be done. "I can't talk at the moment. You can call me in one hour's time. OK?"

"I will. My name's Jack and I will call you back. Would you tell me your name?"

"Katrina. OK, thanks. We'll talk soon." There were yet more accusations from beyond the phone and then the line went dead.

"That was short and sweet!" Cleo turned her head from the view and motioned for Jack to come and sit next to her.

"Sounds like a young French girl. She seems to think somebody called Jason knew Catherine." Jack sat down and scrolled through his contacts. He held the phone to his ear. "Catherine, It's Jack. Does the name Jason ring any bells?"

"It could be one of Paul's sharers. You know, of the plane. His name's Jason, at least I think it is. He's the only person by that name I know." There was a pause. "Well, I don't actually know him only met him very briefly at the inquest. I suppose Paul must have given him my mobile phone number years ago. I think they each had contact numbers for ICE, you know in case of emergency."

"So do you have any other contact numbers?"

"No, it was just the three of them I suppose. Paul didn't give me anyone else's name or number."

"I'm calling the number back soon and I'll let you know what information I get, if any. Bye for now." Jack looked at Cleo. "This could be yet another dead end, getting nowhere fast."

"Well, you're not going to know unless and until you call back." She turned and moved closer to him brushing a lock of hair from across his eye. "We'll have to think of something to do in the meantime." She leaned into him kissing him gently on the lips.

"I've just had a perfect idea." He took her hand and led her slowly to the bed.

* * *

George sat in his deck chair his newspaper on the ground and a mug of coffee resting on his lap. The sun had climbed to its mid-morning position in the cloudless sky and his wide-brimmed hat was shielding his eyes. There was the distant sound of small aircraft taxiing on the runway and the fainter engine noises coming from three thousand feet higher. He felt the warmth of the sun through his shirt and thought there was probably no better place on earth to be. He closed his eyes, taking in the smell of newly mown grass wafting across from the lawn mower as it moved slowly from one side of the vast field to the other. He was thinking about all the changes that had occurred during his time at the small airport. There was the greater security now in place at the gates, the requirement to keep accurate logs of flights. He wondered whether it was now time he should hang up his flying goggles. It was all becoming a bit too much. George preferred the easier lifestyle of bye-gone years. Things were more straightforward then.

He'd only bought himself a mobile phone because all the public phone boxes in the area seemed to have been removed or vandalised. He'd got a simple and straightforward one. He wanted a phone that did just calls and text messages. He didn't want a camera but he'd had to upgrade when his first one had died on him, or rather he'd left it in his trouser pocket when he washed his jeans! The battery was beginning to pack up and wouldn't hold a charge very long. This new phone was all shiny and slim not like the old one! He turned the phone over in his hand marvelling at the rate technology had moved on in just a few years. He preferred things you could take apart and fix. He hated the 'throw away' society that seemed now to be the norm. He looked at it thinking that he'd not have a clue how to repair it if it went wrong. Everything now was solid state, micro this and that. He'd listen to young folk in the pub talking computer language that completely left him dumbstruck! It made him jump when the phone burst into life vibrating and chirping like a demented parrot.

"Hello George, Charlie here. I'm coming over your way this afternoon. Wondered if you wanted a few jars later?"

"I think I could manage that, we could have a pizza back at my place. I have a couple sitting in the freezer." George was suddenly galvanised into planning the rest of the day. "Let's make an evening of it Charlie, stay over. I've also got a bottle of malt that needs the top off!"

"OK, great see you about four at your place?"

George placed the phone carefully in his pocket and leaned back in his chair contemplating the evening ahead. *'There's a couple of films on DVD we could watch if I can remember how to work the machine!'*

* * *

"What are you going to do Jack, with the business I mean?" She was running her hand along his free arm; his other arm was holding her.

"What do you mean?" He turned his head slightly to try and make out her expression.

"Well, you've nowhere to live having lost the boat. You've spoken about folding up the office, the business. And you seem to be finding plenty to do here on the Island, workwise I mean."

"Actually Cleo I've been thinking. I'm wondering whether a new start down here would actually be a good idea. You know a clean break. Set up on my own."

"So am I being made redundant?"

Jack was suddenly aware of the hidden message she was giving out. "God no, I'd need staff, I'd have to find a secretary for a start!"

She'd gone rigid, unable to speak. *Was he trying to tell her something?* She wasn't sure at that moment what to say. She remained silent but her head was spinning, her mind was racing.

"The job would be yours if you wanted. What notice do you need to give on your flat?" He leaned in and kissed her tenderly on her forehead. "Would you like to come and live here on the Island with your boss?"

"Really, do you mean it?" She was looking at him, wide-eyed.

"Really, yes I do mean it, Cleo. That's if you want to."

"Of course I want to Jack!" She wriggled into a crouched position next to him and then threw herself on top of him as he lay there. "Oh Jack, it would be lovely….." They kissed and held each other, each one thinking about their future. A future with each other!

It was Cleo who'd reminded him to call the number. Jack would have spent all day holding her in his arms, drifting in and out of consciousness. They'd been chatting about nothing in particular when Cleo ordered him back into 'work mode', poking him on his arm to galvanise him back into action. He'd made the call. Katrina wanted to tell someone, somebody who knew him and cared about him, what had happened to Jason. She felt she owed it to him. Jack was somewhat confused at first but as he listened to her school level English he started to understand why she'd made the initial call, the first contact. She didn't want to just forget about it, she couldn't. The call lasted probably no more than ten minutes, interspersed with bouts of crying down the line as she recalled the events that had led to Jason's accident. Jack took down the details and where he could contact Katrina. He thanked her and explained he'd pass the information on to Catherine. Jack dropped the phone on the bed and stroked Cleo's arm.

"That sounded a bit heavy!" She turned to face him, resting on her elbows and kissing his shoulder. "What do you think it's about? I mean her interest in him"

"I'm not sure, she's very upset. She sounds quite young." Jack reached up and inadvertently scratched at the wound on his head.

"Stop Jack, you'll make it bleed!" She pulled his hand away quickly and looked at his head. It's healing nicely at the moment you don't want to get it infected.

"I think I need to go and find out what this Jason was doing and why he ended up dead. It may be just another dead end but I won't know until I go." He kissed her and got up. "Can you keep an eye on Catherine? We don't know, whether she's in any danger or Amelia. I know the police are still keeping a watch but if you could as well……"

"I can do that Jack." She smiled and stretched out on the bed feeling the cool sheets against her skin. Rolling again onto her back she turned her head following him as he walked across the room.

"I'll suggest to Catherine that you stay with her while I'm gone. And stop doing that!"

"What?"

"Moving about like that, it makes me….. You know!"

"Oh yes Jack, I know. But watching you is fun ………" She threw a pillow at him. "Go on, go and get ready, now!"

* * *

Charlie's car wheels crunched on the gravel as it came to a halt in the parking area outside George's flat. No sooner had they said their hellos when the bell rang again.

"Come on up old chap!" George pressed the button to release the front door.

Jack appeared in the doorway and was introduced to Charlie and there followed another round of hellos.

"So you're the famous Jack Ramsay!" Charlie held out his hand. "I've heard all about you from George, and Jan."

Jack looked confused. "Jan?" He looked at George for an explanation.

"Jan…. Janet is Charlie's daughter Jack. You'll know her better as DI Hill."

Jack took a deep breath. "Oh, I see." He smiled slightly. "People in my line of work tend to be a thorn in the side of the police. We get accused of getting in the way, slowing up progress and at worst wrecking a case!"

"That's pretty much word for word what she said!" Charlie was laughing. "But she *was* impressed with you helping to get that case solved, albeit in a bizarre way!" By the way, I'm so glad that little girl was found safe. It doesn't bear thinking about if he'd….." He was suddenly aware he was clenching his hands into fists. "Well, you know." Charlie suddenly realised that he'd disclosed information not yet in the public domain. "Janet didn't say much you know……. Sorry, I shouldn't be talking about it at all! ….." He trailed off, not knowing how Jack would respond.

"Yeah, a good result in the end." Jack looked at the two men. "Anyway sorry to call uninvited George but I just wanted to let you know I'm popping over to France for a few days, I'm following a lead. Cleo's staying here, well at Catherine's, just to keep an eye on things, keep me in the loop should anything happen."

"Anything I can do? You only have to say the word." George was looking, hoping Jack would suggest he came too. "I could fly you over Jack, be there in no time. What do you say? Chocks away, what?"

"That's very kind of you George but in fact, Cleo's already booked me on the ferry to Cherbourg" he lied, "leaves late tonight and gets in early tomorrow morning.

She's got a hire car arranged for me as well. Nice thought though George." Jack wasn't keen on flying at the best of times. He saw it as a necessary evil, a way of getting somewhere quickly if the need meant there was no alternative. As an afterthought, he added. "If you could just keep an eye on Cleo for me, give her a call just to let her know you're there if she needs anything. That would be a load off my mind."

"Consider it done old chap!"

Jack said his farewells and left the two men deciding which pizza, which pub and which DVDs were going to form the main performances of their evening's entertainment. He climbed back into the car and started the engine. Jack hadn't enjoyed telling George a lie, it wasn't that he didn't want his company but he wanted to be able to move at his own pace, not to be explaining every step and turn to somebody. Neither the ferry nor the car were booked but would be as soon as he got back to the hotel.

* * *

His hands were trembling, so much so that he almost dropped it as he picked up the phone and answered. At first, he could hear nothing. "Hello............. is anybody there?" The line was definitely open; he could just make out very faint background sounds. He had no idea what they were, he listened, closing his eyes in order to try and focus his hearing. A few more seconds passed. "Hello!" He continued to strain, try and catch some sound that would give him a clue. *'They were playing with him!'* He became angry. "Is there anybody there? Speak damn you!

"It's me!" The voice was distant as if she were speaking from across an empty room. He could tell from the sound of her voice she'd been crying. "Do what they say, please, or they......" She suddenly went silent.

"Maria, are you OK?"

"Of course she's OK.........." The man's voice appeared to boom loudly in his ear. "She's too valuable to damage. Well, at the moment anyway!"

"Don't you put a finger on her, I'll...." Hi, voice trailed off realising the futility of his threat.

"You won't do anything Paul. You'll wait until *we* tell you what *you're* going to do." He heard her shout something, the sound of a slap and she screamed.

"Tell me now; I'll meet with you, anywhere. Just tell me."

"*We* decide Paul, *not* you. You're going to have to be a little bit patient and wait. I've waited a long time Paul. A few hours or even days won't change things now. You've really upset everyone you know that don't you? You've made some very serious enemies who've not enjoyed the way you fucked them off. You can't go around upsetting people like that and expect to get away with it. I think you're beginning to realise that now."

"We can talk. I can make all this good... Just give me a chance to explain."

"Bit late for that! I think I know how this is all going to end Paul. It's not looking too good for you. It'll all end in tears for you, I think you know that now don't you? And remember we hold all the cards."

"Please don't hurt Amelia. Let me talk to Maria, please?"

"No! I'm afraid that your time's up for now."

With that, the line went dead. Paul quickly dialled Maria's number but already it had been switched off. "Fuck, fuck fuck...." He threw the phone back down on the bed and put his hands up to hold his head feeling it was about to explode.

* * *

CHAPTER SIXTEEN

Jack was glad Cleo had booked him a cabin. By the time she'd driven him to Ryde for the ferry to Portsmouth and he'd taxied to board the Cherbourg bound crossing he was ready to eat and sleep. After finding his accommodation he'd made his way quickly to the restaurant and had finished his meal before the ship had left sight of the Island. He'd caught a glimpse of the lights across the water. The seaside towns glowing in the fading light with their promenades twinkling like a distant Christmas tree. Jack returned to his cabin, called Cleo briefly and hit the sack, falling asleep almost immediately.

The crossing had been good. The sea had been kind and the majority of passengers who'd imbibed too freely with duty-free alcohol had managed to keep most of it in their stomachs. Another reason Jack had chosen a cabin to himself! Eventually disembarking, Jack pitched up at the car rental office and, after the formalities of insurance and driver's licence checks, was on his way. He was pleased to be on the move again but this time under his own command. The traffic started to thin as he put miles, '*or should that be kilometres!*' he thought, between him and the ferry port. He had a few hundred to do to reach his destination but he was enjoying the journey. The French countryside was drifting by as he made his way south. With the windows and roof down he was breathing in France's air, its smells and its freshness. The day was still young with the sun still on an upwards travel across the big blue sky spread out above his head. '*I'm glad I paid the extra and took the convertible!*' He mused.

He headed south skirting Rennes and followed the road to Angers. After a while, he decided to look for somewhere to stop, fuel the car and get something to eat. Jack turned off the main road and followed the signs for the town centre. He pulled into a large market square where he found both fuel and a café. He was hungry, it was nearly 1pm and his breakfast on the ferry seemed like a distant memory. Although tempted, he decided against a long glass of Pernod with ice but opted for a latte and a filled baguette. As he sat in the shade watching the town going about its daily routine he began to wonder about his life and how things had changed recently. He thought about Cleo, how she had been a major player in giving him the strength to continue. He'd much to thank her for and he had grown fond of her. '*No, more than fond, he'd found somebody with whom he wanted to spend time, in fact, every second of the day.*' Jack smiled at the realisation that he was on the verge of a new chapter in his life. His current happiness was tinged with sadness remembering what he'd lost all those months ago. He'd never forget but he would carry them with him in his heart.

The sounds of the traffic, the people walking past and the chatter of voices brought Jack back to the present. He made two calls. The first to Cleo, he'd promised to call her and decided that he'd do so now in case he forgot later. The second was to Katrina. She sounded busy and Jack realised she must be working in the café and the lunchtime trade could be clearly heard on the line. He estimated another two to three hours driving and asked her where he might find accommodation when he arrived. She gave him the numbers of two places in the town. They were written on cards pinned up near the counter where she was standing. Jack heard an older woman calling and she said she had to go. She'd wait at the café to meet him. Then she was gone.

The open car became like a hot wok as Jack made slow, and at times no, progress along the main road. In the end, he raised the roof and switched on the air conditioning, the relief almost instantaneous. A serious accident had blocked the road for miles and Jack turned off after about half an hour, following both his satnav and fellow road users to circumnavigate the holdup. The progress was still somewhat of a procession but at least he was moving and headed in the general direction of his destination.

It was nearly five-thirty when he drove into the small village square and parked the car. Jack climbed out and straightened his body. His back ached and his head was now thumping. He cursed himself for not buying a bottle of water. A girl was sweeping the area outside the café across the street and as Jack approached she stopped and looked up.

"Bonjour, Mademoiselle Katrina?" Jack was

desperately trying to remember his French vocabulary but before he could utter anything she smiled.

"Are you Jack Ramsay? You're later than you said, we're closing now but I can make you a coffee."

"Thank you, but may I have some water?"

"Please sit and I will fetch some for you." She gestured to a table and Jack eased himself onto a plastic chair while she vanished back into the café. Within a minute she reappeared with a tray, two glasses and a jug of iced water with slices of lemon and sprigs of mint. She placed the tray on the table, sat at the vacant chair and poured them each a glass.

"A vôtre sante!" She smiled at him and held up a glass, Jack did likewise. The water was good and he felt refreshed, the long drive in the heat had tired him more than he'd imagined.

"So Katrina, tell me what you know about Jason."

* * *

Cleo had dropped Jack at the ferry and driven over to stay with Catherine. Jack having suggested she do so and Catherine agreed, saying she'd feel more secure knowing a trusted acquaintance was staying with her. She'd made a mushroom stroganoff and Cleo had bought two bottles of wine, one white, and one red. Catherine was genuinely pleased to see her and the two women chatted over their meal and well into the evening, Amelia having been dispatched to bed earlier. Cleo felt more relaxed, the return of Amelia had brought cheer back into the Blanchard's household and Catherine was able to release some of the worry and tensions the last few days had wrought. Between them, they'd consumed all but the dregs of the bottle of Merlot. They were talking like friends of long standing. They spoke of past lives, boyfriends and places they'd visited. They discovered things they had in common, music tastes they found similar, books and authors they'd both read and films they both hated. Finally, after a strong coffee, they retired to bed. Cleo was in the guest bedroom, the same one Jack had slept in just days earlier.

The morning dawned slightly overcast but it was bound to turn brighter as the 'chirpy' weather girl beamed out from the television screen in the kitchen. Amelia was downstairs dressed and ready to go and muck out Gypsy. Catherine had issued strict instructions that she was to wait in the kitchen until Beryl arrived.

"Then, and only then, may you go and play with Gypsy!" Catherine had repeated again, reinforcing her argument with the promise that she and Cleo would come down to the paddock and watch her ride after breakfast. Catherine turned to Cleo raising her eyebrows questioningly.

"Oh yes, that would be fun. I'd like to watch you riding Amelia. Mummy tells me you have a whole bunch of rosettes pinned up in your tack room. I'd like to see them." The two women smiled down at Amelia who appeared to be making a remarkable recovery from her recent ordeal. Just at that moment, there was a thump at the kitchen door and Amelia shouted.

"Beryl's here..... Can I go now mummy, please? You said I could as soon as she was here. Yes?"

"Go on, we'll be down shortly."

Amelia flung open the door and Beryl stood there beaming down at her. "Come on my girl, let's go and sort out that pony of yours." Beryl put a protective arm around her and they walked off down the path chatting away, a trail of straw and a whiff of equine odour marking their trail.

The two women sat in the kitchen perched on the breakfast bar stools with their respective coffee mugs. The conversation flowed easily as if they'd been lifelong friends.

"Thanks again for staying over Cleo. You've no idea how much I value your company." Catherine held up her mug. "More?" She poured two more mugs from the machine. "Shall we go through to the conservatory? We can watch Amelia more easily from there."

They took their coffee and sat looking out through the conservatory windows. At the far end of the garden, they could just make out two figures, one large and one small, passing in and out of sight as they went about the business of mucking out Gypsy's stable. Beryl had decided he should have fresh straw and between them, they were busy removing the dirty straw to the muck heap, a fenced area in the corner of the paddock. The two wheelbarrows, one large heavy duty and the other a lightweight garden barrow moved back and forth, laden with straw in one direction and empty in the other. Water and disinfectant were then liberally applied to the concrete floor and allowed to dry before clean fresh straw was laid. While the floor dried, Beryl instructed Amelia to fill the feed bucket and hay net ready for later when Gypsy would be coming in.

"She's having fun; she doesn't seem to have been affected by her abduction." Catherine took a tissue from her pocket and wiped away a tear. "She's not told me much. I hope they didn't....." Her voice trailed away to just a whisper.

"She'll be fine Catherine, after all, she was questioned by the police and they would have picked up on anything she'd said." Cleo placed her mug down and turned from looking out onto the garden. "She'll soon put it out of her mind."

"But I can't forget about it. It was my fault and I should have been watching her!" Catherine screwed the tissue into a tight ball in her hand. "What if they try again? They will, I just know they will....... And I don't know where Paul is. I can't tell them. Everyone thinks he's dead. What if next time she's taken and I can't tell them because I don't know............ What will they do to her?"

"Jack is following up on that phone call and I know it's a long shot but he's of the opinion that there's more to be discovered. Let's allow him a few days to see if he can find anything more."

"I feel so helpless, what if we're being watched right now with somebody waiting to take her again?"

"The only people watching Amelia are us and the police. They told you they'd be keeping a covert surveillance of the house. Just try and relax Catherine, I know it's been very difficult but she's safe and back with you."

* * *

The door had been kicked in again just hours later. Others on the estate had known about Scooter-lad's treasure trove stashed away in the house. They'd waited until the police had completed their initial search of the property and because the thin blue line was always stretched to beyond breaking point; there were no available officers to stay on site. In the time between the police leaving and the locksmith arriving to secure the premises the boxed TVs, computers, microwaves and other assorted received items had vanished to the four corners of the estate along with a quantity of legal and some illegal substances. The scooter was found three days later in the river Medina having been ridden and abused by various under age kamikaze pilots. DI Janet Hill had been furious, slamming the door to her office and sending numerous items flying as she flung her arms across the desk. This simple lapse of security would have disastrous consequences. The crime scene had been totally compromised. Scooter lad would get off the charges made against him, it would be impossible to make a case that wouldn't be thrown out by any court. He'd walk free and she'd be hauled over the coals at best, demoted at worst. She put her head in her hands. "Fuck... Fuck, fuck." She repeated quietly to herself.

* * *

They'd talked for a couple of hours, her mother giving disapproving looks in their direction as she busied herself noisily in the kitchen area of the café. It was clear to Jack that Katrina had fallen for this Englishman. She was sixteen, he was twice her age plus and yet he'd treated her like a woman, not like the other boys in the town. She'd been flattered by his attentions and the promise of more. She described the day of the accident in detail. Jack made some notes, trying to allow her to talk freely without him having to stop her while he hurriedly wrote things down. It was clear that Katrina had been devastated by his sudden and tragic death. Being the first on the scene and comforting him during his last moments had a lasting and profound effect upon her. She welled up and tears rolled down her face as she spoke. Her voice trembled, her words no more than a whisper.

"You said that he asked about the café." Jack decided to change the direction of the questioning away from Jason and his violent demise.

"He asked about the café, yes but he wanted more to know about the owner." She wiped her eyes with a napkin, took a sip of water and continued. "He spoke to Monsieur Michael, the owner. They went off to have a meeting."

"OK, so perhaps he knew him."

"Well no, but perhaps yes. I don't know the truth of the matter, but it was a strange meeting."

"Why strange exactly, can you explain what made you think that?" Jack had become keen to know what Katrina saw in just a meeting.

"I don't know why, but they were not easy in the company of each other."

"Well, if they were strangers……"

"No! That's the point. I think they *knew* each other!"

Jack's mind was beginning to kick into gear. *'He needed to speak with this Michael.'* "Where is the owner, Michael? Where does he live? Is he local?"

"That's the thing, he's gone!"

"Gone?"

"Well taken a short holiday but he's not here at the moment….."

Jack felt he was travelling up yet another blind alley. "Don't suppose you know where he's gone?"

"She cannot tell you, she not know where they go." The voice of Katrina's mother was suddenly close by. Her poor English sufficient to understand the conversation that had been taking place. "She told you all she knows."

Jack decided upon a tactical retreat. "I've taken enough of your time. Perhaps we can talk for a while sometime tomorrow. Thank you, and now I will go in search of my room." Jack stood and looked at both of them. "Madam, Mademoiselle." With that, he left them to finalise their locking up and walked back to his car. The evening air was cool, a pleasant relief from the heat of the day. Jack felt tired, he needed a meal and a shower, and not necessarily in that order! Tomorrow he'd talk with Katrina again. There was something, some piece of the jigsaw that needed to fit. She held the key to how that piece fitted, but Jack realised she didn't know this. Jack didn't know either, but he was determined he'd find out. Mulling over in his head what questions he'd pose to her, he fell into a deep sleep. The hours passed and his body was feeling renewed. The pain from his recent injuries was now just a shadow of what it had been, almost not there at all. But sometimes, when he forgot and moved too quickly or pulled too hard, it would send spears of pain around his body just to remind him he was not yet mended. He dreamt of trying to manoeuvre giant sized chunks of jigsaw while all around him knew where they went but wouldn't tell him. They laughed at him, his incompetence, and his inability to see where the pieces fitted. He was getting angry, he shouted for them to help him but they just faded away. Eventually, he'd placed all the pieces down on the ground only to discover that there were some missing. There was nothing more to be found, he was left with empty spaces, the picture incomplete. He didn't know what to do, he didn't know how to move on. But move on he must, as time was passing, and time waits for no man.

* * *

"Bailed?" Nobody could believe it. Janet Hill sat motionless at her desk. The others in the office were looking on speechless. "The little shit's got bail, there's nothing we can do."

"It's the evidence Guv. The case will get thrown out he'll get off and all because of not having the bloody manpower!" The voice that came from the back of the office Janet knew belonged to DS Anthony Sharp, the new lad down from Winchester who seemed to have much to say for himself. *'He's someone I'll have to keep an eye on.'* She thought quietly.

At precisely the same time Scooter-lad, who'd been identified as Wayne Brooks, walked out of Newport police station, turned slowly and stuck two fingers up at the building before spitting copiously on the pavement and walking off in the direction of the nearest betting shop. Clearly, this was his lucky day and he needed to capitalise on his good fortune with a little light gambling. He swaggered along his jeans half off his backside and his hoody over his head in spite of the temperature. Talking on his phone, he took no notice of others walking along the pavement. An elderly woman pulled at her husband's arm in order to avoid being barged out of the way. He glared confrontationally at them, daring them to speak out but they scuttled past eager to put as much distance between him and them as they could.

Something caught his eye just ahead. A piece of paper at the side of the road fluttered into the gutter wafted by a passing vehicle. Wayne bent down and snatched it up. It was a crisp new twenty-pound note. This really was turning out to be his lucky day!

* * *

He'd left text messages, four of them. His recipient had not acknowledged any of them. '*Where the hell was he?*' There was nothing in the papers and he'd looked online. '*Did he still have her?*' There was only one thing to do. He'd have to go and see for himself, talk to him find out why he wasn't doing as he was told.

The journey had been long and when he eventually turned into the road he was quite weary and certainly not expecting to see police vehicles parked outside. He didn't stop or even reduce speed but drove on by. He continued on for about a hundred yards, pulled into a side road and parked. He got out and walked over to where three women were standing, staring back along the road. Kids were riding their bikes around in circles on the edge of the group, over grass and kerbs, bumping their tyres as they did so. The women were happy to talk and tell him all that had happened. All the details of the police raid on the house. He handed out cigarettes from a packet he carried. He didn't smoke one himself. They told him all about the little girl who'd been rescued and the man who'd been taken away. When he'd gleaned all the information he needed, he made his excuses and walked back to his car. From his position, he could see the house, who came and who went. He waited, he could afford to wait he'd been waiting a very long time.

* * *

Wayne had been back to the house and wasn't surprised to find all his stock had been nicked. The door had been fixed with a new lock. The police had given him a new key when they let him out. He found his black bag and started to throw a few clothes into it, enough to keep him going for a while. He'd won another fifty quid in the betting shop so was feeling good. He placed his hand down through the split in the lining of the bag and pulled out the cheap PAYG phone. He put it in his jeans pocket. *'He'd let him know, leave a message later when he had a few miles under his belt.'*

A few of the kids who should have been at school, but were either suspended or 'hopping off,' acknowledged him as he walked down the road. He ignored a shout of 'Where's your scooter Wayne?' and continued through the estate until he came to the main road where he turned north. He entered a small park with a few swings and a litter bin next to a bench. Wayne sat and took out the phone. He switched it on and waited what seemed like minutes before it eventually fired into life. He had two bars on the battery and three on reception. He waited. The message appeared on the screen demanding that he text, and the time he was expected to do so. He'd missed three times but the fourth message gave him a time of 3:30 p.m. He looked at his phone and saw it was only just after three. He had plenty of time! He placed the other phone in his pocket and sat back taking in the scenery. A woman walking her dog walked by and the dog, a small terrier type, yapped at him while straining at its lead. He kicked his feet towards the dog and the owner pulled sharply at his lead to drag him from harm's way. He had three ciga-rettes left and decided to while away some time with a smoke while he waited. The woman had walked across the park and vanished from sight passing into the alley that ran down to the estate. He'd the place to himself. The sun felt warm on his back but he kept his hood up. The PAYG phone bleeped. Wayne took a long drag from his cigarette and pulled the phone from his pocket. He looked at the message, it was empty! He scrolled up and down but there was no message. He pocketed the phone. *'He'd have to tell him the girl had escaped. He'd tell them he'd been arrested but that he'd said nothing. He'd tell him too that he still wanted to be paid!'*

Wayne was considering how he'd spend his money when he got it! He finished his cigarette and tossed the butt onto the ground. He'd get out of this dump, perhaps go abroad. *'Spain would be nice'* he thought and voiced the words out loud. The phone bleeped again and he cursed as he took it out only to discover another empty message. A man was walking along the path his phone clamped to his ear and clearly in deep conversation. Wayne took no notice as the man sat on the bench still talking into his phone. Wayne was slightly annoyed at losing sole rights to the bench but he wasn't going to argue. The man was well built and could clearly handle himself.

The phone in his pocket started to ring! Wayne didn't understand, he'd been told he'd only get text messages. He looked at the time, it was only 3:10 p.m. Too early! He pressed the button and held it to his ear. It sounded like a recorded message. It was very faint and Wayne had to strain to hear it over the loud voice of his bench companion.

"You've failed us, Wayne. I can't abide failure. I'm afraid we can't continue our contract with you so you'll very soon be receiving a severance from us." Wayne didn't know what a severance was. He had no idea what was going on, he still wanted his payment. *"We no longer require your services Wayne, termination is the only way forward. You see we can't afford to leave any options open to you either, so that's why we have to let you go. I hope you understand our position Wayne...... goodbye.*

The man on the bench finished his phone call and turned to face Wayne who was staring blankly at the phone in his hand. "Bad news is it, mate?"

Wayne looked at the man and then back at the phone. "You're fucking right!" The man moved quickly and took the phone from Wayne's hand. With his other hand, he plunged the knife deep into Wayne's stomach. Wayne's eyes were suddenly wide with the realisation of what was happening, the sudden sensation of sharp biting steel in his body. "What about my money?" He whimpered. Wayne's hands clutched at his stomach as his life blood began to ooze out over his clothes.

"Sorry mate, I just deal in terminations, ending contracts." The man got to his feet. "Oh, can I have my knife back? You don't need it anymore." He reached and took hold of the handle twisting it slowly before pulling it out of Wayne's body.

"Fuck….. Help me!" His voice so weak it was barely audible. He began crouching forward drawing his knees up to meet his head. His shallow breathing was tinged with a sinister gurgling deep in his body.

"Won't be long now, soon be over. You just sit there and enjoy your last few minutes." He walked slowly away.

Wayne was alone again, just him and the park. He had the bench to himself again and the sun was shining. He'd received his severance payment, it was his lucky day!

* * *

Chapter Seventeen

The coffee was excellent. He savoured it and decided upon just the merest dash of cream. Pastries of every conceivable type were available as well as warm croissants. Jack sat listening to the town waking up outside in the street. Voices, conversations, traffic all mingled together to create a truly idyllic backdrop as he drank the last of his coffee. He declined yet another refill having consumed three. The car was parked at the back of the small hotel but Jack decided that a ten-minute walk would be more beneficial that sitting in the car.

Turning left out of the entrance he made his way through the town. The narrow streets and narrow pavements meant constant checking every time he stepped into the road to allow for meandering pedestrians carrying shopping baskets filled with bread, carrying newspapers and steering young children. He arrived back at the café and saw Katrina fixing a tablecloth to one of the outside tables. She was deep in concentration fiddling with the plastic clip and was unaware of his presence until he spoke.

She jumped slightly but regained her composure when she saw him.

"Monsieur Jack. I did not expect to see you so early. Please sit and I will bring you a drink. Would you like coffee?" She smiled radiantly at him and for a second he almost forgot she was only sixteen.

"Thank you but just water." He sat at the table and she vanished inside. The café was quiet. He could hear music coming from a small radio inside and a conversation between two women seated just inside the doorway. He was the only customer outside. She appeared almost immediately carrying a tray similarly laden to the one she'd brought him the evening before. She poured them each a glass and sat on the seat adjacent to his. She pushed the other plastic chair away slightly with her foot making room. "Can you spare time to talk some more now?" The iced water was a shock after the hot coffee.

"It's not busy as you can see." She gestured with her arm. "It may become busier later, but for now I can talk to you."

"Your English is very good. You're fluent."

"Fluent?" She wrinkled up her nose in a most appealing way as she struggled to understand. Then her eyes widened. "Ah, yes I understand. Fluent! I have studied English at school and want to go to England to study the English Language at university when I am older next two years."

"I'm sure you'll do very well." Jack watched as another customer sat down at one of the vacant tables.

"Pardonner, un moment!" She jumped to her feet and took the order. Two minutes later she reappeared with a coffee and croissant, placing it down in front of the customer. She sat down again and Jack was aware of her perfume. He was also aware she'd sat just a little closer to him. "So how can I help you more?"

"When we spoke yesterday evening you mentioned that Jason and the owner of the café seemed to know each other." Trying to continue a conversation now twelve hours old seemed to Jack like relighting a damp bonfire! He needed to get her to remember what she was saying and more importantly what was going through her mind as she was speaking. "Try to recall what you told me. Can you remember what you were thinking as we were talking?"

"You were asking me what had happened. You were nice to me, not making me upset too much." She moved slightly on her chair. Jack felt her thigh brush against his leg. "You asked about the accident and I told you all that had happened." She paused for a few seconds. "Well, not all!"

Jack was not sure what to do. Their legs were still in contact! He didn't want to pull away sharply causing embarrassment. *'Perhaps she was unaware?'* The thought went through his mind that he was making more of this than there was to it. *'She didn't realise and she'd move her leg away in a moment!'* Two more customers appeared and sat down at the table next to theirs.

"Sorry." She gave him a smile and jumped to her feet and, taking the pencil and pad from her back pocket, she took their order and again vanished from view.

"It's beginning to get busy. Would it be better to talk at some other time?" Jack looked at his watch. It was just approaching 10.30am. She'd sat down at his table again, still close but not touching. "Later today, do you have time when we could continue.....?"

"Perhaps that is best, yes." She slipped the pad from her jeans and wrote an address and time. She tore off the sheet and handed it to him. "I can see you there, for an hour." She jumped up again as one of the customers beckoned her for attention. "I must return to my work, sorry." She touched his arm lightly and before Jack had realised what had happened she was gone. He looked at the piece of paper, her writing small but very neat. The address meant nothing to him and the time 2:00 p.m. was just a time. He guessed probably her lunch break or such like. He pocketed the piece of paper and finished his glass of water. Katrina was nowhere to be seen as Jack left his table. He placed a ten euro note under the water jug and made his way back to his hotel. *'Was there any more information he was likely to get from this girl?'* Jack thought about the leg contact, her touching his hand. *'I'm reading more into this than there is, she's just a girl.'* He could still smell her perfume..........

* * *

The wheels slipped on the gravel as the car came to a stop. DI Janet Hill climbed out of the passenger seat. She'd asked DS Sharp to come with her and instructed him to drive. They walked the short distance to the door and rang the bell. It was a while before the door was opened and, although a telephone call had preceded the visit, Catherine was surprised they'd arrived so quickly. She ushered them into the snug and invited them to sit on the large leather sofa. Cleo was sitting at the kitchen table with Amelia and they were practising drawing horses on a large piece of paper. Catherine beckoned

Cleo through to join them leaving Amelia
unsuccessfully to trace a horse outline using a piece
thin baking parchment.

"We thought you should know before the press gets
hold of it. It'll be all over the 10pm news but I wanted
you to hear it from me first." DI Hill cleared her throat
and continued. "There's been an incident today and it
impacts upon our current investigations with regard to
the abduction of your daughter. We, the police that is,
were called to the scene of a fatal stabbing. The victim
has been identified as a Mr. Wayne Brooks. The same
Wayne Brooks bailed this morning for a number of
offences including the abduction of your daughter." She
waited a few moments to allow the information to sink
in. "As of this moment, we're pursuing a number of
leads in order to catch the person or persons responsible
for this crime. We are treating this as a murder."

"What are you saying? Put it into plain English for
god's sake. Is somebody coming after us...... or
Amelia?" Catherine jumped to her feet and ran into the
kitchen. "Amelia, you must not leave the house unless
you are with me. Do you understand?" She threw her
arms around her daughter, holding her tightly.

Cleo caught the DI's eyes. "She's understandably
worried sick. Until this is all resolved she's not going to
be able to relax."

"We'll have this wrapped up quickly don't worry. It's
pretty clear he's been silenced. We're following a number
of leads, bound to get some results very soon." It was
DS Anthony Sharp who'd spoken. He looked pleased
with himself having put the two women's minds at rest.

"Please be assured we're doing all we can to find the
person or persons responsible and bring them to

her head towards her DS and
her eyes. "Thank you for your
ning her head back again to face
tinued. "We'll leave you now.
the house under surveillance day
 She and her DS got to their feet. "But
do take obvious care, vary your routines, that sort of
thing, keep a phone with you and make sure you
lock doors that aren't being used." Cleo saw them to
the front door while Catherine took Amelia back to the
kitchen.

"If you're concerned or need assistance in any way,
here is my card." DS Anthony Sharp pressed a card into
Cleo's hand and he walked alongside her. His hand held
hers for just a millisecond too long and she started to
feel an instant dislike for this man! They stopped as
Cleo opened the door to let them out. As the DS passed
her she deftly placed the card in the top pocket of his
suit jacket.

"I don't think so, thankyou all the same." She looked
him in the eyes willing him to speak, to say something.
He averted his eyes, blushed slightly and continued out
to the car. DI Janet Hill allowed herself just the merest
smile, the two women catching each other's expressions.

"We'll be in touch....... when we have some news."
She climbed into the passenger seat and Anthony started
the engine.

*'I'd love to be sitting in the back seat listening to the
conversation that's about to begin.'* Cleo mused to
herself pushing shut the heavy front door as the car
made its way back down the drive.

* * *

Not a thing. No call, text message, nothing at all. He'd been going out of his mind with worry, pacing the room, checking his phone to make sure the battery was charged. He'd checked the internet for news, bought the local and national newspapers each day just in case there was some mention of abduction. It was a slim chance and he didn't hold out much hope. Not leaving the hotel for longer than he needed, just in case a message was left. But there'd been no contact. It had been two days! He'd tried calling but the phone was switched off. He'd left countless text messages but none had been opened or seen. Paul didn't know what to do. He'd no idea where Maria was being kept, whether it was nearby or miles away he didn't know. He was worried sick about Amelia as well. *'Catherine would most probably have been contacted, should I try and contact her?'* He pondered the thought and decided to wait just a bit longer. *'They may call, any minute now.'* He looked at the phone, willing it to ring.

* * *

Jack had again walked, leaving the car at the hotel, deciding the exercise would do him good. He'd found the address on google maps and using his phone negotiated the fifteen-minute walk through the town to the eastern side. It was hot and the sun's rays seemed to reflect off the buildings and pathways. It was quiet with few vehicles and even fewer pedestrians. He found the address and looked at the door. It appeared to be to a flat above a shop. The shop was closed and with shuttered windows it wasn't clear to Jack what it sold. There was only one bell push at the side. Jack pressed it but could not hear any ringing. He waited for a few seconds and not hearing any sounds from within pressed it again. He heard a bolt being drawn and was pleased that he'd soon be able to get out from under the rays of the relentless sun.

"Please, come in Monsieur." She smiled at him as she stood framed in the doorway. She appeared taller but he saw there were two steps up to the level where she was standing. She moved to allow him to enter and closed the door behind him. "Please go up the stairs and the door at the top is open." Jack trod the narrow wooden steps and she followed, their footsteps echoing as they climbed to the first floor. The open door to the flat was unpainted in that shabby chic way only the French can get away with. Jack entered and looked around, taking in the furnishings and fairly minimal furniture. "Please sit, I will get you a drink, yes?"

"Thank you, Katrina." He sat on the sofa and although the room was small it was just big enough to accommodate it. She vanished from sight into the tiny kitchen and reappeared with glasses and a jug of water. She placed them on the coffee table. Jack could see that the glasses already contained a clear liquid. She sat next to him and poured iced water into the glasses, the water immediately turned cloudy and Jack could tell he was being offered Pastis. *'Should this young girl be drinking? Should he refuse to drink with her? What was he getting himself into?'* Before Jack could come to a decision she'd handed him a glass and taken a gulp from hers. He sipped his drink, it was good he had to admit, but he was very unsure about allowing himself to conduct an interview with her drinking like this. She looked at him over the rim of her glass. "Don't worry Mister Jack I've had this before." She placed the glass on the table. "So, you wanted to talk more, am I right?"

"Yes, we were being interrupted at the café and I do have some other things to ask." Jack reached into his pocket for a small pad and pencil.

"We have an hour............ and nobody will interrupt us." She glanced at him with a knowing look and then laughed out loud. "Oh, you Englishmen are so funny!" She tucked her legs up under her and turned to face him. "Come on, you ask and I will tell you what I know."

Jack looked at the notes he'd made earlier. "You'd said earlier you thought Jason knew the café owner. Who is, I mean what is the name of the café owner?"

"His name's Michael, he comes to the café usually each day." She drank from her glass, Jack noticed she'd nearly finished. "But we haven't seen him for a while."

"What made you think he knew Jason? That they knew each other." Jack watched her drinking and wondered whether this was her first of the day. She placed her empty glass on the small table stood up and walked to the kitchen. Jack watched as she came back clutching a bottle of spirit and sat down on the sofa. He was feeling most uncomfortable with her clearly getting drunk. "Look Katrina." He took the bottle from her and placed it on the table. "I don't think this is helping."

"But it is helping. It is helping to ease the pain I'm feeling. It makes me numb to the pain of remembering Jason and the way he died." Tears were rolling down her cheeks and she wiped them with the back of her hand. "You probably think me stupid, a crush, something like that. But I liked him very much and now he is gone and I wanted to......." She dissolved into tears, shaking uncontrollably and spilling her drink.

Jack, without thinking, placed his arms around her and she clung to him tightly sobbing. They sat there for what to Jack seemed ages but was probably just half a minute. He wasn't comfortable with the situation. This young girl, not really a woman, drunk and the two of them alone in this flat would be a very difficult thing to explain should the need arise. Jack had visions of the mother suddenly appearing and finding them locked together in what appeared to be an embrace. Just as Jack's mind was speeding into overdrive she stopped sobbing and let go of him. Relief flowed through him as she appeared to be composing herself once more.

"You are right, about the drinking I mean." She stood up again. "I will make us some coffee, yes?" Without waiting for a response she vanished again into the kitchen, where after some opening and closing of cupboards and water being poured she reappeared with two mugs. "It's only instant I'm afraid. And there's no milk!"

"That's fine." Jack took the mugs from her and placed them on the table. "Are you OK to carry on?" He smiled and tried his best to show he cared about how she was feeling without causing her to dissolve into another round of tears.

She sipped at the hot liquid. "I'm a bit better now." She paused before saying. "You perhaps think I'm a silly girl but I really cared about Jason. I know that I only knew him a short time but I hoped that he and I might become...." She stopped, took a deep breath, closed her eyes for a second and continued. "I hoped we would become more than we were. But now it's all over I must carry on. You understand Mister Jack?"

"Yes, Katrina. I understand all too well." Jack's memory flashed back eighteen months to the time his wife and baby had been hit by the car, killed outright. Two lives wiped out in a second and the driver never caught. "You have my deepest sympathy Katrina. I do understand the pain you're feeling." He reached for the glass and downed the remains of his drink. "I too suffered a loss. It was a while ago but the memory and pain still are still strong. You learn to cope, to deal with it. You have to, and over time it does become easier to bear. You never forget........" Jack closed his eyes just for a second worried he might not be able to talk about it. He could picture her face the morning she kissed him goodbye as he hurried to make the work meeting. He had been running late and he'd hardly said a word as he grabbed his jacket and keys. Jack opened his eyes, suddenly aware he was headed down a dark hole. He fought his way back to the present, to the here and now with this girl in a French flat. She was looking at him intently.

"Are you OK Mister Jack?" She touched his arm and he almost jumped with the shock.

"Yeah, just remembering that's all." He took two or three deep breaths, reached for his coffee and sipped at it trying to conceal his emotions. Jack paused before continuing. "You say you haven't seen this Michael for a while?"

"Not since the accident. And now Maria, she is gone too!"

"Hang on! .... Who's Maria?"

"His partner, I don't think they are married but they have a small flat not far from here. She left too. My mother says they were having a few days away."

"You're not so sure?" Jack was making notes in his book.

"Well after Jason met with Michael, he seemed very unsure, how do you say….nervous. I am talking about Michael now. And then he was gone."

"When did you last see Michael?"

"It was before the accident with Jason. Not just before but a while before, hours I suppose." She was calmer now and sipped at her coffee, her elbows resting on her knees and perched forward on the sofa.

"Do you have an address? The flat where they live, you say it's not far from here."

"You passed near to it when you came here. I can show you, I've visited it a number of times when I have taken things. How do you say, run errands?"

Jack smiled. "Yes, 'run errands' is correct!"

"I have to go back to the café soon shall I take you and show you their flat?" Katrina got to her feet. "We have time if we go now."

* * *

Didier was bent over the engine cursing the obstinate spark plug for refusing to budge. The other three lay patiently in the plastic tray awaiting their recalcitrant sibling. He stood with a start upon hearing his name, missing the edge of the raised bonnet by millimetres. Katrina accepted a kiss on the cheek as he wiped the oil from his hands ready to be introduced to Jack. Jack was glad Katrina was with him, Didier spoke no English other than being able to tell him the names of various English football players and teams, none of which interested Jack in the least. With Katrina's help and translation Jack was able to ascertain that Michael had called Maria and Didier had taken her to the railway station to catch a train. He seemed to spend ages recalling the destination before agreeing it was most definitely Vivonne.

Jack noted the town in his book, Katrina and Didier continued to talk for a while longer. To Jack, they both appeared to be talking at the same time and he had no idea what they were talking about. Eventually, Didier waved his hand at the car indicating he'd better get back to the job in hand. Jack and Katrina thanked him and they continued their walk back to the café.

"He said she was upset. Michael had phoned her and she'd packed a bag to go and meet up with him." Katrina brushed her hair from across her eyes as they walked on. "I asked if they were having a short holiday. He said it didn't seem like it, she was agitated, angry with him, Michael that is. She was annoyed he'd gone off without telling her and then expected her to follow on. He'd taken the car so she had to get the train."

"What make of car, do you know?"

"An old Citroën, like Didier's but a dark colour, blue or green I think. So dirty, they never washed it!" She laughed. "It was a bit of a wreck, one day he took mama and me down to the market and it broke down. We had to push it the last three hundred metres to a garage and get it fixed before we could drive back again!"

"So do you think that's where they are, Vivonne I mean?"

"Maybe, it's a pretty town, not very big but a nice place to spend some time." They walked up the steps to the flat and knocked on the door. It was clear no one was at home. Didier watched them for a few seconds and then returned to extricating the plug. Jack peered in through a shuttered window, the small gap offering little or no real view inside. Katrina knocked again but the flat offered no response. "They're not here, the place is empty."

"Can you describe Maria, what does she look like?" Jack was making a note of the address and ready to write Maria's description.

"I can do better than that." She took out her phone. "Here, these are pictures I took when we had a small party just two months ago." She scrolled through a series of pictures. "This is Maria. And this one is Michael."

When Jack looked at the image on the phone he knew he'd seen that face before. Although he'd gone some way to alter his appearance, it was Paul Blanchard. Jason had found him and now Jason was dead! Various scenarios flash into Jack's mind. *'Paul Blanchard had killed Jason to maintain the secret of his true identity. Was that realistic? What if Jason had blackmailed Paul? This was yet another possibility?'* A whole raft of 'what ifs' swarmed through Jack's head.

"Can you send these to my phone?"

They walked along the narrow streets back towards the café, Jack trying to glean as much information about Michael from her as he could. Both she and her mother had worked for Michael for about eighteen months. Katrina had started by washing up after school in the small kitchen but more recently had taken over the waitressing. She enjoyed it and Michael had been a good boss to work for. Maria could be difficult. Katrina wasn't sure whether she was protective of Michael, envious of other women's attentions, or just plain awkward. She would be demanding whenever she came to the café, nothing would be good enough. Jack was beginning to get a picture. Turning the corner the café loomed into sight. They both stopped at the side of the road.

"Katrina, thank you for all the information you've been able to give me." He handed her one of his business cards. "If you remember anything, or you just need to talk you have my number." He kissed her lightly on the cheeks catching a scent of her perfume again.

"Thank you, Mister Jack. I hope you find the truth." She sighed. "And perhaps the reason for Jason's death may be solved. I hope it is." She touched his arm, just a light touch but sufficient to send a tingle. "I must now go back to work." Without a backward glance, she walked across the road and disappeared into the café. Jack stood for a moment taking in the views, the sounds, and the smells. Diesel and coffee, the clatter of an occasional moped and voices of locals as they walked passed by, all going about their lives and oblivious to this Englishman standing, watching.

* * *

CHAPTER EIGHTEEN

Jack's journey had been straightforward. He'd headed south on the N10 and soon found he was approaching the outskirts of the town. Vivonne's town centre was old. The streets were very narrow and progress in a car almost impossible. Jack had passed the railway station and had considered parking. After becoming lost, he'd wished he'd done so. More by luck than judgement he found himself back on the main road and headed for the station. He decided to park the car and continue on foot. The town seemed busy and Jack saw it was market day. Turning the corner he found himself in the middle of a large square, stalls everywhere and the place was crowded. He'd no plan in mind but was now quite hungry. He found a stall selling street food, then another! His senses were being overpowered by an array of different scents all tempting him in different directions. In the end, Jack settled for a filled baguette and coffee and eased his way to the edge of the market where he found some benches. He tucked in eagerly while watching the world go by and thinking how on earth he was going to find Michael or Maria, if in fact they were still in the area. He finished his coffee quickly when a particularly nasty mini swarm of wasps started circling the waste bin next to where he was sitting. *'I wondered why this bench was vacant!'* He swatted at them and discovering the futility of his actions quickly gave up deciding retreat was the only option.

Fuelled by his meal Jack walked on through to the main street where he found a hotel. It seemed to be the only one in the town so he ventured inside to take a room. He was in luck and within ten minutes had the key to a room on the third floor. He hoped Catherine would cover the expenses as it was more than he really wanted to pay. The advantage was that there was a space at the rear of the hotel to park and so Jack decided to walk back to the station to collect the hire car. On his way down the stairs to the foyer, he met a man coming up the stairs, his head down and striding quickly. As he passed by Jack glanced in his direction expecting an exchange of pleasantries but none were forthcoming. Jack was about to speak but the moment was gone and the man hurried on up the stairs and out of sight. Jack shrugged. *'Sometimes people just don't want to talk!'* He continued on out into the street. It played on his mind all the way to the station. *'Some people just seem to want to avoid contact, talking, or even just exchanging the time of day! So wrapped up in their own little worlds they want nothing to do with anyone.'* Jack was the kind of person willing to pass the time of day and talk to people. He became agitated, annoyed when he didn't receive the same back. He got into the car and started the engine. *'Why am I getting so worked up over a complete stranger ignoring me? He clearly didn't want to talk, so why should I worry? Get over it Jack!'* But

Jack *was* worrying. He couldn't let it go it was like a dripping tap! There was something, and he didn't know what, that kept nagging away at the back of his mind.

* * *

He was going crazy with worry. He'd still heard nothing, nothing at all! He'd left countless messages, tried calling but the phone remained switched off. He sat holding his phone, his lifeline to Maria and Amelia, but it was like holding one end of a rope with no one at the other end. He could do nothing and they knew it! He sat at the table in the restaurant having come down from his room. He'd been going stir crazy just sitting and waiting while he looked at the four walls! He wasn't hungry, the half-eaten meal on the plate bore testament to the fact. Paul made the coffee last as he watched the comings and goings both inside and outside in the narrow street. The room wasn't particularly busy it being still too early for the evening patrons to make an appearance. The sudden vibration and chirping startled everybody in the room. Paul grabbed the phone clutching it to his ear and listening intently. When he spoke it was with clenched teeth in a forced whisper.

"Let me speak to Maria, please?" Paul's hands were shaking. Others in the room were glancing in his direction. "I need to know they're safe, unhurt, Amelia as well."

He'd been aware of the others in the room disturbed by this man but the names hit him like sledgehammers! He looked at the man sitting at the table across the room. He could have passed him in the street and not recognised him. The picture he had on his phone, the one Katrina had sent him bore little resemblance to the man now talking. He'd cut and dyed his hair and was now sporting a beard, albeit short. But Jack knew now he'd found Paul Blanchard!

Jack watched as he scribbled something down on a piece of paper, the man's hand trembling as he tried to write and speak at the same time.

"Yes... OK, I'll be there." He spoke very quietly. There was a pause. "Will you bring her, can I see her?" There was another pause. Paul spoke again. "Are you there?... Answer me!" He looked at the phone, the call had been ended. He sat with his head in his hands, his elbows resting on the table.

Jack quickly rose from his table and moved silently across the room to where Paul was still sitting motionless. He placed his card alongside the coffee cup and sat at the vacant chair at his table. "I may be able to help you."

"Who?...." Paul lowered his hands and looked at Jack. "How did you find me?...." He looked around the room and then back at Jack. "You know who I am?"

"Paul Blanchard presumed dead three years ago. He died in an aircraft crash." Jack held his phone to show Paul the picture Katrina had taken. "I heard you mention Amelia. She's your daughter."

"They've got her! Bastards, if they do anything..."

"Hold on! They haven't got her, relax Paul." Jack raised his hand to quell both Paul's raised voice and his gesticulations! "She's safe and back home with Catherine." Jack was aware of the relief on Paul's face on hearing the news. "The police got the guy responsible and they're keeping the house, your house, under surveillance." He saw no point in elaborating at this stage although he knew Scooter lad had been merely a pawn.

"But they've got Maria, I'm so worried for her, she's pregnant. We were here and they took her, just a couple of days ago. I don't know what to do. And now they've told me I have to meet them." Paul was visibly shaking while he poured out his troubles to Jack. "I have to make sure she's safe. They won't hurt her if I give myself up to them. They'll let her go won't they?"

Jack wasn't so sure. All this information was overloading him but he didn't want to commit to making a comment until he knew a whole lot more. "We need to go somewhere a little more private than here in the restaurant. We need to talk and not be heard."

"My room, let's go up to my room." Paul stood and without waiting headed for the door. Getting quickly to his feet Jack followed, having first scanned the room, nobody else was taking any notice, and looking out of the window to the street beyond there was nobody to be seen. Paul was waiting in the foyer and the two men made their way in silence up the stairs to his room.

* * *

Cleo received his message and read it three times, at first not believing what she was seeing. He'd tried to call but phone reception was almost non-existent. He'd sent the text message hoping it would eventually get through. She tried Jack's number on getting the message but it went straight to answerphone. Cleo looked at the time. She knew Catherine would be still awake as they'd only just made their way up to bed minutes earlier. Both women had talked well into the late evening over a bottle of red. They'd become good companions, friends even, which surprised Cleo who'd been rather wary of Catherine at first. She wrapped her kimono around her and knocked on Catherine's door.

"What is it? Is everything OK?" Catherine looked startled as she opened the door. "I'd almost drifted off when I heard you. Come in." She held the door open for Cleo to enter.

"Jack's found him!" Cleo looked at Catherine who seemed not to understand. "He's found your husband, Catherine. He's with Paul." The sudden anger which erupted took Cleo by surprise. She knew it would be traumatic whatever the outcome but she was fondly imagining Catherine would be pleased.

"The bastard, I want to talk to him! Phone Jack, I want to speak to Paul, now! Phone him Cleo. I want to give that little shit of a husband a piece of my mind!"

"There's no signal there, where he is. I've already tried." Cleo was somewhat thankful that Catherine wasn't able to call and speak. It might make an already bad situation worse! Catherine was in no state to make reasoned conversations, the half bottle of red wine and the anger were a dangerous combination.

"What did he say, Jack, I mean? How did he find him? What's Paul's excuse for putting everyone through hell for three years?" Catherine was calming slightly although Cleo could clearly see she was incandescent with inner rage.

"The message was very short." Here. She handed Catherine her phone and she read what Jack had sent. "So he's with him now, they're talking. Paul's no doubt giving him some bullshit about why he's done the dirty on us. He'll be blaming everyone except himself. What a bloody waste of space!" She sat down on the edge of the bed, putting her head in her hands and dissolving into floods of tears. "I accepted his death. I could deal with that. But now that I find he's still alive........"

Cleo sat next to her and placed an arm around her shoulders. "It's the shock, Catherine. It was going to be whichever way it turned out."

"This way is worse, much worse!" She sobbed. "I almost wish now that Jack had never found him........ Christ Cleo, what do I tell Amelia? How do I explain this all to her? And what do I tell his parents? God, it'll kill them! It would have been better for all of us if he'd died, killed in that plane when it crashed three years ago!"

* * *

Paul and Jack sat in the two chairs which were positioned to view the river from the hotel room window. Paul had placed two glasses on the table and a bottle of Jack Daniels stood between them.

"Do you want a drink? I need one." Paul didn't wait for an answer but poured two generous measures. "I've tried but I can't find any proper scotch in this town." He handed a glass to Jack. "How did you find me? Who sent you, was it Catherine?"

"It was pure luck. I'm in the room above." Jack pointed up. "I'm on the third floor, directly above this one." He took a drink and wished there'd been some Coke to go with it. He'd forgotten how raw it tasted. "Catherine now knows you're alive. I texted a message a few minutes ago. I've been working on her behalf."

"I see." Paul looked beaten, his head inclined forward and staring blankly at the floor. "She won't understand why I did it....... Did Jason tell you where I was? I expect he did. I left the flat before he came back. I just had to get away, do some thinking. I had to have a bit more time to think things through."

"Jason's dead Paul, or didn't you know?"

Paul's eyes widened. "God no, I had no idea. How, what happened? He's really dead?" He downed the remains of the Jack Daniels and poured two more large measures. Jack noted his hand was shaking as the bottle was placed on the table. "I thought he was following ......" His voice trailed off. He took a drink from his glass and continued. "So Jason told them? He told them where I was?"

"I don't think he did Paul. It seems Jason was killed when he'd served his purpose. He'd found you, but it would appear somebody was following him!"

"Amelia, she's safe though isn't she?"

"She's safe, as I've said. But tell me about Maria. You'll have to tell me precisely what happened. Tell me every minute detail of your journey down here, and hers, from what you know. And what you did when you got here. It may just give us some clues."

"I was careful, I didn't drive straight here. I stopped twice, doubled back a few times. Checked to make sure I wasn't being followed. Then the bloody car packed up! I had to get a lift here to Vivonne. I was lucky and got a lift in a van. It's not where I was headed. I was going to go to Spain, drive on down and get Maria to fly down later when I got somewhere for us to stay." Paul emptied his glass and reached for the bottle. Jack grabbed his hand.

"This isn't the way forward Paul. We both need to keep clear heads and be ready for what may come next."

"You're probably right Jack." Paul suddenly remembered. "I have to meet them Jack, tomorrow evening. I have to get the money, to give them, from the bank tomorrow. I don't have it all. Some I can draw tomorrow, and I have about half I brought with me but it won't be all of it.

"OK, slowly. Who are you meeting?"

"I don't know. That's the point, Jack. I have to meet with them to make sure Maria is safe. They'll let her go if I meet with them and give them the money. The money I owe them, and *my* share as well, all of it, Jason's as well!"

"But you say you don't have it all."

"I don't, I've spent just about all my share in the three years. The café just about broke even, paid the rent on the apartment." Paul looked at Jack quizzically. "If they don't get it all back, if I can't pay in full. What will happen?"

"Christ only knows Paul, I've no idea who these people are, what they're about, what they're capable of. You must know more than me on that front, surely!" Changing the subject slightly, Jack continued. "Where are you supposed to meet tomorrow evening? Have you been told?"

"No. Apparently I'll get a text message to tell me where to go." He took out his phone, checking to see if anything had been sent. "I've had nothing yet, no messages or anything!"

"Give me your phone." Jack didn't wait but took Paul's mobile and keyed in his number. A muffled beep emerged from Jack's pocket. "There, you have my number." He handed his phone back. "Is the money somewhere safe?"

Paul nodded. "Do you want to see it?"

"No, just as long as you can lay your hands on it quickly." Jack stood up. "I'm going back to my room. Don't go anywhere without letting me know first. Try and get some rest, sleep if you can." He picked up the half empty bottle and walking to the basin poured it away. "You don't need this!"

"Thanks, Jack." He sat with his hands cradling his head.

"I've done nothing yet. Let's hope that together we can sort this mess out. Our priority now is Maria and getting her back unharmed. If you're contacted I need to know immediately, do you understand Paul? The moment you hear from them let me know."

Paul nodded and rose wearily to his feet. Jack could see he was at the end of his tether. He looked broken, all that could have gone wrong, had gone wrong. The only saving grace was that his daughter was home with her mother and safe. As Jack took the stairs back up to his room he wondered how on earth he was going to help him. It was a waiting game. The problem was nobody had told Jack the rules of engagement, and he'd joined the game just as it was about to get complicated and dangerous!

* * *

She was in a small space, a room of sorts, but Maria was comfortable enough. She was terrified of what may happen at any minute but she was being regularly brought meals albeit packaged sandwiches and tins of drink. She was alone. She had no phone, they'd taken it! They'd taken her watch as well so she had no idea of the time. The walls and floor seemed thin but however hard she banged on them she could not get any response. It was dark, with just a small and very grubby overhead roof-light shedding a meagre light down on her surroundings. On the floor, she had a mattress and a sleeping bag. They were both relatively clean for which she was grateful. In the corner, a plastic bucket and on the floor alongside, a toilet roll. She'd slept in snatches ever since being taken from the hotel. Without her phone and having no watch she'd no idea what time of day, or even what day it was!

At first, she imagined she was being held in a building, but the movements, though small, soon brought her to the realisation that she was locked inside a lorry container. Not the enormous type at the ferry ports and on large trailers. This was a small one, probably no bigger than two metres by three. She was chained by her left wrist to the corner of the container furthest from the small door. She could lie on the bed, she could reach the bucket, but she couldn't reach that door! When meals arrived, the door would open and the food would be brought in. It was always the same person, or at least when she'd been awake she could tell it was the same person. Food had arrived twice when she'd been asleep.

She'd slept, for how long she had no idea. When she woke she was cold. The walls of her prison felt cold and clammy. She shivered pulling the sleeping bag over her shoulders. She imagined it must be early morning, she remembered it being dark or at least there'd been no light coming in from the roof light when she'd last looked up. Now there was a faint lightness in the sky, tinged with red. Sunrise, but on what day she had little idea.

Maria kept telling herself that she'd be freed soon. They'd let her go, she was of no value to them whoever they were. A terrifying thought percolated through her as she sat on the mattress. *'What if they did decide she was of no further value to them?'* She tried to stay positive. She had to stay positive for the sake of her baby but she often found herself dissolving into floods of tears. She kept telling herself it was her hormones. *'Pregnancy does strange things to you!'* She kept saying to herself. She spent hours listening, trying to make out where she might be and where the container was. She was convinced it was on a vehicle because of very small barely perceptible movements every so often. *'What was causing them?'* Maria said to herself out loud. Suddenly Maria's world shook! The vibration of the big diesel engine as it stuttered into life caught her completely by surprise. Suddenly she was moving! The lorry was moving, where she had no idea, and where from she was equally ignorant. She pushed herself into the corner on the mattress, her feet angled out for stability as the vehicle lumbered slowly over the undulations. The big diesel engine growled as, in first gear, it made its way first up a steep incline then down again. The tears were rolling down her cheeks, she cried out loud but nobody heard her plea, her voice lost, consumed by the loud throbbing diesel which seemed to shake her whole world.

* * *

CHAPTER NINETEEN

Jack's sleep had been broken. He'd spent hours thinking about what to do. He was unable to plan anything. He'd no idea what was likely to be the next move by a person or persons unknown. The next stage and when it was likely to happen a mystery. How would it happen and what notice would they get? *'How on earth do you plan for something you know nothing about?'* He showered and dressed but still felt tired. The bed beckoned him. The thought that he could just lay his head for a few more minutes was tempting but he resisted the urge. Looking at his watch he decided to wait a while before phoning Paul. He imagined he'd probably also lain awake best part of the night himself! Jack made a coffee from the kettle and tray on the small table in the corner. He decided caffeine might just bring him to a sufficient state of preparedness. He stood looking out through the open window, watching the town below slowly come to life. Cars and vans moved back and forth over the road bridge while a commuter train crossed the river further upstream, snaking its way through the trees and buildings. It was still sufficiently dark for the lights of cars moving along the road to appear to twinkle. He sipped the hot coffee savouring the quiet, the peace and the view that lay before him. The hot liquid seemed to revive him. Jack was suddenly brought back to earth as his phone shattered the relative tranquillity in which he was enveloped. Almost dropping the coffee cup, he grasped at his phone.

"A text, I've had a text. I've got to go Jack. I have to go on my own, it says so." Paul's voice sounded terrified.

"Wait! Paul, listen I'll come to your room. Wait there!"

"No Jack...... I *have* to go on my own. They'll hurt her if I'm not alone! You can't follow, they'll know!" The phone went dead, Paul had rung off.

"Shit!" Jack cursed and took the stairs two at a time to get down to Paul's room. The door was wide open and Jack entered calling Paul's name. He was too late, the room was empty. He looked around for signs, anything that might give a clue as to where he'd gone. There was nothing in the room, Paul had packed his bags. The wire basket into which Jack had placed the emptied half bottle the evening before was nestled up against another empty bottle of Scotch. "Shit!" Jack cursed again. He turned and quickly made his way back up to his room where he grabbed a bag into which he'd placed everything he thought he may need. He praised himself for preparing it the previous evening. As he made his way down the stairs and out through the main entrance he was aware of a car's engine starting. He turned just in time to see Paul behind the wheel of his VW heading down the side of the hotel and turning right into the narrow street.

Less than a minute later he was in his car and turning right desperately trying to see Paul's car somewhere up ahead. The narrow streets made progress difficult and Jack was beginning to give up any hope of seeing the VW when he caught a glimpse of a car turning left some way in the distance. He was unsure if it was Paul's car, but it was the same colour. Eventually, he reached the turning and, seeing no other cars on the road ahead, turned left. He put his foot down and pushed the hire car as fast as he dared along the road. A long way ahead Jack could make out a VW moving quickly. It was travelling too quickly for safety along the road. Jack recalled the empty bottle in Paul's room, the contents of which were in the driver of the car in front. *'Shit!'* he said out loud as he watched it veering erratically left and then right.

Jack considered the pros and cons and decided to call Paul on his mobile. To Jack's surprise, Paul answered. "Paul, we need to discuss what, and how, we do! I'm here to help. Let me help." He didn't want him to know he was following. "Come back to the hotel and we can talk this through, get a plan together." Jack was thinking fast. "Or meet up somewhere? You say where and I'll come to you."

"I can't. I don't have the time Jack. I have to get there now!"

"Where are you meeting them?"

"You can't come! I have to meet them on my own or the deal is off. I have to for Maria's sake, don't you understand Jack? If anyone else turns up......." The phone call ended, Paul had rung off again.

Jack eased back slowing the car and allowing a greater distance between him and the VW. The last thing he wanted now was for Paul to know he was following him! They were leaving the town and appeared to be headed roughly southeast. Jack took his phone and brought up a map before placing the phone in the suction holder in the corner of the windscreen. The battery was low, showing around 20% charge. He could see there was no way he could connect the power lead whilst driving. To do so while trying to watch the car, now three hundred metres ahead, at the same time was impossible and dangerous. Jack toyed with the idea of stopping briefly but, weighing up the pros and cons, decided to drive on, he was sure to lose him if he stopped. He was cursing himself for not thinking to connect the lead when he set off.

The road was fairly busy, cars turning in between him and the VW meant he was less obvious should Paul check his mirror. It also meant that keeping the VW in sight was becoming more difficult with each passing minute. A white van turned across from a side road causing Jack to stand on the brake pedal. He turned the wheel in an effort to avoid a collision and slewed the car to a stop sideways in the road. The driver and his equally thuggish passenger seemed to entirely fill the cab space of the van. They simply glanced at Jack with disdain before speeding off up the road. Jack found himself now the cause of a minor traffic jam. His car was blocking the road in both directions! As irate drivers tooted their horns, Jack quickly got the car back on track and pulled away. He could see the white van in the distance and it was moving quickly. Jack strained to see but could see nothing ahead of it. Paul's VW was out of sight. Jack floored the throttle and the car leapt forward eagerly, closing the distance on the van. He glanced at the speedometer and judged a line to overtake. There were no cars coming the other way and the road was clear and straight. He was closing the distance on the van quickly. He indicated and flashed his lights to warn the driver he was about to pass. He turned the wheel to the left and pulled out, pressing down on the accelerator pedal. He estimated the van to be moving at about sixty and he was doing seventy plus. Just as he was level with the van the driver moved over, not to the right but to the left! Jack instinctively planted his foot firmly on the brake in a vain effort to avoid another collision, his heart in his mouth! The van swerved across the road just brushing the front bumper of Jack's car. As the van's brake lights came on, Jack knew that this was not just 'white van man' on a bad day; these two were on a mission! And it was just about to get nasty!

* * *

The rolling motion was making her feel sick, or it could have been morning sickness. Either way, she knew she was going to throw up. She sat on the mattress and held the plastic bucket ready, the contents of which did nothing to quell her nausea. The smell of urine and excrement, albeit her own, from the previous day and night slopped around, agitated by the vehicle's lumbering movements.

Just as quickly as it had started, it stopped again. Maria had no clues as to why it had stopped. *'Where are we now? What's going to happen?'* For all, she could tell, the lorry could have just been driving in a circle around a big field. She thought about it carefully.

The slow rocking movements and the labouring engine noise all pointed to a vehicle moving slowly over soft terrain, not roads! Maria was convinced they were in a field or along a track. The engine had stopped and all was quiet again. She strained to listen but she could hear nothing. She'd forgotten all about her sickness and placed the bucket back down in the corner. Maria concentrated, closing down all but one of her senses in an attempt to hear anything. She listened intently for any small sound which may just give a clue to where she was. The air was getting hot and stuffy she guessed the sun was up. Soon the temperature within the container would quickly rise, the only relief being when the door was opened and the food was brought in. When that might be she couldn't tell.

Maria knew food and drink were being brought to her on a fairly regular basis. She was convinced it was the same man each time. *'Could she be sure, absolutely sure?'* It was important, little pieces of information added together would give her a picture and information was power. It would give her an edge, not the upper hand but something!

As she sat she looked closely at her prison, the container that had held her captive for how long she couldn't remember. The walls were lined with sheets of plywood, sharp splintered edges where one board met another. The floor was the same, the wood untreated and marked with years of use. There were scuffs and marks, scars indicating its use in another life and another time. Maria looked up, the roof was different. It had been lined with metal. It was a thin shiny metal which seemed to be held in place with small round screws. She couldn't reach it to tell. The door was lined with wood. She knew it opened outwards but she couldn't reach it as her chain was too short. She studied the chain. It was heavy and where it was fastened round her wrist it had left dirt and bruising to her skin. In one place her skin was bleeding. The chain was padlocked around her wrist and the padlock looked new and strong. It was made of brass and appeared impregnable. The chain was dull steel but the links looked strong, too strong to break. Her eye followed the chain to its fixing in the corner of the container. A metal bracket with a ring was fixed to the wall. It was too dark to clearly see but Maria felt with her hand. The bracket wasn't completely in the corner but about a hand's width away from the edge of the wooden panel. The wood was damp in the corner. A roof leak over the months and years had stained the plywood as the water had run down between the outer metal skin and the board. Maria touched the bolts holding the bracket. They were covered with surface rust but otherwise looked secure. She pulled at the chain but it had no effect. The bracket remained firmly attached!

* * *

Paul continued to drive along the unfamiliar road. He had no map and no Satnav. But he knew the road headed approximately south. The traffic had all but evaporated with just the occasional car passing in the opposite direction. He looked in his mirror. There was a vehicle behind but it was a very long way behind. He couldn't tell what it was, car or van. He couldn't even be sure of the colour. The vibration of the mirror and the distortion of the surface made accurate analysis impossible. He gave up and watched the empty road ahead as it ploughed on through the countryside. There were open fields on the left and a forest of tall pine trees to the right. Paul fumbled for his phone to check the text message again. *'Park in the town centre, Champagne-Saint-Hilaire and wait.'* He was nearly there, he was sweating. It wasn't the heat as it was still early morning, the temperature still below twenty degrees. He was scared and beginning to panic. *'I should have told Jack! It was too late they'd be waiting in the town now. Why choose the middle of a town?'* Paul thought it rather strange to be conducting this sort of business in the open street. There were cars parked in the town centre. The small car park was busy with people going about their business using the small shops around the main square. The sun was shining, the sky already a deep blue and birds were still singing. Bunting of red white and blue adorned the buildings and even some of the cars were decorated. It was clearly Champagne-Saint-Hilaire's annual celebrations. He eventually found a space and parked the VW noting a strangely sweet, hot, familiar smell coming from the front of the car. "Fuck!" he said out loud and banged his hands on the steering wheel. A small cloud of steam oozed through the front grill and rose up confirming a leak.

His phone bleeped another text message. He looked and slowly read the words out loud. *'Drive west and follow signs to Anché. Wait by the church... Ten minutes!'* Paul's blood ran cold. They knew where he was! They were watching him, could see him! He furtively looked around. It was just a small village centre with people doing normal things, leading their normal every-day lives. Nobody was taking the slightest notice of him sitting in his car, steam rising. He tried to look in all directions not sure what he was expecting to see. *'No time to sort the car, I have to go now!'* He picked up his phone, dialled Jack's number and started the engine.

* * *

Standing on the pedal, Jack had managed to avoid a serious collision. What happened next took him completely by surprise. With the two vehicles now stopped in the centre of the road the rear doors on the van burst open. Jack had assumed the van had two occupants. He'd seen the driver and his heavily tattooed passenger as the van had turned in front of him. The two that emerged from the rear of the van were of equal size and threat. One was swinging a baseball bat and the other carried a coiled length of dark heavy oily chain. As the baseball bat hit the windscreen and the chain slammed down on the bonnet of his car Jack decided upon a tactical retreat. With the car in reverse, he floored the throttle, watching both the now running figures wielding their weapons. In his rear view mirror was a thankfully empty road! Jack pulled the wheel around while applying the handbrake causing the car's momentum to carry it in a neat 180 degrees slide. Quickly he engaged forward gear and again planted his right foot on the accelerator pedal. His final view in the mirror was of two exhausted figures slowing and eventually stopping as they became diminished in size by the increasing distance.

The road was straight and clear. Jack pulled over and stopped by a farm track that vanished off to the right.

He'd be able to see if he was being pursued. He waited! Nothing! There was a star-shaped crack in the middle of the windscreen through which Jack peered to view the damage left by the chain on the bonnet of the hire car. *'Expenses, it'll have to go down as expenses!'* He voiced his thoughts out loud to the otherwise empty car.

* * *

Faint, so very faint but she was sure she heard it. She listened, eyes closed and concentrating. She could hear the blood pulsing through her head, ringing noises in her ears but there it was music. *'It's the radio in the lorry cab!'* Maria was certain that's what she could hear. Then it stopped! She strained her ears but there was nothing, the music had stopped. The radio had been switched off! *'Knowledge is power!'* She said quietly to herself. Now she knew that there was somebody in the cab. Then she heard a voice, someone talking. They were talking quite loudly but what they were saying she had no idea. The cab was insulated from the container, her prison cell. The sound was muffled, a foreign language for all she could tell. She could hear the voice, then silence. Then the voice again, again silence! It was a conversation but she couldn't hear anyone else. Then she understood, it was a telephone conversation. The man, it was clearly a man she could tell that, was talking quite loudly on his phone. The next sound she heard was a bang as the cab door was slammed shut. *'Just the one door so just one person!'* She figured. *'Knowledge is power!'* She reminded herself. Maria moved quickly into the corner and lay down on her side. Her head was facing the door. She semi-closed her eyes so it would look as if she were asleep with her hands close to her head. There was a rattle as the door was unlocked and a shaft of light tore through the gloom as the door was opened. He stepped in quietly and pulled the door shut behind him. Maria lay as still as she could, trying desperately to make her breathing slow and deep. She needed him to think she was asleep. He stepped slowly towards her, his trainers sticking on a patch of oily stained floor.

"It's time for some fun before we say good-bye Lady!" He knelt down his head closing on hers. He came closer still. *"Come on girl, wake up. More fun if you're awake!"* She could smell him, sweat, nicotine, and alcohol in equal measures. She wanted to run, to get away but she was trapped. She *had* to let him think she was in a deep sleep. His hand touched her hip and gave her a little push. He moved even closer, his face now only inches from her. He slowly rolled her onto her back and started to unbutton her thin blouse. Maria forced herself to appear to be asleep. He ran his hands over her breasts pinching tentatively at her nipples. She pretended to moan and took an extra deep breath. She was ready! She could visualise him crouching over her. She formulated a mental picture of where he was in relation to her. His hands quickly moved to her jeans and before she knew, he had them unzipped and started to pull at them.

She moved! She opened her eyes and with all her strength she swung her left hand making only a minimal correction in the direction of her aim. His eyes lost focus and his mouth gaped as the heavy chain and padlock connected with his temple. He went down as if he'd been shot, instantly unconscious. Maria quickly stood up and kicked him in the side of the head for good measure. She quickly unlaced his trainers and with the grubby once white laces tied his wrists tightly behind his back. Next, she removed his leather belt from his jeans and with the belt looped through the buckle tightened it around his ankles. With her prisoner on his side, she brought his feet up to his wrists and then looped the spare belt through his arms before returning it to the buckle where she fastened it as tightly as she could manage.

He started to groan, the blood oozing from his temple now running a line down into his eye socket and down his nose. "You fucking bitch! ....." He snorted while trying to focus his eyes on her. Maria zipped her jeans and fastened her blouse while watching him, making sure he was no threat and that he was securely hobbled.

"There is more I have for you." She smiled at him as she emptied the bucket slowly over his head. "This!" He tried to scream out but needed to keep his mouth shut to avoid the bucket's contents. He desperately tried to move but to no avail. Maria placed the now empty bucket down and turned her attentions to her prisoner's pockets. "Keys...... Where are your keys, tell me?" She checked his jeans and pulled out the contents of each pocket in turn. Cigarettes and a lighter, some chewing gum but no keys!

"Release me and I'll get them for you."

"You think me that stupid?" She stood up and tried to think, avoiding eye contact with him. '*I am in control, I must stay that way.*' "I want the key." She held the padlock so he could see. "Where is the key to unlocking it?"

"I ain't telling you and you can't get it unless you let me go." He pulled at the laces. "Fucking untie me. We're both stuck unless you untie me."

Maria didn't respond. She stepped past him and sat down on the corner of the mattress. She didn't look at him but listened to his laboured breathing. Something she had once heard when she was a little girl came into her head. '*You have a tiger by the tail!*'

* * *

CHAPTER TWENTY

Jack was not expecting his phone to ring. Paul's voice sounded hollow as if he were sitting in a large metal dustbin. "Jack, I need help, I need your help. The car's fucked, overheating. I have to get to Anché. I only have eight minutes!" There was a crashing noise that to Jack sounded like Paul trying to select a bunch of gears at the same time! "Can you get there Jack and watch my back? Don't let anyone see you Jack, but just to be there if it gets tricky."

"Paul, wait a minute." Jack found himself speaking to nobody the line was dead. Paul had rung off. He tried to reply but the signal was poor and wouldn't connect. He checked the map on his phone, it had frozen! He knew the general direction and remembered seeing a sign back along the road. He couldn't be absolutely sure but Anché sounded familiar. He turned the key and headed north. The crossroads loomed into sight and Jack turned left. He'd been right, his memory hadn't failed him. Anché was just 4kms west. A quick mental calculation reassured him he could be there in just a few minutes.

He was making good progress and was congratulating himself on that very fact when the road in front was suddenly blocked by a slow-moving tractor and trailer carrying an enormous load of tree trunks. It had just completed a turnout of a forest track and was lumbering along at a snail's pace. It was wide, wider than the carriageway and as a result straddled the centre line. Jack couldn't see any way to safely pass. There were deep ditches at the very edge of the road both sides. It was impossible! He looked at the time. He had about two minutes and at this speed, he'd not make the deadline! Jack drummed his fingers on the steering wheel willing the slow moving road block to turn off. Another minute went by. *'If I could get by now I'd just make it.'*

Two things happened at once! One was a good thing and the other one not good at all. The tractor and its loaded trailer started to indicate to turn right into a farm track. At the very same moment, a fast moving white van appeared in the rear view mirror, getting bigger and more menacing with every passing second. Suddenly the road ahead was clear and Jack floored the accelerator pedal. The car leapt forward but the van was already travelling at a considerable speed and was alongside before Jack's car could gather momentum. Jack gripped the steering wheel. He felt his shoulders tense, his knuckles showing white with the strain. The sound was strangely muted but the impact sufficient to send the car offline. He turned the wheel to the left, his foot still pressed down. Again the impact came, this time with even more effect. Jack fought to control the car, the deep ditches threatening to pull a wheel down. His mind was racing. *'These guys won't give up I have to do something, it's them or me!'* He eased the car closer, closer until just a few inches from the van. Both vehicles were now moving at some fifty plus miles per hour. Although the van was heavier, Jack's sudden movement caught the driver off guard. It happened in an instant, the car nudged the van. The van moved left and dropped a wheel into the ditch. There was no coming back!

* * *

The temperature gauge was hovering dangerously near the red sector. Paul put the heater on and switched on the fan in an attempt to stave off the inevitable. The church was clear to see from a way off and Paul turned into the small parking area to the side. He reversed the car into one of the marked parking spaces so he had a clear view of the road and the entrance. There was only one other vehicle in the car park and the single female occupant was checking her makeup in the mirror oblivious to the VW spewing steam. A car pulled in and parked at the far end of the parking area. Paul took a deep breath as two men climbed out of the car and opened the boot. He watched them as they took out large bags and slung them over their shoulders. They were talking quietly unaware of Paul's observation and walked into the small fenced area adjacent. Paul took a breath; he'd been holding it whilst watching them. He turned to follow their progress as they started to prepare for a game of tennis on the single marked out court. Watching them tensioning and adjusting the net height Paul felt a degree of envy for their apparently carefree existence. He felt he'd all the troubles of the world on his shoulders.

He jumped as his phone beeped another text message. *'Follow the black car, stay 100mtrs behind.'* Paul swallowed his throat was dry and his pulse racing! *'What black car?'* He said out loud expecting the text to supply an answer. He looked around and saw the car. It had appeared at the top end of the car park. Paul realised there must be another entrance. He hadn't seen it when he stopped but then again he wasn't looking. It drifted past in almost total silence, the blacked out windows giving no indication as to the number of occupants. They could see him, but he couldn't see them! They had the upper hand, he was helpless! Paul counted five, ten seconds and then started the car, pulling out to follow.

* * *

As if in slow motion Jack witnessed the van slide and dig into the long grass and brambles that lined the bottom of the ditch. Its forward motion now considerably impeded, it inevitably flipped over landing roof down and facing back the way it had come. The ditch sides were steep and held the van perfectly inverted clamping the side doors firmly shut. The rear doors had suffered also. The sudden impact to the roof had effectively pushed the roof panel into the rear doors jamming them shut.

Jack had no intention of returning to help them out, but the tractor driver had stopped and he could be seen running over to the stricken van. Jack pushed on and eventually the sign for Anché appeared. A wall to the left and houses to the right told him he was approaching the village. Braking hard as he passed a 30 kph sign he was almost immediately confronted with a junction. Jack looked to the right down the hill. It appeared to be a very small village. The houses seemed to thin out and he could see open farmland beyond. Looking to the left he caught a glimpse of a stone building, the church! He spun the wheel over and headed up the hill.

Jack pulled into the small parking area alongside the church. There were two vehicles parked. He stopped and turning the engine off climbed out of the car. He surveyed the battle scars his car had endured during the last few miles and slowly shook his head. Explaining this to the car rental company was going to be interesting! Two men were playing tennis in the small court to the side and Jack assumed they owned the green saloon parked near the fence. In the other car sat a woman speaking animatedly into her mobile phone. Her window was open and he could tell she was local. Jack walked over to the fence and excused himself for interrupting the game. A brief exchange with the players told Jack they had no idea if a VW had arrived and gone. They'd been totally engrossed in their game and had noticed nothing. Jack slowly walked back to his car passing the open door window of the car whose occupant had been busy on the phone.

"Excuse me but you missed him." She called to him in very good English.

"The man in the Volkswagen waiting here, you saw him?" Jack stopped in his tracks.

"Yes, I saw them go. I'm here because it's the only place I can get a signal." She held up her phone as proof. "The man in the Volkswagen, he followed the other car when it left a minute or so ago. You only just missed them! I think they were together."

"Them? He was with somebody else?" Jack moved closer to the open window. The woman was probably in her mid-forties, Jack was hopeless at estimating a women's age. She had shoulder length dark hair with just a few silver threads running through. She was casually dressed in tan cropped cotton trousers, sandals and a white linen top which was revealing to the point of distraction. Jack averted his eyes and concentrated on her face which carried minimal makeup. "You saw others?"

"Well, only the other car, the man in the Volkswagen watched the other car and then followed it....... He was on his phone too, but not talking, texting I expect. Naughty of him, texting while driving!"

"Did you see which way they went when they left?" Trying not to sound as if he were part of the Spanish Inquisition he added.

"No, I was here, on the phone!"

"It's just that I was supposed to meet them and go with them too. I got held up, arrived late."

"I see an accident was it?" The woman nodded in the direction of Jack's battered car. Smiling at him she pointed back to the junction. "That way, but beyond that I afraid I can't help, sorry."

"Thank you. You've been very helpful. Good day."

"Glad to help." She smiled as if sizing him up.

Jack felt slightly overwhelmed by her and left her making another call. He made his way back to his car and sat for a few seconds analysing the information. *'The woman had pointed back the way he'd come, towards the junction. He'd not passed them on his way so that ruled out the road he'd approached the village by. They had to have gone down the hill at the junction!'*

Jack headed back to the junction and turned left down the hill and out of the village.

* * *

She sat there for what seemed like ages but probably no more than a few minutes. He'd been shouting, threatening all kinds of retribution. Now he'd gone quiet and had remained so for the best part of ten minutes. When he spoke the next time he was clearly trying a different tack. Speaking with a softer, more relaxed tone he explained he'd no intention of doing her any harm, something Maria did not believe for one second! She jiggled the chain, playing with the end attached to her wrist. The links were too strong to break. She turned the nearest link over and rested it on the next. Then she did the same again, then again. She studied the chain. By twisting them the chain went from being slack and floppy to being rigid, so long as she kept tension on it! She jumped to her feet and started turning the chain, each time she had to duck under the links and by the time she'd done so about thirty times she had to stop because she was feeling giddy! Resting for a minute she regained her balance and started again. All the time her prisoner watched, trying to fathom out what was going on, the spinning ritual seemed to be going on for ages.

Maria stood, now much closer to the corner but with a rigid length of steel chain in her hands. She carefully turned the last link so that it formed an angle with the bracket and keeping tension all the time pulled down. It was difficult with the bracket being so close to the corner. She would have liked to have had a flat piece of wall to deal with. Working in the confines of the corner made the job just that bit tricky. She listened! Nothing! She pulled down again with all her strength. The wood was giving way. There was a splintering sound as the bolts chewed their way through the damp plywood. Eventually, the bracket fell to the floor and in doing so the tension in the chain suddenly was lost. She was free, albeit with two metres of chain and a steel bracket attached to her wrist!

Her prisoner, who'd been watching the performance, closed his eyes in defeat.

* * *

Paul followed as directed, the car in front was not going fast and in normal circumstances, this wouldn't have been a problem. These were by no means normal circumstances as Paul kept a constant eye on the temperature gauge. The heater, he'd switched on earlier to act as a second radiator was now blowing cool air. This was not a good sign. It meant the water level was now so low it wasn't circulating properly. It was only a matter of time before the engine would go into meltdown! The smell of hot engine was permeating through to the interior of the car. Paul opened the two front windows, not that it would help the engine but he needed the fresh air!

* * *

Turning down the hill and out of the village of Anché Jack was confronted with a junction. Workmen had started digging and temporary signs had been erected. A detour sign pointed to the right. Jack had no choice and turned off the main road and up the hill. Assuming the workmen had been there more than ten to fifteen minutes it was a pretty sure bet he was headed in the right direction. Going as quickly as he dared, Jack followed the narrow road twisting and climbing its way northwards. No more than a single track in places, he watched the road snaking off into the distance. It was a vain hope but he imagined he'd see the Volkswagen at any second and would be able to follow. As the minutes passed he was becoming more and more unsure that he was going the right way. He'd passed a couple of turnings, entrances to properties set well off the road. He wondered whether they could have turned off. Jack was now heading away from ever finding them. A mixture of desperation, frustration, and irritation was, in the end, the reason for Jack pulling off the road across a farm track and making a call. He had a signal; all he needed now was Paul to also be able to pick up. Jack listened holding the phone close to his ear. It was ringing and after a few seconds, he heard Paul's voice.

"Jack, thank god! Listen, where are you?" Paul sounded rattled.

"I'm headed north out of Anché. I was held up getting there. A woman said you'd left and I deduced you were headed this way."

"Jack, I've no idea where they're taking me. They just told me to follow them. This bloody car's playing up Jack. It's got a water leak!" There was a momentary pause. "Turning left off the road onto a track, it's very narrow, hardly even a ...."

"Paul, is there anything to identify it? I'm following;

261

I need to see where it is." The signal was starting to break. Paul's voice was coming and going.

"White.... on trees... Each ...." The line went dead. Jack threw the phone onto the passenger seat and concentrated on the road ahead, looking for any tracks leading off to the left. It had to be close. *'They can't be too far ahead of me!'* He said out loud. The sun now shining through between the trees was strobing, making it difficult to see without blinking. His sunglasses were in the glove box, out of reach and time was pressing. Squinting against flashes of light Jack was forced to reduce speed. *'I mustn't miss the track!'* He saw a sign nailed to a tree, then another. He stopped the car and backed up. Whatever was written or painted on the signs had long since faded rendering them unreadable. There was a space scarcely wider than a car's width between the trees. Jack peered at the grass and assorted herbage, he lowered the window in order to get a clearer view. Something *had* made two distinct flattened paths. The wheels of a vehicle! He looked around. There was nowhere to leave his car other than on the road. *'That's probably not a good idea!'* He said to himself. Slowly he edged the car between the trees hoping that first, he'd not get stuck, secondly, he'd be able to turn the car around, and thirdly he was actually going along the correct track! It seemed to go on for ages and as Jack edged deeper all sight of the road behind was lost. It felt strange to be so close to the trees and bushes, the engine noise was reflected back and seemed very loud.

About 100 metres in Jack was confronted with a choice. The track went off in two different directions. He turned off the engine, opened the door and got out. Jack looked up the track to the right. He studied the grass. It hadn't been flattened, at least not recently. Looking to the left he could see that a vehicle *had* been along there. The long grass had been flattened and swept with a car's passing.

Leaving the car, Jack jogged along the nearly invisible track. It curved around to the right after a short distance and as he reached the end of the curve he could see that it continued straight. In the distance was a dense forest of pine but what caught Jack's attention was the sight of two cars stopped by the side of the track. At that distance, he couldn't see how many people there were and they weren't standing still for him to try and do a head count! His immediate instinct was to crouch down. If they'd been looking in his direction he'd stand out against the natural colours of the wooded and densely-leaved surroundings. Taking to the side of the track offered greater cover but reduced the rate at which he could close the distance. He needed to be closer. He had to find out what was happening.

The right side of the track offered the better cover. Jack closed the distance sufficiently to allow him to hear voices, one of whose was Paul. He couldn't make out what was being said, he had to get nearer. Paul was standing next to his car, the front of which was steaming. He had his back to Jack. The cars were about fifty feet apart. There were two other men, one was clearly the driver. He'd just got out of the black car and was standing next to the driver's door. He was wearing casual tan coloured trousers and a darker shirt. The other man was partially obscured as Paul's car was in direct line of sight. Jack could tell he was in charge. He wore a pair of cream linen slacks and a crisp white shirt. Both men were tanned and muscular and clearly capable of looking after themselves. Jack was still recovering from cracked ribs and, although healing well, he knew that in spite of the fact that it would be two against two, the odds of him and Paul coming out the victors was poor at best.

The meeting had clearly not progressed very far. Jack, from his now nearer vantage point, was able to capture the majority of what was being said. The man in the white shirt was doing the talking for the black car party while his accomplice remained mute, staring at Paul.

"You know why you're here?"

"Yes, let's just get on with it. Where's Maria?"

"All in good time Paul. And assuming, of course, I'm satisfied that you kept your end of the deal." He started to walk slowly towards Paul. The other man had his right hand at his back, Jack instinctively knew why and his blood ran cold. He pictured at any second the whole scene erupting in a mass of gunfire. The man was only feet from Paul when he shouted. "Remain exactly where you are!" Jack thought it strange that he should then walk directly past Paul. He was heading towards him! *'He was well hidden, he couldn't be seen.'*

"Do as he says, remain exactly where you are!" The woman's voice came from directly behind him. The cold metal end of the handgun at the back of his neck reinforced the request. Jack obligingly froze and waited for his impromptu meeting. He remained motionless but his brain was working at warp speed!

* * *

CHAPTER TWENTY ONE

Having spent what seemed like days in the dark confines of the container, Maria was almost blinded by the brilliance of the sun now high in the cloudless sky above her. She looked around, there was nobody, the place was deserted. She'd not really expected to see anyone but the sudden loneliness was frightening. The lorry was half covered by a canopy of trees. She walked further out into the open area, a small clearing, *'almost idyllic'* she thought. Dragging the chain along, she decided it was her first priority. *'Let's get this off!'* She told herself and climbed into the lorry cab. It was a mess with drink cans and sandwich packets strewn about over the passenger seats. There was a small area behind the seats where a sleeping bag had been placed forming a cramped bed. On the sleeping bag, she found a phone, not hers, and a bunch of keys. Maria grabbed the keys and started to try each one on the padlock. Some she disregarded as being too big or too small. There were five that could fit and she tried each in turn. Of the five only two actually slid into the barrel of the padlock. Try as she may she couldn't get either of the keys to release the hasp. She cursed and struggled for five minutes before throwing the keys down. She was angry, she wanted to shout and scream but clearly, the only person who'd hear was her prisoner in the container. She picked up the mobile phone and looked at it. It was switched off and she pressed the button to turn in on. She waited while it chirped and went through its opening repertoire before displaying the message 'please enter your passcode'. She tried all the default codes she could think of and in the end she found herself locked out for 30minutes. The phone joined the keys while she searched the entire cab area for anything that might just be of some use. She started to cry, tears running down her cheeks as she looked fruitlessly through the litter before her. She considered going back into the container and threatening her prisoner with violence if he didn't tell her where the padlock key was. She knew she could hurt him; she couldn't kill him that was a step beyond which she would not, and could not, go. She toyed with that as her next step and looked around the cab. Her eye was caught by an air freshener, the green tree no longer emitting a scent being faded and curled up. It was what was hanging on the thin elastic string that caused her heart to leap. She grabbed the tree and its metal adornment. The key was the right size. She fumbled dropping it in her haste and had to search on the floor amongst the litter until she found it again. It slid into the barrel of the padlock. She took a deep breath and tried to turn it. Nothing, she tried again, nothing! Then she turned it the other way and as if by magic the hasp snapped open.

* * *

She pushed the gun barrel to gain his attention as if it needed it! "Slowly get to your feet and keep your hands where I can see them. Raise them up please!" Jack recognised the voice. She'd spoken to him earlier. It was the woman in the car park in Anché. He complied but remained facing the man now standing in front of him. Her gun-less hand checked each pocket in turn eventually removing his wallet which she tossed to the man before him. "You can lower your hands but keep them on view."

"*Jack Ramsay – Private Investigator.* He read the card he'd taken from the wallet. "Tell me, Mr. Ramsay, what the fuck are you doing here?"

Jack had considered the options open to him in the seconds between having the gun at his head and the question placed before him. "I've been tracing the whereabouts of Mr. Blanchard on behalf of his wife. I'm working for her. Mr. Blanchard was unaware of my existence until now. I've been following him." Jack hoped Paul would fall in with Jack's story, it being the only way he could think of protecting Maria. He knew that if this man thought that Paul was crossing him in any way things could and probably would get very nasty for her.

"And we've been keeping tabs on you!" The man shifted his weight before continuing. "Four of my helpers, men who work for me, were watching you Mr. Ramsay." He paused to let the information sink in, watching Jack's expression. "They were in a van, a white van." He paused again and Jack's skin felt suddenly clammy. "I suggested they try and persuade you to desist from following Mr. Blanchard here." He turned and pointed to Paul who was visibly shaking.

"Apparently you were not sufficiently encouraged by their methods and drove them off the road." The man smiled. "They're on their way by foot as their van is upside down in a ditch. They'll be here soon and I'm sure they'll want to reacquaint themselves with you. I believe they have unfinished business and the like."

"Who are you? You know my name and why I'm here." Jack eyeballed him. "What's your name?"

"Sorry if I appear rude Mr. Ramsay but I'm afraid I'm not going to give you that information. Knowledge is power and all that. I could tell you, but then I'd have to kill you as they say! And I really don't want to do that." He smiled a disconcertingly false smile. "Now, do you *really* want to know my name?" Jack remained silent. "I thought so. Suffice to say that although we have never met, Mr. Blanchard here knows exactly who I am and what I want. He has been working for me, logistics shall we say. Unfortunately, he has mislaid my plane plus a large sum of money and he needs to address that shortfall. He also needs to repay a three-year-old outstanding debt. Now you're going to stand there while I finish my business with Mr. Blanchard. It rather depends on how our business discussions go. If all is well then we go our different ways." He looked at the woman who'd moved to stand and to form a perfect triangle with the two men. "If he moves shoot him! A knee will do, either knee it makes no difference." With that, he turned and walked back to Paul who'd frozen to the spot.

Jack watched Paul, he tried desperately to hear the conversations but both parties were talking very quietly. He caught snippets of things said and managed to get an idea of what was being discussed. Paul reached into the

Volkswagen and pulled out a small leather bag. He handed it to the man. He could see Paul touch the man's arm. The man turned and looked at Paul who withdrew it immediately. The man and the driver walked towards each other and the bag was passed between them. The man returned to stand with Paul while the driver took the bag back to the black car and checked the contents. After an agonising wait, the driver returned minus the bag and spoke very quietly in the man's ear before returning to the car.

Paul started to speak. He tried to explain but the man raised his hand to quell him. They stood motionless for nearly half a minute before the man spoke again to Paul. Paul nodded and with that the man walked back to Jack and the woman.

"I do apologise for keeping you standing around waiting. I'm a reasonable man Mr. Ramsay and I don't go around killing people without a good reason. However, we have a little problem. You see Mr. Blanchard here has not entirely kept his part of the bargain."

"He knew nothing of my existence. He didn't know he was being followed, that I was following him." Jack was to trying to mitigate on Paul's behalf. He did, however, have a fairly clear idea of where this conversation was headed.

"Just as you didn't know you were being followed, Mr. Ramsay! White van man or in this case *men!* Not forgetting our lady on the phone in the church car park." He nodded towards the woman who was still holding the gun. He laughed. "Not such a 'private investigator' are we, Mr. Ramsay? A few schoolboy errors made don't you think?"

"So what's going to happen now?" He nodded towards Paul. "Mr. Blanchard has given you what you wanted. I saw you take a bag."

"Ah yes, but unfortunately our Mr. Blanchard here has fallen a long way short of his promised agreement, which in turn means I'm under no obligation to fulfil my side of the agreement." He turned to the ashen-faced Paul. "Would you be so kind as to come over here and join us, Mr. Blanchard. And let's see if we can resolve this tiresome matter." He looked at the woman. "I think we can dispense with the hardware, my dear. Just for the moment put the gun away." Paul hurried over and stood next to Jack making no effort to acknowledge him or make eye contact. Jack could sense his fear and almost see him physically shaking. "Now Mr. Blanchard, let me call you Paul as it's so much more informal. You've only given me three-quarters of the money from the plane. That's not what we agreed. Plus, I need this debt of yours settled."

"You've got all the money I have. I've spent some during the three years I know but please, that's all I have. I had to live!" Paul surprised himself that he was actually able to speak. He'd wished however that it hadn't come out in quite such an accusatory manner.

"The agreement, Paul, was that you'd pay me in full and then you and the lovely Maria, currently being entertained by one of my assistants, could walk off into the sunset. Yes?"

"But I, I've spent my........ "

"Excuses Paul, I've heard nothing but excuses! This is not going to get us anywhere, is it? I'm becoming somewhat impatient to find a way to satisfy both parties here. You have to understand I'm being very reasonable but please don't expect me to forget all that has happened. I'm not prepared just to wipe the slate clean. He paused and they all stood in silence before he spoke again. Let me see, how about this as a solution? You've paid me 75% correct?"

"Yes, 75% that's right." Paul was eager to please this man.

"So, it's settled. You've withheld 25%, therefore, I should do the same! "What do you mean?" Paul suddenly looked confused as well as scared.

"You can have 75% of Maria back! It's simple Paul. Decide which arm or leg she could do without and we'll return the remaining 75% to you at our earliest convenience!"

The colour drained from Paul's face in an instant. Jack thought he was going to collapse right there and then. "No! Please give me just a bit more time. I can get you some more money!"

"Time is something you no longer have at your disposal, Paul. I'm afraid that it's run out for you." He cleared his throat. "OK, here's another solution to our problem. Well, actually it's your problem. I'm just trying to help you out here don't you see Paul?" Paul was still imagining Maria minus 25% of her limbs. He was numb, beaten. He'd have agreed to anything, not understanding the consequences. "Suppose that I release Maria into the capable hands of Mr. Ramsay here? He'll look after her."

"Yes! Please do that." Paul nodded, watching the man like an obedient puppy. "Good, we'll do that then. I'm not a vicious man Paul and I don't take pleasure in inflicting pain and suffering.

"Thank you, thank you very much!" Paul's colour started to return. He took two or three deep breaths and looked towards Jack. "Mr. Ramsay, thank you. You'll look after Maria for me?"

"Good, then there's just one more thing for us to wrap up Paul." The man was speaking again. He smiled another of his fake smiles. "You'll need to come with us. We can't have you becoming lost again. I don't want to spend another three years searching for you? There's the matter of the remaining 25% you see. You've paid me 75% of the money you stole from me. In addition Paul we also have to consider the loan you have with us, I want that money back. As you know it's a considerable sum we're talking about. Plus interest of course at a percentage yet to be agreed. We need you to arrange this payment as soon as and for that we require you remain with us until ……. well until the matter has been resolved." He turned to the woman. "Escort Paul over to the car, will you my dear?" The woman responded and poked Paul with her finger, Paul turned to face her and still somewhat shell-shocked started to walk, glancing briefly at Jack in wonderment. Paul looked like a lost soul, drained of colour and quivering as he walked slowly away.

"Where's Maria? You said you'd let her go." Jack said quickly.

"And that's exactly what I will do Mr. Ramsay." He handed Jack his wallet. "I am a man of my word in every way, Mr. Ramsay. Do I make myself clear?"

"Yes. You've made it very clear indeed." Jack took the wallet and looked the man in the eyes. "Where is she?"

"Back the way you came there's a track off to the left. Follow it and you'll find a container lorry. My driver here has already sent a text. You'll be expected.

You may have to wait until my man has finished having his entertainment. He's been very keen to give Maria something to remember him by. I'll leave that to your imagination Mr. Ramsay." He started to turn and then remembered something. He turned his head. "Oh, I nearly forgot. Be quick Mr. Ramsay. My other men, the four in the van, remember? They're due to arrive very shortly at the lorry. They won't be very happy at having had to walk all that way but I'm sure they'll be pleased to see you! They may wish to entertain Maria as well. They may, of course, wish to beat the shit out of you Mr. Ramsay. I expect they'll want to do both!" He turned again. "I'll say good day Mr. Ramsay. You'd better hurry!"

Jack started to run, the uneven track and the long grass made it difficult. His mind was full of one thing, damage limitation! His side was hurting with the sudden violent exercise, *'bloody ribs!'* he cursed under his breath. He arrived back at his car. The woman had parked her car just off the track to the side. He checked the gap, there was space! He reversed a short way and turned the steering wheel following the track which was little more than a space between the more dense bushes and trees. Progress was slow but eventually Jack could see the area ahead was more open. There was a small clearing in the wooded surroundings. He could see a figure standing next to a large lorry. How the lorry had made it down the track Jack had no idea, it looked as if it had become part of the forest, its drab paintwork blended like camouflage. As he got closer he could see the figure was a woman. She started running towards him. He noticed she was swinging a length of chain around her head and screaming.

"Are you Maria? ...." He swung the car around in the small space and shouted through the window. "Quick get in, I've got to get you out of here!"

"Who are you? I do not know you." She held the chain ready to slam it down on the car or Jack if he chose to get out.

"We don't have time Maria. I will explain it all when we're out of here. But please, you must trust me!"

"I'm not sure if you're a safe person. Where's Paul?"

In desperation, Jack shouted at her. "Get in the fucking car, *now!* There are four men on their way to rape you and probably kill me so please will you get in?" Jack flung open the door.

"OK, don't use that language at me. Take me to Paul!" She quickly climbed in and Jack put the car into gear. "So who are you and where are you taking me?"

"I'm sorry, but we have to get out of here pronto! I'm taking you back to the hotel first, to get you cleaned up. Then I'll explain what's happened." He urged the car forward and out of the small clearing. "My name is Jack Ramsay and I'm trying to keep you and Paul safe OK?"

"Is he safe? Tell me, is Paul safe?"

"At the moment he's OK."

"Is he at the hotel waiting?"

"No, he's not Maria. Please, just trust me. I'm here to get you to somewhere safe, out of here." She seemed to settle and eased herself back in the seat. "Put your seatbelt on, it may get a bit bumpy!"

Driving as quickly as he dared, Jack drove down the track back the way he'd come. He'd gone almost fifty metres when he saw them! They were headed directly towards them walking in single file. They didn't look a particularly happy bunch! The leader made eye contact with Jack and alerted the other three. As one they started to run, towards the car! Jack locked the doors although it seemed a futile and token effort. Throwing the car into reverse he quickly backed the car into the clearing.

"Go there, that way!" Maria pointed to the opposite end of the clearing. "I saw before you came, the track goes that way too!"

"Where does it lead?"

"How would I know such things, I only saw it just before you got here!"

Jack had no choice and gunned the engine across the open space and into the narrow opening at the other end, the car appearing to vanish, absorbed by the foliage. The car bounced along grounding and leaping with equal measure. A thick branch neatly removed one of the door mirrors as Jack tried to judge the spaces between the trees. The four were still following and, for a while, gaining. The distance between them was decreasing with each passing second. He could go no faster and risk damaging the suspension rendering the car undrivable yet to continue at this speed meant they'd be caught within the next minute. The car was protesting, bucking and crashing down as it left the ground and landed again.

"Watch them, tell me what's happening!" Jack couldn't allow himself the time to look in the mirror he needed to watch the track ahead. Maria swivelled round and peered out of the rear window.

"He's gone down!" She suddenly shouted. "I think he has fallen, tripped over. The man at the front has fallen down." There was a further pause. "The others, three of them are still chasing after us … But now they're longer back, how do you say?"

"Good, but keep watching." Jack began to relax just a little and eased the throttle by just a small degree. *'Don't get complacent!'* A small voice in his head made itself heard.

"They've stopped, they've all stopped running!" Maria was shouting at Jack. "Did you hear?"

"Yes, but we have to carry on. We don't know where this track goes." They continued, now at a more sedate pace. The terrain was still undulating but with a slightly reduced speed, it was less damaging to car and occupants.

It seemed ages but gradually the track became wider and flatter. It was a relief when gravel took the place of grass! Eventually, they came to a junction and took the road leading back to Vivonne and the hotel. When they arrived back at the hotel, the receptionist gave them a strange look when they walked into the foyer. First, they climbed the stairs to Paul's room where Maria collected a few items.

"I want you to stay here. I will be safer if you are here." Maria pleaded with Jack. "Please, stay with me!"

Jack looked around the room which was identical to the one he was in. "Better if we stay in my room for the time being. They know you were in this one should anyone come looking."

"Who Jack? Who will come looking?"

"I don't know exactly Maria. It seems Paul has got himself into a mess, he owes a great deal of money to somebody and they want it back."

"That's why I was taken, how you say abducted?" Maria was looking directly into Jack's eyes. "So I am free if Paul pays them the money he owes, yes?"

"That's how I see it!" Jack looked around the room. I'd feel better if we didn't stay in here too long that's all." She nodded and they decamped to Jack's room where she took a long bath while Jack sat in the window watching the traffic, trains and boats below.

"Now you tell me everything, yes?" She called from the bathroom. "Come and explain it all to me please!" Jack heard her moving in the bath, the sounds of water splashing. Jack moved one of the chairs across the room and placed it just outside the door. He sat down. "Just open the door a small way, so then I can hear what you are going to say." Jack opened the door a few inches and sat back down. The door and Jack's chair discreetly positioned for Maria's modesty.

It seemed a daunting task, explaining all that had happened. Jack started from the very beginning with how he'd been asked by Catherine to find her husband. Maria listened to all he had to say. She occasionally asked him to repeat or clarify parts of the story but in the main she allowed him to speak without major interruption. Then it was her turn and she spoke about the man with whom she fell in love and who later she discovered to be Paul Blanchard. She described their life together and how happy she was. Maria talked about the café and how it was her desire, her dream to someday open a chain of cafes all over France. Jack didn't ask any questions, he just sat there listening to her speaking in faltering English. Sometimes there would be periods of silence when she would be struggling for the right word or phrase. Other times Jack sensed her silence was a quiet tear. He felt as if he were seated in a 'confessional' listening to a person's innermost secrets. In a way, that's exactly what he was doing. It was both humbling and empowering having another human being share so much. *'The water must be cold by now.'* He thought as he heard Maria stand and step out of the bath. She appeared at the door wrapped in the white bathrobe that had been hanging behind the door. She crossed to the bed and collected the few clothes she had brought with her from Paul's room.

"I will only be a little bit longer!" She smiled and vanished back into the bathroom where she dressed in the clean clothes. She appeared within a minute her hair towelled and held with a band at the back. She wore no make-up but as Jack could see, none was needed. Her skin glowed and her eyes sparkled. Considering her recent experiences she looked amazing.

Jack wanted to ask her but did not know how to broach the subject. He stumbled over his delivery. "When you were being held in the lorry, Maria ...." He cleared his throat and tried again. "Did you... I mean were you, in any way hurt or molested?"

"Molested, what is that?" Her eyes widened.

"I mean, did anything happen to you? Were you attacked in any way?"

"I see, you mean was I raped?" She was blunt and to the point. Jack wasn't sure whether it was due to her command of English or her Latin temperament. "No, I am as you say OK!" She smiled. "Thank you for asking."

They discovered they were hungry but didn't want to stay in the hotel. They walked the short distance to the centre of the small town where they found a discreet but expensive restaurant. *'What the hell!'* Thought Jack and they found a table for two at the rear, overlooking the small rear courtyard. It was pleasantly cool. Maria really wanted wine but her condition forbade alcohol. She settled for grape juice and, so as not to be disadvantaged, should there be the need to make important and quick decisions, Jack concurred. Although some distance from the coast, fish featured conspicuously on the menu. They both opted for the sea bream and were not disappointed when ten minutes later two enormous plates were laid in front of them. The fish, beautifully cooked, was sitting on a bed of salad accompanied by couscous. Maria was feeling more relaxed and they were able to eat and make small talk. It was inevitable that before the meal was finished they topic of conversation had returned full circle and Paul's name featured largely.

"What will happen now? They will let him go soon when he pays them." Maria was hoping that by saying it, it would come to pass. She knew she was being naïve. Deep in her heart she knew the truth, but knowing and accepting were at opposite ends of the dark room in which she found herself.

"Maria!" Jack extended his hands across the table and she held them, tears forming in her eyes. He felt totally helpless as she dissolved into floods. She grabbed at the napkin and held it to her face. "The truth is I don't know what may happen!" He hated the cliché but used it anyway. "We just have to hope for the best." '.....and expect the worst!' The words went through his head.

"What can we do to help?" She was looking earnestly at Jack. "We find some money and we take it to them. Yes, that's what we can do!"

"Where do we *find* some money? And exactly *how much* money are we going to find? And *where* do we take it? Certainly, these people aren't going to be standing exactly where we left them." Jack didn't enjoy wrecking her plan, shooting it down before it was airborne but he was being realistic. "I don't have any money, certainly not the amount we're talking about. Do you?"

"No, I don't have any money." She looked at the tablecloth, defeated. "There must be a way!"

"We have to wait. Paul's phone has my mobile number on it. If they want to talk, they'll contact us. I'm sorry Maria but there's absolutely nothing we can do other than go to the police and tell them all that has happened. It's gone beyond anything we can do, it really has."

"But Paul will be in danger."

"The police have to become involved now Maria. Paul is in danger but this is really the only way we can help him now."

"OK, you are right, correct I know. That is our way forward. That is how we can help to get Paul back." She stood up abruptly. "Come on then, we will go now. We strike hot irons in the fire as you English say, yes?"

"Something along those lines, yes." Jack had a quiet smile and motioned to the waiter to pay the bill.

* * *

Chapter Twenty Two

Jack had experienced red tape and bureaucracy many times before and at all levels. He'd not encountered anything to compare with the twelve hours they subsequently spent explaining together and individually their stories to the various departments at junior, middle and senior level! Eventually, at around 3:00 a.m. they arrived back at the hotel physically tired and mentally exhausted. Jack's room was pleasantly cool. The windows had been left open and the breeze caught the voile curtains wafting them with an almost ethereal motion.

"You have the bed and I'll sleep here on the chair." Jack took a spare blanket from the cupboard. Maria went to the bathroom and reappeared wearing her bra and knickers. She slipped into the bed and closed her eyes. Jack sat in the chair. He went over in his head all that had happened in the previous 24hours. He was about to call Cleo. *'She'd probably not want to be woken at this time of the night!'* He mused and placed the phone next to the bed, where he plugged it in, to charge.

He tried sitting with his legs out straight, it was no good. He tried turning on his side but the chair was really too small. He placed the other chair in front and experimented with putting his feet on it. He'd tried a whole assortment of positions and eventually let out a gasp in defeat.

"For goodness sake come, get in this bed with me!" She raised her head sufficiently to look him in the eyes. "You're keeping me awake with all of your tossing about. Get in and we both get to sleep, yes?"

"Well, if you......" Jack was taken aback by Maria's forthright decision. The comfort of the king-size mattress certainly beckoned.

"You English, you are so funny I think. Come on, you will be more comfortable and be able to sleep. But there will be no hanky or panky. I tell you that now. Do you understand?"

"Right, no hanky-panky, that's fine!" Jack smiled but in the dark of the room, she missed it.

* * *

Paul's car had died, a haze of steam still clung in the air.

"Leave it where it is. Get in the car." The rear door of the black Mercedes was held open. Paul climbed in and sat next to the man. He was nervous but was trying not to show it. The bag, Paul's bag, had been placed in the boot. He knew he'd fallen short. The money he was required to give them and the amount in the bag, were not the same. He was about a million euros short. He knew he'd never get the money. He didn't have it anymore, it was all gone, spent on living, existing and hiding for three long years. His life had changed, dramatically and irreversibly during that time. He had a new life, of sorts! Most of the time looking over his shoulder, making sure he'd a plan, a way out, an escape! Up until very recently, he'd imagined he would eventually become free, his new life would take over and he'd become this new person. The clichés *'You only live once'* and *'Life is not a dress rehearsal'* ran through his head. They were all just ways of trying to justify not making a total mess of things. But he had made a mess of things, big time! Paul sat there in the car, the engine noise and car's movements so cushioned by the opulence within he wasn't aware they were on their way.

He was in a world of his own. He'd started to collapse in on his very being. *'Life's like playing a games machine. It's all a gamble, taking risks, some players get on, make it big. Others don't do quite so well, they get to the end but they survive! Then there were people like him. He was a risk taker, played the high stakes. He didn't need to, he should have settled for what he'd had. He'd wanted more, that was his big mistake!'* He thought about the one big difference. *'Life doesn't allow you to start the game over again when you get it wrong......... Or start again when you die!'*

Paul peered out of the window. The passing scenery seemed so far beyond the tinted glass. It appeared now beyond grasp, like a place he'd never get to visit. The air in the car was cool but sterile. There was nothing, no smell to tell you that you were alive! The land beyond the window was real, you could smell it! *'This wasn't real!'*

* * *

283

Jack listened to the birds chirping, the sounds coming in through the open window. It wasn't quite light. The sun was just about to break the horizon. He was aware of an orange glow in the eastern sky. He felt her move slightly. She was on her side with her arm across his chest. He'd moved his arm during the night, she'd turned and the result was the sleepy embrace that Jack discovered himself in as his eyes opened. The birds were chirping again, Jack listened. *'No, they're not birds!'* He grabbed his phone!

"Cleo. I was going to call you. When we, I, got back to the hotel it was very late. It was early morning actually!" He paused to allow her to fire questions at him. "We have to go to the police station again today. It's a long, very long, story but the bottom line is I found Paul. Yes, yes I know! But listen, he's now with some people. People he owes money to. A great deal of money!"

"Jack. Who is it? Is it Paul, tell me!" Maria's voice sounded sleepy.

"Jack? Who's that with you?" Cleo was raising her voice just a little.

"It's Maria."

"Who the hell's Maria, Jack?"

"Jack, tell her you are calling her later. I need to sleep a bit more, you too I expect."

"Cleo, it's not what you think. She's just here... Because, she..."

"I know exactly why she's there Jack, I'm not stupid." Cleo cut him in mid-explanation. "Then next time we speak you'd better have thought of a bloody good reason!" The line went dead.

"Oh fuck!" He said burying his head in the soft white pillow. "Fuck, fuck, fuck....... What am I going to do?" He spoke so quietly Maria didn't catch all that he had said. Jack was upset, he was choked. *'She'd totally misread the situation, jumped to conclusions. Not given him a chance to speak!'* He started to sob quietly tears were welling, wetting the pillow.

She leaned over and placed her hand on his shoulder, caressing lightly. "Don't worry Jack she will call you back when she's settled herself up!"

"Down, you mean down!" He sniffed, his head remained buried.

"OK, as you wish. Up or down, she will settle!" She continued to caress his shoulder. She rested her head on the pillow looking at him, her hand still lightly touching his shoulder. The sobbing and sniffing became less as he sank deeper onto the bed as his body began to relax, the tension in his muscles ebbing with each deep breath. She watched as he drifted off into sleep. And when she was satisfied, she too closed her eyes.

* * *

Catherine had made coffee. Hot black coffee! Cleo didn't want coffee, she wanted answers! She'd been going out of her mind, thinking about what had happened.

"Listen to me, Cleo." Catherine was now taking control. Cleo had been her rock all this time, now it was her turn! "You've put two and two together and come up with five!" She handed her a mug of the steaming liquid. "You know Jack, and I know Jack, and he's a perfect gentleman. No way is he up to anything. There'll be a perfectly reasonable explanation."

"But I heard her Catherine, a woman in his room, I heard her talking!"

"And you jumped to the wrong conclusions. You didn't give him a chance to explain did you?"

"No, because….."

"Because of what, you'd already made up your mind he was guilty?"

"Because I ….." She broke down sobbing into an already wet tissue.

"And for all you know Cleo, Jack is most probably doing exactly the same thing right now over in France!"

* * *

Maria had showered and was sitting on the bed wearing the white robe. Jack was asleep as his phone rang. She shook his arm. "Wake up, she's calling you!" Jack woke with a start, staring blearily at her.

"Hello?" Jack took a deep breath. "Cleo?" He waited, the silence at the other end of the line was deafening. He wanted her to speak, say something. "Cleo?"

"Yes. I wanted to talk to you, Jack." She sounded strange, distant. It worried him.

"Yes, and I wanted to talk to you too. I wanted to explain all that has happened. I wanted to tell you how much I've missed you. How I've longed to get back to see you……… Cleo, there really is nothing to …….." He was lost for what to say, how to start."

"Jack just please explain it to me, tell me all that's happened, I'm listening!"

He told her whole story, the chain of events. What had happened, how it had happened and even his thoughts on why it had happened, leaving nothing out and including how and why Maria had ended up in his room. "I'm concerned for her safety Cleo and she didn't want to be in her room in case they should return."

Cleo had listened, there was much to digest. She didn't interrupt or question, she just allowed him to finish, to bring her up to speed. "You said Maria's pregnant? Has she told you who?"

"It's Paul, he's the father!" Jack had lowered his voice to a whisper. Maria was in the bathroom, just out of earshot.

"Oh, Jack! Catherine needs to be told, she has to know, she has to know Paul is the father. She'll have to be told that Amelia will have a half-sister or brother soon. There'll be implications, Jack, with Paul's estate, his assets." Cleo's mind was racing.

"Let's take it one step at a time Cleo." Jack considered his next request very carefully. "Cleo, do you think you'll be able to tell….."

"Yes, Jack. I'll break the news to her."

"Thanks for that. And by the way, thanks for listening to me, letting me tell you everything….." He trailed off not knowing how to finish. Conversations like this were not his strong point.

"Talk soon Jack, take care. Love you… Sorry!"

"Love you back!" He placed the phone on the bedside table just as Maria walked into the room.

"I can see you have a cheerful face on you, not the sad face of earlier. That's good. All patched up now?"

"All patched up!"

* * *

They'd breakfasted and were waiting in the lounge area. The two men entered the hotel and walked over to where Jack and Maria were seated. They discreetly took out their identification to confirm they were from the gendarmerie. The plain clothed detectives were now dealing with the investigation. It was Jack and Maria's job now to assist with their enquiries as best as they could. The journey back out to the fields and wooded areas caused Maria some anxiety. She clutched Jack's hand, holding tightly as the car bumped its way along the track.

It all looked different, there were police officers everywhere! Jack was impressed with the speed and expense that had been lavished on gathering as much information before the trail became cold. Unfortunately much cleaning up had already taken place before the police arrived. A fingertip search was under way in the small clearing. The lorry had undergone a major transformation. It hadn't been much to start with but now it was a completely burned out shell. The number plates had been removed and chassis, as well as engine numbers, had been ground off before the whole thing doused in petrol and set alight. Tracing the vehicle's registered owner looked unpromising! Maria confirmed this was the container in which she'd been imprisoned. She was reluctant to look inside but when told that no bodies had been found her relief was instant. Although she'd left him a prisoner in the container Maria was sure he'd been rescued by the four who'd chased them just twenty-four hours earlier!

They discovered Paul's car back on the other track. It was parked up exactly where Jack had last seen it. There were marks where another larger vehicle had turned around. The grass and small shrubs bore testament to having been flattened in the process. Again there were officers peering in, around and under the vehicle. The smell of coolant still clung to the engine and underside of the open bonnet. The key had been left in the ignition and they'd tried to get the car started with no avail. The engine had internally haemorrhaged. It had made it thus far, and its next journey would undoubtedly be on the back of a breakdown vehicle, to be tested by forensic experts should the missing person investigation turn darker!

Back at the gendarmerie, there were questions and yet more questions. Jack and Maria had repeated their stories both, together and separately, giving them their versions of events over and over again. Eventually, it seemed that no more questions were considered necessary. Investigations would continue but they were free to go. They both left their contact addresses and numbers. They'd phoned the mobile provider and Maria, having had her mobile taken had cancelled the current sim card. Replacement phone and card were on their way and a courier would bring them to the hotel before the end of the day.

"Where have they gone?" Maria repeated her question over and over. Jack's response had been the same one. "I don't know Maria. We have to wait to see if Paul contacts us! He has my mobile number as you know. Jack had tried Paul's number a few times. Each time it had failed to connect. He knew he'd be the first to hear if there was any news. If Paul wanted to speak, or *could* speak! He tried not to think too much!

Waiting is a practiced art. Not one that many people find easy to achieve. Maria paced the room, stopping to look out of the window occasionally. Huffing and checking the time on the cheap watch she'd picked up in the market on their way back to the hotel. They'd taken her other one. It had been a present to her from him on their first Christmas together. She so wanted that watch back, and the person who'd bought it and wrapped it up in smaller and smaller boxes until she became angry with him! Only to be thrilled when she eventually saw the gold Rolex nestling inside that last box!

Jack had texted Cleo, giving her another update on the trip out to the scene with the police. She called him back just minutes after he'd sent it. She'd wanted to hear his voice and Jack was so pleased that she did! Catherine had taken the news of a baby better than Cleo had expected. She'd been almost philosophical in her response and reactions. Cleo talked about the day to day happenings. They'd both taken Amelia to school in the morning but Catherine was going to collect her later. Cleo had been out and bought the makings of a Jamaican dish, a recipe of her grandmother's. She was going to cook their supper.

The hotel phone in the room beeped and Maria dashed to pick it up. "It's reception, Jack. The courier's here with my replacement phone. I'm going down to get it."

"Wait! I'm coming with you." Jack made his excuses and pocketed his phone.

They went down to the foyer where a leather-jacketed motorcycle courier stood waiting for a signature. Maria duly signed for the package which was handed to her. The box looked to be about the right size and weight. She smiled and thanked him.

"Let's go and get it charged up. That'll take a few hours!" Jack carried it for her and they made their way back up to Jack's room. Jack searched for something sharp to use. The black plastic covering the box was tough. While he was looking, Maria, managed with her nails to slice through and started to peel away the outer wrappings. Removing the plastic now revealed the box. She looked at the graphics printed on the top and sides. She didn't pay them any them any real attention and removed the lid. Wrapped neatly in the paper was the phone. She picked it up and held it close to her chest. It wasn't her new phone. It was her old one!

Maria sat on the bed rocking slightly and with tears streaming down her face. Jack suddenly became aware of her distress and quickly sat down next to her placing his arm around her quivering shoulders. He looked into the box which was on her lap and in imminent danger of falling to the floor. There were three more items in the box. She placed the phone on the bed and took out the next wrapped item. Carefully she removed the paper and when she saw it she gasped! The gold Rolex's face looked back at her, its second hand sweeping away the passing minutes. The next paper bundle was more obvious. It was held with an elastic band. There were five thousand euros in a roll. Jack took it from her and placed it on the bedside table. Maria took the remaining item from the box. It was an envelope with her name. She immediately recognised the writing and with a shaking hand passed it to Jack.

"Please. I can't do it! Open it for me Jack!" He carefully opened the envelope and withdrew the single sheet of A4. He unfolded it.

"It's a letter....." He looked at the bottom. "It's from Paul!"

"Read it to me please!"

Jack held the sheet of paper as if it were some long

lost ancient manuscript. It was a plain sheet of A4, the words handwritten in ballpoint pen. He scanned it quickly and turned to face her. "Are you sure you want me to read it? It's a personal letter addressed to you. You should be the one to read it."

"Please, I can't! You read it to me!" She was breathing deeply and Jack could tell she was having difficulty holding on to her emotions

Jack took a deep breath and started to read out loud but his voice was subdued, just sufficient for them both to hear the words. He read it slowly.

My darling Maria,

I've been allowed to write you this letter and to give you the money that was in my jacket. They said a small amount makes little difference to the amount I still owe them. They have sent back your watch and a phone that were taken from you when you were abducted.

There is no easy way to say this Maria. In reading this letter you understand I am never coming back. I would give anything to be able to hold you and be with you again but that will never happen.

I have been foolish, stupid and tempted by greed Maria. My life has been ruined and now there is no way out for me. This has all been of my own making and I am blaming nobody but myself. The choices I have made over the last few years have led me to where I now find myself.

In the box, you will find your phone and your watch. I so much wanted you to have the watch

back. I remember the look on your face that Christmas when you opened the present and saw it. You'd told me you had always wanted an expensive watch but could never afford or even justify having one. I will always remember your smile when I placed it on your wrist.

The money, use it for you and for the baby. When our baby is born, please tell him, or her, about me. I wanted to be there but you know I can't do that now. This will be difficult but my wife, Catherine Blanchard must be told of the baby. Jack will help sort that out for you. Trust him, Maria, he is a good man.

By the time the box is delivered to the hotel I will be dead and my debts will all have been paid.

Don't cry for me Maria, I am not worthy of your tears.

I will love you always,

Paul Blanchard

She took the letter from him and held it close. "So he is dead?" Maria's tears ran down her cheeks as the terrible realisation hit home. She sat down on the bed in silent acceptance.

"It very much looks that way. I am so sorry." Jack took his mobile phone from his pocket. "Excuse me Maria but I have to do this now, Catherine has to be informed." He scrolled down to Cleo's number and made the call.

* * *

EPILOGUE

The journey back to that small café was subdued. Maria said very little during the trip, each of them with their own thoughts. Yvette and Katrina took charge, fussing and comforting as best they could. The flat was as it had been left. It had only been a week but it seemed to Maria a lifetime. Didier came out from his flat to meet her. He looked a little confused but in the fullness of time He, Yvette and Katrina would eventually learn the fate of Maria's partner Michael. There Maria stayed and when Jack felt he could leave her continued on his journey home.

Jack arrived back at the car hire office and after long and protracted discussions they accepted Jack's offer to buy the car. It was easier to do than go through the arduous paperwork involved in claiming for repairs. He needed a car any way, the 'Bee' was really just for occasional use! He booked himself and the car on the ferry back to Portsmouth.

Cleo was as pleased to see him, as he was to see her.

Catherine had closure, of sorts. She'd discovered more, got some answers to questions that had played on her mind for all that time. Not all the answers she wanted! The gambling and the loans to try and pay what he owed had spiralled out of control. She knew now why he'd vanished, faked his own death, but still she was bitter. She now knew of Paul's fate. She knew she felt something for his eventual demise but the loss was not as great as the one she had endured for three long years.

Jack could only confirm the arrival of the letter to say Paul was dead. He'd made a photocopy for Catherine. He could only respond with the same answer, the one he'd given to Maria when asked if Paul Blanchard was dead. There was no body found, one may turn up in the fullness of time but a death without a body never seals a fate!

There would be more to deal with as the years passed. Amelia and her half-sister/brother would grow up and the questions they asked would have to be truthfully answered!

Drawing a line under this case for Catherine, Maria and all concerned would be difficult. Perhaps a line would never be drawn.

* * *

Lightning Source UK Ltd.
Milton Keynes UK
UKOW02f1236131216
289878UK00001B/3/P